WHAT DREAMS ARE MADE OF

WHAT DREAMS ARE MADE OF

Autumn Dawn

Writers Club Press
San Jose New York Lincoln Shanghai

What Dreams Are Made Of

All Rights Reserved © 2002 by Autumn Dawn

No part of this book may be reproduced or transmitted in any form or by any means, graphic, electronic, or mechanical, including photocopying, recording, taping, or by any information storage retrieval system, without the permission in writing from the publisher.

Writers Club Press
an imprint of iUniverse, Inc.

For information address:
iUniverse, Inc.
5220 S. 16th St., Suite 200
Lincoln, NE 68512
www.iuniverse.com

Any resemblance to actual people and events is purely coincidental.
This is a work of fiction.

ISBN: 0-595-22436-9

Printed in the United States of America

CHAPTER 1

"I've always wanted to be famous," she told the man with the long dark eyelashes and beautiful brown eyes. They were the only two in the bar now, happy hour hadn't started yet and the rest of the regulars were still at work. Her name was Sam and she had only been bartending at the White Rhino for a month, and even though it had a bad reputation, Sam enjoyed it. It got her away from her insane cousin and she had finally found someone to supply her with some good meth. It had taken almost a month. When she found him she hadn't been high in a week and she had been at her wits end. She couldn't remember how to function sober anymore. The drugs had all but taken over her life.

"When I was little all I could think about was being an actress. I just wanted to be somebody. I would play out my favorite scenes from the movies I had watched in the privacy of my bedroom. I would do it over and over until I got it just right. Just like I'd seen it in the movie. That's all I've ever wanted—to be somebody different—to play another part-someone other than me." She continued to wash the glasses from previous customers and wipe the ashes off the bar.

"So what are you doing here in this dump?" He asked her.

"You have to know people. The only person I know is my best friend, Bob. The last I talked to him, he was a production assistant with his uncle who produces commercials in LA. We don't talk that often, I'm bad about staying in touch with people." The memories of that remarkable person were too much for her now. He was the only man who hadn't tried to get a piece of her and he meant so much to her. They could talk for hours on end and still have so much more to say to each other the next day. She missed his presence in her life terribly.

"I have a half sister who lives in L.A. I haven't talked to her in over five years though. She just kind of took off one day." He flicked more ashes onto the bar completely missing the ashtray.

His name was Greg Fiori and he was good-looking, nothing exceptional, but he knew where to get the drugs. That was all that mattered to her now. She'd had to flirt with him a little to get him to trust her and when she had offered him cash for the supply he'd given her, he brushed her off. Told her he would take it out in trade. Whatever that meant. Sam wasn't about to sleep with him for drugs. Hell, she wasn't about to sleep with him period. There was just something about him that made her skin crawl and she was starting to get a little uneasy about the way he looked at her. He always came in when nobody else was around, so she sort of had no choice but to pay attention to him.

People were starting to filter in. Despite the brightness outside, the inside of the bar was dim, creating an almost sad and lonely atmosphere. For the people that came in everyday at 3:30 p.m., after the first shift was over at the manufacturing plant across the street, this was their church, their place of worship. Seeking her advice on why they couldn't find a job or why their lover left them, confessing their simple sins, asking for forgiveness from the bottom of a bottle. They threw out intimate details of their lives for her to sort out. These people had become like a distant family to her. They were the regulars. Tim, the blonde haired, raspy voiced painter who always had a cigarette hanging out of his mouth and played pool with his legs spread wide, Mike, the biker with his leather jacket and lack of cash, John the computer geek with his fine strawberry blonde hair and mustache who always drank a Bloody Mary, he'd been the one to show Sam how to make them. Then there was Jerry, he was a short, stocky man who worked construction and did a lot of drugs. He always ordered a 7/seven and never drank anything else. These were the people that made her job interesting and she enjoyed seeing them everyday. The night crew was a different story. The old drunk men seeking solitude from their wives. Always trying to hit on her. She hated nights.

"Will you bring me my stuff before you go to work?" Sam whispered as she mixed a White Russian for Theresa, an older Hispanic woman who hadn't liked Sam at first but Sam had eventually worn her down.

"Yeah, I am getting some more today," he said as he stood up from the bar to walk outside. She had run out that morning and was trying to survive on the fumes of her earlier high.

And off he went. Happy to have him out of her hair for the time being, she mixed and mingled with the rest of the people. These were good people really. They had warmed up to her after just a few days. Her gorgeous chestnut curls with golden highlights, creamy white skin and beautiful eyes threatened the women. The men were intimidated by her sassy attitude. Now they knew her though, and they just ignored it. The real jerks came in at 6:00 when happy hour started. And the bitches that came in on Friday and Saturday night. Were they a lot to handle. Then there were the minors who were downstairs in the bowling alley always trying to buy beer. They came upstairs because they knew their chances were better with Sam. She hated carding people and she knew she should do it more. But she had a fake ID when she was 20 and had only been denied getting into one place.

Why she ever agreed to come to this hokey Midwest town she would never know. Her mom sent her here to get away from the bad crowd she had gotten mixed up with and to get her back on her feet after her boyfriend of four years dumped her. She still couldn't get over him. Although, they never got along and she knew it was better this way, it still tore at her immensely. It was a comfortable, yet volatile relationship. They were never in love with each other at the same time and she was incredibly jealous of his friends and the relationship he had with his family. A relationship she didn't have with hers.

It was 6:00 now and she needed to get ready for the rest of her shift. She worked 14 hours a day here because all of the other bartenders had quit. It was great because when she was high she could do anything forever. But when she ran out—that was a whole different story. When she had lived by herself she only slept every three days. Now she had to go home after work and pretend to sleep while she lay awake in bed until boredom sunk in and sleep would overcome her. She always had to be on guard because her cousin was really nosy and constantly on her case about everything.

So she waited to get her nightly fix and it was a long, long wait.

"Where the fuck have you been?" Sam's cousin screamed. Shelly was not at all subtle about anything. "It's four o'fuckin' clock in the morning. What the fuck have you been doing?" Control Freak! *Do you know any other words besides fuck*, Sam wondered.

"I had to work late and we had to restock the bar." It was a lie but what was she going to say? *I did about three lines of coke and went to some guy's house, who I have never met, and stayed up with four other guys playing gin rummy.* No, that was probably not a good idea. Shelly was a total hypocritical bitch. 'Sam shouldn't do drugs because they are bad'. No it was really more like 'Sam shouldn't do drugs because Shelly can't control that'.

Shelly was screaming and carrying on. She looked like she was doing some sort of Indian rain dance in the middle of the cramped living room of their apartment. She was way out of control.

"Look," Sam held up her hands to defend herself and stop Shelly before she fell onto the ground laughing at her cousin's antics. "I am sorry I didn't call, but I knew you were asleep." Another lie. Trying to play it off as innocent didn't seem to work with Shelly. She saw right through Sam.

Sam walked into her small bedroom and locked her door leaving Shelly to finish her parade. Her bedroom had nothing that belonged to her except her clothes and her cherished Marilyn Monroe bust that she had bought for herself from the money she earned at her very first job. Everything else belonged to Shelly. The double bed with the orange and yellow quilt. The small worn out dresser that was probably an antique. The ugly lamp with those flapper girls on it. Sam hated it here. It was pure misery. She just wanted her old life back, however pathetic it was.

She stared at the calendar for a long time thinking she had only been there a month yet it seemed like a year. It was late February and it was cold and the apartment reeked of welfare. Sam always got on Shelly's case about that. She didn't work, she didn't cook or clean, and she hardly paid any attention to her four-year-old daughter, Maxine. The government pretty much paid Shelly to be a mother. It was sad, really. She hadn't always been like that though. When she and Rick, Max's father, first got married they had it all. They both loved each other very much and they both had great jobs. When it came time to start their family, Shelly couldn't get pregnant so they adopted. The first three years were good for them, but after that, Shelly decided she didn't want to be a mother or a wife anymore. She cheated on Rick, got involved in drugs and lost her job. From there it all went downhill. Talk about dysfunctional families. Sam's made the top of the list. She loved Maxine to death though and spent as much time with her as possible. If it weren't for her father, Maxine would be totally fucked up. Or more fucked up than she already was.

Piss on another night in this godforsaken town.

She walked down the street in the pouring rain. No cares in the world. When she was high she could handle anything. She didn't have to be to work for another two hours, but she slipped out while Shelly was getting high in her bedroom in order to avoid a confrontation. No use in starting off the day like that.

She had walked this street a few times in the last couple of weeks always ending up in the same place. In front of this beautiful house with the white picket fence and wrap around porch. It was fairly new and it stuck out like a sore thumb in the midst of all the other run down houses. She didn't know who lived here, in fact she had never seen anyone around it. It could've been a vacation home, but she doubted anyone vacationed on this side of town. The large maple tree blew gently in the morning breeze. It had stopped raining at the moment and the almost green grass sparkled with water droplets. There were white adirondack chairs on the porch, the kind you saw at the east coast beaches. A wind chime hung from the soffit and played a light musical tune. The whole house was white with a sage trim, freshly painted. It gave Sam a sense of belonging and just looking at it and imaging the wonderful family that lived there filled a void that had been inside of her ever since she was little. She wanted so badly to go and ring the doorbell and ask to come in and see the house. But she turned and walked away knowing that the life she was throwing away only made it greater that she would never own a home like that.

🍁 🍁 🍁

Bob was in the middle of a commercial shoot. Some young punk kicking around a soccer ball while a voice behind him told of the wonderful things sports drinks could do for you. He could tell a lot about an actor just by their attitude. This kid obviously had his parents wrapped around his finger and used his jobs to manipulate them. His mom was on the side smiling nervously, obviously ashamed of her son's behavior but not knowing what to do about it. After all he was probably putting food on the table. He suddenly thought of Sam. Not that she was like that but she had a way of getting people to do what she wanted. Especially guys. She didn't use that to her advantage though. She always pushed guys away, and when they got too close that was the end of them. He never pushed her or tried anything with her. Their relationship was truly platonic. Probably one of the best relationships he had ever had with a woman. They once joked about getting married to each other, but he told her he didn't think he could handle sex with her. It would be too much.

No, he had a crush on her roommate when they were all in college together. It was just a small community college on the northern west coast and they had lived in the dorms together. Taylor was her name. She was the epitome of innocence. Soft-spoken and gentle while Sam was outgoing and vivacious. He never understood how their friendship came to be, but maybe it was true in the old saying, "Opposites Attract".

Taylor'd had a boyfriend and maintained her faithfulness to him the whole time. She'd never thought of cheating on him. Sam was a different story, always looking in out of reach places for a good time; the places she thought were safe but often turned out not to be.

He missed those girls so much. They'd had a lot of fun together. Sam had kept in touch after they left school and called him on occasion. He never spoke to Taylor again. He assumed she had gone back to her small hometown and married her high school boyfriend and maintained a comfortable and stable life.

He was thinking of Sam so much today because two years ago to the day had been the day their friendship had really began. It wasn't the way most people come together but the life-shattering secret they stumbled upon this day had been a bond for them. As he was getting ready to go on break his cell phone rang.

"Hello?"

"Mr. Bob?"

"Sam! Oh my God! I can't believe it's you. I was just thinking about you. How on earth did you get this number?"

"Is that a 'Why are you calling me'—Oh my God or a 'I am so happy to hear from you'—Oh my God?"

"The latter of course."

"Well, in that case, I called your mother in Baahston and she spilled the beans. By the way congratulations on your promotion."

"Thanks. You know I worked hard to get here." Bob had been promoted to a Director's Assistant at his uncle's studio. He had been working there for several years as a go-fer and had reaped the rewards.

"The last time I talked to you in L.A. was when the police were chasing OJ. I think you were watching it from the street weren't you?"

"Yeah, it was pretty crazy down here for awhile." He smiled at the memory of that phone conversation. She was so hyped that his uncle lived down the street from OJ Simpson.

"Well, I just really missed you and I wanted to say hi to the only man in the world I could give a shit about."

They talked for an hour. He told her whenever she wanted to come out, she could stay with him. All she had to do was call. He had broken up with his girlfriend and was not tied down at the moment. *Probably not for long though,* she thought. He was a good catch. He wasn't so much good looking, but it was his personality that made him so wonderful. He always made her laugh, even when she was on her last leg and thought her world was ending.

After their phone conversation, she counted up her money and made a few phone calls. The world was looking better already.

The night was winding down. There were only four people in the bar. It was Wednesday, not a real hot night for partying. Sam went downstairs to the bowling alley and into the bathroom for a quick fix. She always carried a small wooden box in her pocket with a bindle, a blade, and a straw. She went into a stall, got her line ready, flushed the toilet and snorted. The rush was awesome; the drip was so bad that it tasted good. She stuck a piece of gum in her mouth and walked out smiling at the junkie who was fixing her hair at the sink.

CHAPTER 2

Two Months Later

Her bags were packed. She was leaving this pathetic excuse for a town. She left her niece Max a little card with a teddy bear. No details, just goodbye. She hated leaving that little girl with the life she had been dealt, but she couldn't take care of her. She didn't tell anyone else she was leaving or where she was going. She didn't even let work know. Her manager was a dick anyway, let him cover for her for a few days. The airport shuttle pulled into the cul-de-sac and she walked out the front door and locked it behind her. It was five a.m., and her plane was set to leave later that morning. She had plenty of time but she wanted to leave while it was still dark. She sat in the front of the shuttle because the back was full. She listened to the conversations of the people behind her as she watched dusk turn to dawn. She was so happy to be leaving this town and it's trash.

At 10:15 she boarded the United Airlines flight leaving for Los Angeles. She would be there in a little over two hours and her new life would begin.

As the flight landed at LAX, Sam was so jazzed. She could barely hide her smiles as she walked off the plane and into the airport. This was it. This was where she was going to make her dreams come true. She knew the stories of the hundreds of people that came to L.A. daily, hoping to fulfill their dreams, but she also knew only a small percentage made it. She was determined to be a part of that small percentage.

She found a payphone and dialed his number. After two rings he picked up his cellular phone and yelled, "Hello?"

"Hey you," she said. She couldn't stop smiling, she was so happy to be there.

"Hey you! What's up? You sound like you're a mile away."

"Well maybe about 30. I'm at LAX."

"What? Are you kidding? Please tell me you aren't kidding."

"No, actually I am just sitting on my couch wishing I was there."

"Oh." He sounded so disappointed that she kind of felt bad.

"Just Kidding! Come and get me!"

"You are a brat! Give me about an hour. I will meet you at the bar near the United Terminal." Knowing what she was thinking, he added, "and yes, I will hurry." He was already running out to his shabby gray pickup before the call was disconnected.

She sat at the bar and ordered a frozen fuzzy navel. $18.00 later she watched Bob walk in. Bob was one of her best friends from college. They didn't start out that way though. They were both Irish with redheaded tendencies and a dry sense of humor. He had actually been infatuated with her roommate, Taylor. A sad day for Taylor had turned out to be a turning point in Sam and Bob's relationship. This secret they held had been a bond for them and had turned their muddled acquaintance into a beautiful friendship. Bob had been exactly what she needed in her life. A great guy friend who didn't want to get down her pants.

"That was fast," she smiled.

"Hey, I had something to look forward to." He gave her a big bear hug noticing how good she smelled as he buried his face into her neck.

"You smell great."

"Biolage on the head and vanilla on the bod." She felt butterflies in her stomach as she said it. She felt almost shy like she was on a first date. She wasn't accustomed to that feeling around Bob, after all they were just old friends. He definitely wasn't anybody she needed to impress yet she felt like she should.

"You've lost weight!" She noticed, as she pulled back from him, that he had been working out. His stomach felt firm and he actually had muscle showing in his biceps. Bob was your typical Irish stereotype; red hair and freckles. He wasn't ugly by any means and he was the nicest guy Sam had ever known in her whole life. He had smiling green eyes and the greatest laugh ever.

"Yeah, I've lost about 20 pounds and I have been working out at the gym after work. I also quit smoking pot. It didn't look well on me." He was always high in college. They had all smoked a lot of pot but Sam figured he was a lifer.

"I figured you could come back to work with me for the rest of the day and you can stay with me until you figure out what's going on," he said, grabbing her suitcase and leading her out to the parking lot. "What is going on by the way?"

"I just sort of picked up and left. I decided I am going to make my dreams come true. I am not going to sit on my ass, in that horrible place, and be surrounded by a bunch of losers waiting to make a pass at me. I want to be where the action is and where the sunshine is," she said, as she tilted her head back and soaked up the April rays. It was a warm day in LA. The hot sun felt good on her nervous and chilled body. She was so sick of the cold, Midwest temperatures. It was so exciting to be in this town. The endless possibilities and the breathtaking risks she was ready to take, all had her head swimming.

"You didn't tell anyone where you went?" Bob asked.

"Nope, I didn't want to listen to anybody tell me I was making a mistake and my chances here were slim and blah, blah, blah." She also figured no one else really gave a shit where she was.

They were on the freeway heading to the studio. She let the wind rip through her hair. As of this moment she felt like a new woman. Hell, she could be a new woman. She could be whoever she wanted to be. This was new territory and these were people who knew nothing about her. Except for Bob, but he wouldn't try to stand in her way. He knew her to well.

When they arrived at the studio she was almost in shock. It was nothing like she pictured. It was more like a small warehouse in the middle of a parking lot.

"I know what you are thinking. But you have to remember that this isn't NBC, it's a private studio."

"I knew that," she said trying to hide her disappointment. This wasn't the place she was going to run into anybody helpful. But, she reminded herself, you never know.

They went inside and he introduced her around. The inside was more of what she had in mind. The bright lights, the cameras, the people running around shouting out directions and orders. Bob told her about what he did and let her stand beside and watch and even help out during the day. By the end of the day she was exhausted, yet still enthralled with the whole scene. She had a feeling she was really going to like it in L.A.

CHAPTER 3

That night, they feasted on lobster and shrimp. Sam was so full at the end of the meal that she felt like she would explode. After dinner they went dancing. It felt like old times for Sam because almost every Thursday night in college they all went to a dance club near the campus. She saw a few low profile celebrities. A few guys with small parts in Soap Operas and a couple of girls she had seen in music videos. She was a little disappointed, after all this was L.A., and movie stars should be swarming the streets and clubs.

They left in the early a.m. Sam would stay with Bob until she got her agenda figured out. Little did she know someone else had an agenda already planned for her.

Saturday morning proved to be difficult for them both until about noon. Sam had taken the bedroom and Bob had slept on the couch. He didn't really have his own apartment. He lived in his uncle's guesthouse free of charge, which allowed him to save up most of his money. By the typical bachelor atmosphere, Sam guessed he must have a lot of money in savings. Luckily she had quite a bit of her own money, but she knew it wouldn't last long there.

After lunch they went downtown. Bob knew a guy who did some photography on the side, and he figured it would be a good place for Sam to start. She would get some head and body shots at about the third of a cost of a professional, but with the same quality. But first they went to the studio and had Anna, one of the makeup artists, fix Sam up to be photo perfect. Then the hairstylist went to work. Her hair was already a beautiful chestnut color with some natural highlights from the sun so no color was needed. He just put some mousse in her curls and teased it for a glamorous look.

When they walked toward the small, second story studio in a rough part of town, Sam was hesitant. She immediately noticed the hookers standing on the corner and the dealers looking for buyers. This certainly wasn't a place that gave the impression of professionalism. But her thoughts changed as she walked up the stairs and into Jimmy Berg's studio. The pictures on the wall declared otherwise. Pictures of Christy Turlington, Niki Taylor, Kate Moss and a few select others graced the walls. The camera equipment was incredible and Sam reminded herself of the old saying, "Don't judge a book by its cover".

Afterwards, Bob asked her opinion of Jimmy.

"He was great, but I kind of felt weird posing and all. I actually felt like a dork," Sam laughed.

"That's what this place is about, Sam. You have to do things that make you feel that way and you have to be good at not showing those feelings and being totally into the moment. That's what will separate you from half of the other people out there trying to get into this business. The rest depends on your looks."

"Seeing those pictures of all those models on his walls really made me feel average and plain. I don't compare with what is already out there." She was starting to get depressed just thinking about what she was up against.

Bob stopped her and grabbed her lightly by the arms.

"You have it, Sam. You are beautiful, you aren't plastic like those girls and you don't suck dick for a living either. Be yourself, and promise me you won't fall into the Hollywood trap."

"Okay I promise." He was so serious the way he looked at her that she felt almost whole for a minute, like someone actually cared about her well-being.

After a few minutes of an awkward moment for both of them they went on their way. He decided to take her to the Chinese Theater so she could compare her hands with her long time idol, Marilyn Monroe. Little did she know that her hand size wouldn't be the only thing she had in common with Ms. Monroe.

CHAPTER 4

She hadn't been to work for a few days and nobody had heard from her. He couldn't remember that girl's name she was always hanging out with. He went to her house and her dope head cousin was so out of it that she probably didn't even know Sam was gone. He couldn't believe that she vanished. That nobody knew where she went.

Not a word to anyone. It figured that she would turn out to be just another typical bitch, only after one thing. Well, she took him for granted and this time it really pissed him off. He was going to make her pay for what she did to him. Nobody made a fool out of him.

He was trying to remember that guy's name that she had told him about. Bill, no. Bryan, no. Bob, yeah, that was it, Bob. He knew just who to call to find Bob.

It had been at least a week since she had been high and she was feeling it now. She was sluggish and she didn't want to get out of bed. At least it was Monday and Bob had already gone to work so he wouldn't suspect anything by the way she acted. It was almost 11:00. She had been asleep since 9:00 the previous night, but she felt like she could sleep another 10 hours. That's what drug withdrawal did to you. She really needed to find a connection here. It shouldn't be to hard, all she had to do was walk down the Sunset strip and she could probably get anything she wanted. She threw some clothes on and decided to do just that.

❧ ❧ ❧

Bob took his lunch early and decided to call Sam. She didn't answer the phone at his home and he didn't know if she was just not answering, or if she was out looking for a place to live. He hoped it was not the latter, because he really enjoyed having her around. It was just like old times. They got along so well and it was great to have a real friend around again.

Ever since he, and his latest girlfriend Jennifer, had broken up, he had been lonely. The decision had been mutual, after two years together their goals changed. They finally just grew apart and he knew he would never be happy unless he was doing what he was doing now. Working behind the scenes and bringing it all together was like having an anonymous success. He was proud of every commercial he had worked on and it really was a boost for his ego to know what he had done, even if nobody else did. One day he knew he would take over the studio and have the name to go with the success but until then he was happy where he was.

CHAPTER 5

After hanging out in one of the sleaziest bars she could find, the bartender, of all people, finally hooked her up. She bought a gram of crank and figured she could make it last for a while. She couldn't wait to get home and cut a line. She grabbed the bus and ran the quarter of a mile home from the bus stop. It was like being a child again and getting a new toy. She opened the door, slamming it behind her and threw her purse on the couch. She pulled out her bindles and looked at it. The stuff was pure white, which meant it had been cut with something. She had been ripped off. This was not a good time for this to happen. She was going through withdrawals and this was not what she needed right now. If she had a gun she probably would've stuck it in that bastard's mouth for fucking her over. But being that she didn't, she was going to have to go back down there and take care of this problem some other way. She picked everything up and ran back to the bus stop. When she got to the bar she was out of breath and the bartender was gone.

She went outside and slid down the side of the brick wall and cried. She really needed to get high and above that, she really needed it so Bob wouldn't know anything was wrong. How could she do that if she couldn't get high? She had no energy and she felt like shit all the time. Sooner or later he was going to catch on.

"Is something wrong pretty lady?" The voice came from overhead.

"It's a long story." She tried to smile as she stared up into the shadow that was blocking the sun but she started to cry again.

"Boyfriend or girlfriend problem?" You never knew these days.

"I just moved here and I was looking for something and when I found it I got ripped off. Now I can't find the guy who ripped me off." At this point she was so upset and angry that she didn't care who she told.

"Aha, you must've bought something from Joe in there." He pointed to the door of the bar referring to the bartender who had ripped her off.

She looked him in the face, not sure if he was a cop or not. But he didn't look like one. She couldn't see his eyes through his dark glasses but he was well built, about 6'1" with short, kind of spiked, coppery brown hair and a goatee. He wore black jeans and a black t-shirt-through which Sam could see his very toned abs. He had a beautiful smile and wonderfully straight white teeth. She figured he was either a weight lifter or a musician.

"Well, if you are looking for what I think you are looking for, then I have a really good contact who won't rip you off."

"You aren't going to kill me or rape me or kidnap me are you?" She half laughed as she said it but she was getting desperate. She might as well consider this a lucky break. After all if it came down to it, he was definitely fuckable.

He held out his hand and smiled at her, "I'm James. I promise not to do any of those things."

"My name is Sam. Short for Samantha." She took his hand and he pulled her up off the ground. "Thank you." He had a nice strong grip and he put his hand on her back as she stood up. He seemed too nice, and actually gentlemanly, to be getting her hooked up with some crank. Of course it could be a farce. He didn't actually say he was going to get her some.

They walked to his car. He had a black '69 Mustang Fastback.

"Wow! That's a really nice car for a dive like this," Sam remarked as she inspected the car. The license plate said *Cruel* and she hoped it wasn't a nickname given to him for the way he treated women and animals.

"Yeah, well I'm into classic cars and classic women. Besides I like the atmosphere and the people here, with the exception of Joe." He pulled out of the parking lot and headed north. "So what did he give you anyway?"

"Wha-who?" She was still in sort of a daze. "Oh, Joe?" She hadn't even known the kid's name until James told her. She pulled out one of the bindles and unwrapped it slowly as not to spill it on the seat. He licked his finger and dipped it into the mixture then he stuck his finger on his tongue.

"Painkillers." He replied.

"How do you know that?" She asked him.

He looked at her with one eyebrow raised. "Experience."

"Well, when I ran into my living room and opened this up you can imagine my shock. I knew by the color," she stated.

"Yeah, good ol' Joe. He did that to me once. I came back after closing and fucked him up so bad he's still trying to make it up to me. He's just a piece-of-shit kid trying to be a big time pusher. He really doesn't know his head from his ass." Seeing that had made her feel worse he added, "He talks a good talk though if you don't know him."

"Yeah," she sighed.

She was so pretty. Her chestnut locks blew in the wind. Her bright green eyes still sparkled from the remnants of the tears. Her freckles just dotted her nose and her cheeks ever so slightly, adding to her innocence. He felt sorry for her, yet he wanted to take her home and make love to her like there was no tomorrow, even though he hadn't known her for more than 15 minutes. Women rarely had that effect on him. He was so careful because most of the women in this town were either insane, or just plain crazy. She did drugs, but so did he and she obviously wasn't a junkie or the signs would be showing. You just couldn't hide that pitiful need for drugs.

As if she could read his mind she said, "I don't want you to think that I am some major drug addict, its just that I got the feel for speed several months ago and I like it-you know? I came here a few days ago and I am staying with my best friend from college and I ran out. I have been trying to fake my energy and pretend that I feel great but it's getting difficult. I don't want to get out of bed and I feel like shit all the time. I want to quit, but now is not a good time."

"I take it your friend doesn't know about this little habit of yours?"

"No, he doesn't and I'd like to keep it that way. He has done a lot for me and I would hate to disappoint him." It was bad enough she felt that way about herself.

"He?" He asked, as hope flew out the window.

"Yeah, we are the best of friends and I think it's because there is no more interest than that for each other. I love him to death but not in that way."

"Oh." Hope flew back in. The guy must be gay to not want to fuck this woman sitting next to him. "Well, here we are." He pulled into the driveway of a charming little home in an even more charming neighborhood. It somewhat resembled Pleasantville.

She looked at him and he said, "My parents are in real estate. Fortunately for me or I would be living in a dump."

"Oh, so you are a rich kid with a drug habit."

He laughed at her as he got out the car. He came over to open her door but she was already out. He unlocked the front door and she walked into an even more incredible three-bedroom house. The entry stepped down into a sunken living room. He had two coffee-colored leather couches that complemented the beige carpet and an enormous entertainment center with a full surround sound system. The kitchen was off to the left and the bedrooms and bath were on the right. Straight through the living room was an outdoor patio with a hot tub and a small, but nicely groomed yard.

"No girlfriend?" She asked, hunting around for signs.

"Not in two years." He answered proudly.

Great, she met another loser. If he were wonderful he would already be hooked up.

"No, I am not a loser," he said reading the disappointment in her eyes. "My last girlfriend was a real bitch and she left a bad taste in my mouth. So I am very careful. I do date though."

"Well, that's good," she said, a little bit relieved but still cautious.

Bob came home later that afternoon but she wasn't there. He was a little worried because he thought she would have left a note. He had to go out and do a late night shoot. Before that he was going to go to the gym and then to dinner with some friends. He was hoping she would be able to go, but maybe she was out breathing in the life in the big city. She had always been an adventurer. He left her a note saying he wouldn't be back until late and that he would see her tomorrow. Could they get together for lunch? He left the note on the bar and walked out stepping on the bindle that was on the floor.

CHAPTER 6

"Do you want something to drink?" He asked. "I have soda, iced tea, water, beer."

"A bachelor with iced tea? Unheard of, but I'll have that," she said, as she took a seat on the sofa.

"Quit stereotyping," he said, as he brought her a glass and set it on the table. Then he reached into his entertainment center and took out what looked like a normal shelf but was really a hiding space for his stash.

"My parents come by unexpectedly sometimes so I have to be careful." He put down the shiny mirror and poured out some crank. It was a nice, butter cream yellow with lots of rocks. He cut it up and made it smooth and then formed a long line for her. She snorted half of it, with the glass straw, through one nostril and the other half through the other nostril. She lay back on the couch and asked him if he had a cigarette.

"I don't smoke."

"Neither do I but when I'm high, I love the taste of a cigarette."

"We can go down to the liquor store and get some," he offered.

After he did his lines, he put the stuff away, grabbed a bindle and shoved it into his pocket. "Lets go have some fun."

They left the house and she felt so wonderful she wanted to do anything-including him. On the doorstep she kissed him and told him thanks. As she turned toward the car he gently grabbed her arm and kissed her back. Her mouth was so soft and she sucked on his lips ever so gently.

"Unlock the door, let's go back inside," she whispered, her lips just brushing his.

He did as she asked and she put her hands on his face and kissed him again. He unbuttoned her shirt, as she did his, and before long they were in the bedroom. He kissed her whole body and when he reached her wetness, he devoured her. She shuddered as she came, never remembering an orgasm that intense. She rolled him over and took him in her mouth, sucking with all her strength. He pushed her off and then sat up, leaning against the headboard. She straddled him and brought them both to full orgasm within minutes. After a small pause, he rolled her over and entered her again. She wrapped her legs around him and they moved to a silent beat until immense pleasure took them once again. This time worn out, he rolled off of her, watching her as he traced the outline of her breasts with his index finger.

"That was incredible," he said, his breath heavy.

"Yeah, I feel wonderful," she replied. She hadn't had sex like that in a long time. She kissed him again biting his lip ever so gently as she pulled away. "Let's go do something almost as fun as that was."

"What happened to the energy-less sap I found less than two hours ago?"

"My batteries have been recharged, my hard drive has been rebooted," she laughed, getting out of bed and throwing her clothes on.

"Right behind you," he said, knowing this could be the start of something very exciting for him.

CHAPTER 7

They went to a pool hall downtown and before Sam was even ready to go home, it was already midnight. She decided, rather than risk waking up Bob, she would just stay the night with James. He was so cool and fun to be with. Of course, once again, it could be the drugs that led her here, but she didn't think so. There was something different about him. She actually found herself genuinely having a good time, plus she was so attracted to him. She couldn't wait to get home and have him again.

They headed home and before the car even hit the street, she unzipped his pants and brought his hardness into her mouth. He had never had anybody do it quite the way she did. It was more sporadic than rhythmic. He could barely stay on the road he felt so good. When he came he thought for sure he had died and gone to heaven. When she got back into her seat and put her seatbelt on she said, "I hope you saved some of that excitement for me."

"There's plenty more where that came from."

They pulled into his driveway and before he could even get out of the car she straddled him.

"I can't wait another minute, make love to me now."

He unbuttoned her blouse and she unzipped his pants once again. She was surprised to find that he was ready to go again. She rode him fast and hard like a cowboy on a bull. His strong hands gripped her back and helped move her body to the rhythm she had created. Then she put her mouth on his and they both came with such intensity that had anybody walked by the car they would have seen it moving.

"You are so incredible," he breathed, reveling in the bliss that he felt.

"Hmmm, you too." She was completely fulfilled and absolutely exhausted. She put her head on his chest and was so comfortable that she could have fallen asleep in his arms right there.

"C'mon, let's go to bed." He lifted her up and carried her inside the house.

"You wouldn't happen to have a t-shirt I could borrow, would you?" She was so shy and innocent in the way she had just spoken to him, that had he not known otherwise, he never would have believed he had just had wild, incredible sex with her five minutes before.

He threw her a t-shirt from the oak dresser under the window. "Judas Priest, huh? The only people I know who like Judas Priest are wanna be guitarists."

"Well, it just so happens that I am a guitarist in a heavy metal band."

"Really?" She smiled at him as she removed her clothes and slipped the t-shirt over her naked body. "Have I heard of you?"

"Not yet, but you will." He couldn't take his eyes off of her. "We are getting ready to cut a record. We meet with the label execs next month."

"That is way cool. Will you forget about me when you become rich and famous?" She asked, hoping he was about to embark on something big because she had always wanted to be with someone famous.

"Never, ever, could I forget you darlin'."

She snuggled up to him and was asleep within minutes. She hadn't felt this good in a long time.

❦ ❦ ❦

Bob walked into the house at a quarter past one. He was careful to be quiet and not wake Sam, even though he was dying to talk to her. He thought about waking her up but he figured he would talk to her the next day. He was exhausted and he had to be back at the studio at 7:30. He curled up on the couch and fell fast asleep.

CHAPTER 8

❈

James took Sam home in the morning. He had to go practice with his band and then go to work. She found out that he was a bartender at a place called *HotShots*, a local and very trendy bar. She kissed him a long goodbye when they pulled into the driveway.

"Will I ever see you again?" He asked, as she pulled away and opened the door.

"Do you want to see me again?"

"I'll call you when I get home from work," he smiled as her long legs lingered between the car and the driveway waiting for his answer.

"Okay. See ya." And with that, she bounded out of the car. She smiled and waved at him and after he drove off she ran into the house and opened the bindle, cut a line and took a snort. He had given her some crank to take home and last her awhile. She figured it would be gone in two days.

She noticed the note on the counter and called Bob at work. When she reached down to get the phone she saw the bindle on the floor. She picked it up, flushed the contents down the toilet and burned the paper in the sink with her lighter. Hoping he hadn't found it, she dialed his cell phone.

"Hey what's up?" She asked.

"Not much, how are you today? I'm sorry I didn't wake you last night but I got home late and figured you were tired."

So, he didn't even know she hadn't been there. Nothing to explain then. "Oh, that's all right I was pretty tired anyway but I feel great today. Do you want to go to lunch?"

"Why don't you come down around 1:30. I'll send a driver from the studio to pick you up."

"Sounds good, see you then. Bye." She hung up the phone wondering what she was going to do with herself for the next four hours. She started cleaning the house and before she realized it, it was already noon. She took a shower and fixed herself up and by the time she was done the doorbell rang.

"Just a minute," she called as she headed toward the door. She opened the door and there was a bouquet of red and white roses on the doorstep. She reached down to pick them up and when she stood up again, James was standing in front of her.

"I missed you already," he said. "I have to go to work now, but I want to see you later."

"Call me when you get home."

He had a better idea. "Here's the key to my house, be there at 11:00." He dropped the key into her hand, folded it up and kissed her wrist.

"The key already huh? You don't even know me, but you trust me?" She stood there stunned. She was hoping this wasn't moving too fast. She didn't want this to be another relationship based on good sex with nothing else to offer. No, she'd had her fair share of those. She was so intoxicated with him though, that she couldn't say no.

"I know where to find you if you do anything crazy." He was already at the car opening the door.

She walked inside and put the roses on the counter, luckily they had come in a vase because she knew she wouldn't have found one in the apartment. They gave the atmosphere a nice touch especially after she had cleaned so thoroughly. It looked like a whole new place.

The doorbell rang again. Half expecting James to be standing there again she swung the door open. Unfortunately, this time it was only the driver. She grabbed her bag and locked the door behind her. It took about 25 minutes to get to the studio with all the traffic. When she got there, Bob was outside smoking a cigarette.

Her mouth watering, Sam pulled it out of his hands and took a drag.

"Since when did you start smoking?" He asked. She had always given him a hard time in college for it.

"Since I wanted to," she said as she inhaled it. Man, she loved a cigarette when she was high.

"Well, I thought we could go across the street to *HotShots* and have lunch there, if that's okay with you."

Almost coughing up a lung, Sam turned around and sure enough, kitty corner to the studio on the main street, was the bar James worked at.

"Well, I..."

"C'mon I'm starved," he said grabbing her hand. "Besides I know the bartender and I think he's right up your alley."

They walked in and James was just opening up the bar.

"Hey bud," Bob said to James. "I have somebody I want you to meet."

"Actually, I already..." James looked up and saw Sam standing in front of him. The look on her face showed him that he shouldn't finish his sentence.

"Hi," he said to Sam. Trying to act as if he didn't know her from dirt.

"Hi, I'm Sam," she said in that sweet, shy 'little 'ol me' voice she sometimes used.

"Can I show you guys to a table?" He asked, grabbing some menus. He sat them at a table near the bar so he could look at her. He pulled her chair out for her and then handed her a menu.

"Can I bring you an iced tea?" He asked, and winked at her when Bob wasn't looking.

Later when Bob went to pay the bill, and ask James what he thought, James asked if he could take Sam out that night.

"Don't ask me, she's the one who would have to go."

"Well, just don't expect her home tonight," James said, and smiled a devilish grin.

※　　　　　※　　　　　※

He had two leads from some junkies through a contact of his own in California. Neither had panned out though. She had to be there. He knew that was the only place she would have gone. She was so big on becoming famous. He had been so sick of hearing about her dreams. He just wanted her to want him and to want to be with him. Was that too much to ask? She had turned him into the cops and then she had drained his bank account while he sat in a cell for five days. He had gotten out because she skipped town and there were no witnesses who saw him do what she accused him of. Of course, it was a small town and that didn't stop the rumors. His reputation was ruined now. He would find her though and when he did she would be sorry.

CHAPTER 9

❀

She awoke drenched in sweat. Her fists were balled up so tight that she couldn't unfold her fingers for a few minutes. James had grabbed her and held on to her because she was screaming and cursing so loud that she had startled him awake. When he finally got her to calm down and take deep breaths, she was fully awake but couldn't remember anything.

"Shhh," he said as he rocked her in his arms and brushed his fingers through her hair. Her sobs were stifled now and she was completely relaxed in his arms.

She had been having the same dream frequently but this was the first time she had woken up screaming. She was really embarrassed because now she would have to explain this to James and she didn't want him to think badly of her. Fortunately, she wouldn't have to explain it tonight, because before long she was asleep again, folded safely in his strong arms.

🍁   🍁   🍁

He awoke to the smell of breakfast cooking. Before he could even get out of bed, she had brought a plate into him with bacon and eggs and juice. She was wearing a purple g-string and nothing else. Her round breasts were so firm and so beautiful. Her nipples were hard, and as she bent over to give him his plate he grabbed one with his mouth. Putting the plate and the glass aside he grabbed her and rolled her over into the middle of the bed. He devoured every inch of her glorious body. He brought her to orgasm with his magical fingers and then he grabbed her hips and pulled her down on top of him and she rocked him so hard her head was spinning when they were through.

"Holy shit," he said.

"Was it as good for you, as it was for me?" She huffed, nearly out of breath.

"Better."

After gaining her strength, which had been all but drained out of her body, she got up and grabbed the box off the nightstand. While he was still lying down, she poured the powder onto his stomach and formed a line with a credit card. She took the straw to her nostril with one hand and, while plugging her other nostril with a finger, she snorted. She threw her head back and swallowed the drain.

"Want some?" She asked, rolling onto her back and handing him the supplies. He snorted a small line and when he was done, he ate his breakfast.

"How can you eat when you are high?" She asked, wishing she had a cigarette.

"It doesn't affect my appetite." He looked at her body. He hadn't realized how thin she actually was. "I wish you would eat something, though. I haven't seen you eat since I met you."

"I eat all the time," she said. "Besides, you've only known me for two days." It was true though, she hadn't eaten much since she'd been there and she already had lost another five pounds.

When he was done with breakfast, she asked, "care to join me in the bath?"

"A bath?" He mocked her. "I haven't taken a bath since I was seven."

"It's good for the soul. Plus it reduces stress."

"You should be one to talk about what's good for you. Did you know that drugs aren't?"

"Yes, silly. C'mon. I'll wash your hair."

She ran a bath and poured bubbles in.

"Obviously you had this planned because I don't believe I keep bubbles in the house."

"Yeah, I bought them yesterday. When I first saw your bathroom I wanted to live in it."

They got into the warm bath. He had a two person jetted tub that was surrounded by deep aquamarine tile and glass block on two sides. He also had a corner shower with a clear glass door and two pedestal sinks with oval mirrors hanging above them.

"The whole time I've lived here I have never used this tub."

"There's a first time for everything. Maybe we should christen it."

She sat on his lap facing him and poured water over his head with a pitcher she had found in the kitchen. Then she poured shampoo into her hands and lathered his head up. She washed his shoulders and his chest and then moved her hands below the water to wash what lay beneath. He was instantly aroused but she didn't give into his temptation this time. She rinsed his head and kissed him on his eyes and his nose then finally his mouth. He grabbed the pitcher and washed her hair, massaging her scalp so well that despite the speed that was in her system her whole body went limp with relaxation. He ran his hands up and down her belly and her chest fondling her breasts ever so gently. He loved to touch her body; it was so firm and so soft. He knew he was falling in love with her, which was crazy to him because he had been so careful not to do this again.

It had happened this way with his ex-girlfriend. Everything happened so fast that before he knew it they were living together in an apartment in North Hollywood. She was great at first but then after a year everything went to hell. She was jealous of the band and the girls that hung out at the clubs after the shows. She started going crazy every time he talked to anyone with tits. She had threatened one of the cocktail waitresses at the bar he was employed at before *HotShots*. They were just friends but she was so damn jealous. He ended that relationship and then moved to this house in a smaller subdivision just outside of Brentwood. As far as he knew his ex didn't know where he lived or worked and he hoped to keep it that way. She never showed up at any of the performances they did which were mostly at *HotShots* on Saturday nights for Battle of The Bands.

Sam turned around and straddled him, which wasn't hard because he had been ready for her since they got in. Hell, just looking at her made him hard. Before long they both came with intense pleasure.

CHAPTER 10

❀

"Do you get the newspaper?" Sam asked.

"Which one?" He was watching her rub lotion over her body. "Do you need any help with that?" He asked, grabbing the lotion out of her hand and rubbing it on her breasts.

"Any one with the employment ads," she said, grabbing the lotion back and finishing her job.

"Do you need a job? I thought you were just a little rich girl with an unlimited cash flow."

"Hardly. My cash flow will run out very fast in this city."

"I'll bring you down to *HotShots* when I go to work. We're looking for a cocktail waitress. Can you dance?"

"Why?"

"You'll find out tonight. You need some short skirts too."

"I have a few of those."

"I figured."

Before they left for work, she called Bob and told him her plans for the day. He told her he would stop by after work.

"How come you never told me that you knew Bob?" Sam asked when she hung up the phone.

"Because I didn't know that you knew a Bob and I didn't know that you and I knew the same Bob. There is more than one Bob in the world. I think I may even know two or three."

"You are such a smartass," she looked up at him with a smile on her face. He had such a perfect face, so symmetrical. It was the kind of face that gave a person a warm feeling inside just by looking at it. She threw her lip-gloss into her purse and then remembered she needed to get something else. "I need to take some stuff to work with me."

"What stuff?"

"Drugs."

"No you don't."

"Why not?"

"I don't do drugs at work and neither should you."

Her Irish temper came to face. "Since when did you get designated my guardian? I'm a big girl and I will make my own decisions." Her cheeks were flushing and she could feel them getting redder by the second.

He gave her a slightly condescending look, "not this time darlin'. Be ready in five because we have to go by Bob's so you can change. I'm gonna go get the mail."

She hated guys like that, willing to give her anything to get her into bed then BOOM-no more. *Well, fuck him*, she thought. She hurriedly grabbed a bindle from his stash and put it in her purse. She went out to the car and got into the passenger seat.

"Ready?" James asked.

"Looks that way."

"Gotta love those strong, independent women," he smiled, pulling out of the driveway.

CHAPTER 11

❀

"Where did you find this one, James? She's gorgeous." Ronnie picked up a glass and wiped it dry. "Let me guess, you must be fucking her."

"Hey now that's not nice. Besides, we make love," he laughed, joking with his buddy who also bartended. He wasn't going to get into explicit details with Ronnie. He was known to have a big mouth and this time James didn't want his life story thrown around the bar. This time it was special.

She was wearing a short, black mini, platform sandals and a sheer white top with the bottom three buttons unbuttoned exposing her silver naval ring. You could see her white lace brassiere through her shirt but it looked chic on her instead of slutty like it would on most girls. She had a little color from the sun she had soaked up the past few days in L.A. and it looked great on her. Her legs were a mile long and she had firm curves from her breasts to her buttocks.

She was currently talking to the manager, Lonnie. He was a really great guy with style and class, and she was immediately drawn to him. He had short blonde hair, blue eyes and he wore khakis and loafers with a blue polo.

"Can you dance?" He asked her.

"James asked me the same thing. What's with the dancing?"

"Every two hours, starting at 6:00, the waitresses get up on the bar and do a little dance. It's part of the happening atmosphere around here. We also have air bands on Friday night, in which I encourage the staff to participate. On Saturday nights, we have Battle of the Bands, and as you probably already know, James' band has won every time for the last three months. I shouldn't even allow them on the bill anymore since they're pretty much professional now, but he has a great voice and they really get this place rockin'. I have to admit I'm very proud of him."

James hadn't told her he was the lead singer. Come to think of it, she really didn't know much about him, but it was time to change that before she got any more involved.

"Well, I happen to dance very well and I am sure I won't disappoint you. When do you want me to start?"

"Today, but you don't have to dance tonight. I'll let you watch for a while, at least until you get the hang of it. You can train with Amber today." He pointed to a girl with about the same stature as Sam. She had long brown hair, which she wore pulled back giving emphasis to her big, brown eyes and full lips.

"I don't think I need any training, but thanks for the offer." She went over to the bar and grabbed a small apron. Immediately, she went over to the first table she saw, which happened to be a table full of good-looking guys and James found himself a little jealous.

"She's a keeper, James." Lonnie walked by and put a hand on his best bartender's shoulder. "Definitely gonna keep you on your toes, though."

"Thanks, Lon," he sighed as he watched her flirt with her customers.

※　　　※　　　※

She had only been working for three hours but she already had $60 in her pocket from tips. A little after five, Bob walked in with a package under his arm. He knew just where to find her, because she had called him and told him about her new job.

"Jimmy dropped these off today. I already opened them 'cause I couldn't wait. They are fabulous, Sam."

Sam opened the envelope and stared at the proofs. They were pretty incredible. She shouldn't have a hard time getting a job with these.

"Wow!" Amber came up behind her. "Those are incredible."

James walked over, curious as to what was going on. By now, several people were hanging over Sam's shoulder.

"What's goin' on?" He asked. Then he saw the pictures in Sam's hand. "Holy shit! Is this you? You didn't tell me you had these done."

"And you didn't tell me you were the lead singer in the band," she snapped at him, still a little ticked off from earlier and feeling a little tired. In fact she hadn't had a pick-me-up in awhile and she was definitely due for one.

"Amber, can you cover for me for a few? I need to go freshen up."

"Sure," Amber said as she took the proofs from Sam's hand.

She walked away and grabbed her purse from the bar. She went into the bathroom and, making sure nobody was in any of the stalls, she chose one and pulled her box out. Once she snorted the line, the tension started to drain, and she felt more energetic. She checked herself in the mirror, reapplying her lip-gloss so it would look as if she did go in there just to freshen up.

She found Bob on her way back from the restroom and asked if they could go have a cigarette.

They walked out to the side of the building and Bob inquired about her date with James.

"The sex was good," she was emotionless as she took a drag off the cigarette.

"You slept with him?"

"Yeah, so what. He is pretty irresistible." She smiled at the memories she had with him. Careful not to reveal any more she said, "How is work?"

"Good, we got another production assistant today. She is really cute, but already involved." He had attempted to ask her out, but she had mentioned a boyfriend. "Oh, and by the way the house looks fantastic. Thanks." He decided not to mention the flowers.

"No problem, I didn't have much to do yesterday anyway. But, now that I've found a job, I can start looking to get out of your hair."

"No hurry." He was a little disappointed that she was talking that way. He enjoyed having her there even though he hadn't seen much of her.

Before they walked back into the bar, she sprayed herself with perfume and put a stick of gum in her mouth, not only to hide the cigarette smell but also to get rid of that nasty drain in the back of her throat.

🍁 🍁 🍁

For the following week and a half Sam stayed at Bob's place. She was afraid she was wearing out her welcome with James and she wanted to keep from losing him. They hadn't spoke much since her first day at *HotShots*, but they saw each other at work and every time James tried to get a moment alone with her she avoided him like the plague. However, she was miserable not being with him. She was high most of the time and she was not sleeping at night. She didn't want to sleep anyway because she kept having nightmares about Greg, and what he'd done to her.

There was a note and a bouquet of roses on the front doorstep. She picked them up and went inside. Before she could even close the door and turn on the light he grabbed her and the groceries and the flowers fell to the floor.

"Sam," his voice was hoarse like he had a cold.

"How the hell did you get in here?" She demanded. It was pitch black but she knew it was Greg without even seeing his face.

"I just wanted to talk to you."

"Look, you need to leave. I'm not interested in you that way."

"Why do you say that? You don't even know me." He backed her up against the wall. His face was about two inches from her but it was so dark she couldn't make out the features.

"I know you've been following me around and to be perfectly honest, I think it would be best if you found a new hangout."

"Got another man? You know, you are nothing but a whore." He had been watching the way she pranced around the bar. She was so friendly with every guy that came in. No, it was more like flirting.

"You have to at least fuck someone to be called a whore and I wouldn't touch you with a toad's dick." She regretted it the moment it came out of her mouth. She had a way of always saying what was on her mind in the heat of the moment. She really needed to quit that.

"Bitch," he yelled grabbing her shirt and pulling her back, and then shoving her into the coffee table.

She looked at him through fear-ridden eyes, pulling herself up off the floor. She finally understood what he wanted, what he had come to her house for. "Now I get it. You thought you were going to get laid for the drugs. That's why you're here. You thought we'd have a little payback session. Do I look like I have to fuck somebody to get what I want? You are fucking crazy, you know that?"

"I won't let you go, Sam. I'll make you see that we were meant for each other. If I can't have you, nobody can."

"I am not yours, you fuckin' freak. Now get the hell out of my house!" She pushed him as hard as she could but he was too strong for her.

He pushed her to the floor, pulled her skirt up and unzipped his pants all in one motion. She could tell he was high by the way he kept snuffling and wiping the sweat off of his brow. She knew he used, but this was a little more extreme than even she had expected of him. After *spilling himself into her he looked into her eyes one last time before taking off. She was so filled with rage that had she had readily access to a weapon she would have killed him. All she could do was lie there and fight back the emotion that was ready to burst out of her. She had shed only one tear. He wasn't worth even that one.*

Just remembering that incident brought tears to her eyes. She got even though. She had made him pay for what he did to her. Then she left. Just took off without warning to anyone. That was it, end of story, and end of her life in Oklahoma.

CHAPTER 12

❀

Saturday morning James finally called Sam.

"Before you hang up on me, let me say something. I'm sorry for whatever I did to make you mad but I need to see you again." He pleaded with her over the phone.

"You didn't do anything wrong." She was so happy to hear from him now that she felt like a fool for being mad at him. "I thought I was wearing out my welcome with you and I was afraid of losing you."

"That's so stupid, Sam. I miss you so much. You have hardly said anything to me at work. It was just one little argument."

"I know, I am just so afraid." She paused, "I just…" With that he cut her off telling her he was picking her up in fifteen minutes.

"I am going out with James." She called to Bob as she slipped her hip slung Calvin Klein's on and a tight white tee.

"Good, will that make you in a better mood?" He had sensed her grumpiness and tried to cheer her up. She was so different now then when they were in college, now she wouldn't even talk to him about her problems.

"Yes." She kissed him on the cheek and then smiled at him. "You know you are my best friend, right?"

"Yeah."

"I am sorry I've been acting so weird. It's just that chic thing and new flings and all that."

She rushed into the bathroom to do a line before James picked her up. She was starting to feel better about life.

When she heard James pull up, she ran out the door and before he could say anything she jumped into his arms and kissed him fully on the mouth.

"I missed that especially," he said referring to her kiss. "Go pack some things so you can stay with me for a while."

They walked inside together and James asked Bob if he was coming to *HotShots* that night.

"Yeah, I may go with the boys and bring this girl that I just met."

"Cool dude. It's about time you meet someone. I've known you for a year now and I haven't seen you with anyone. I was beginning to think you were gay."

The look he gave James showed that he wasn't pleased with his comment. "Thanks a lot, but she has a boyfriend."

"Dangerous territory dude."

"He's out of town and she didn't want to spend the weekend alone. She's new to the city."

Sam came back in the room. "I need to drop my proofs off at the photographer's so I can tell him which ones I want."

"Oh yes, my aspiring actress. We can drop them off on the way."

"Good. Where are we going anyway?"

"It's a surprise. But hurry up because we have to be back by seven."

"Oh yes, for BATTLE OF THE BANDS," she announced.

They dropped off the proofs and went on their way. Within an hour they were at this quaint little beachside restaurant. The outside was very charming. It had a cottage appeal and there were flowers everywhere, in big pots and little pots, crawling up the side of the restaurant. Covering the arbors that led to the eating area out back, which was right on the beach. All in all it was very romantic.

They sat down and Sam had the biggest and best frozen fuzzy naval she had ever tasted. James drank an import and they relaxed in the sun.

"I'm sorry," Sam said as she looked out over the ocean. "I don't have much luck with men. I either chase them away or I can't get rid of them."

"I want you to not get rid of me, Sam." He leaned closer to her and stared into her deep emerald eyes. Even though he was afraid of her response, he blurted it out anyway, "I am falling in love with you. I know it sounds crazy, we haven't even known each other for two weeks but I can't get you out of my mind. You do something to me. It's something that I can't explain because I've never felt this way before about anyone, but I need you."

Tears welled up in Sam's eyes and before she could stop them, they were spilling down her cheeks. James put his hands on her face and wiped them away. She wanted to tell him she loved him but she was too scared, so she bit her tongue. Everyone she had ever loved had left her.

Their food came and they ate. Sam found, in spite of the drugs, she was famished. She had been doing them all day for the last four days and she had never gone that long without giving her body a break.

"I am glad to see you eating. I was beginning to think you were anorexic or something." He smiled breaking up the seriousness that had passed between them minutes before. He noticed how bad she was shaking and how her eyes screamed from lack of sleep. He wanted to tell her to quit using, but he didn't want to make her mad again. He cared so much about her, but he knew this wasn't the right time to bring it up.

"I don't do it that much," she lied pushing the food around on her plate. It was something she did when she wanted to avoid confrontation. "It's just a recreational thing."

"Recreational my ass," he dropped his fork on his plate and leaned back in his chair. "You've been high every day for the last week at least, and I know you've been using at work."

She looked up at him, "it was noticeable?"

"Only to me, I'm sure. But the point is that you can't live on it."

After lunch they walked on the beach for a while hand in hand just happy to be near each other again. Then they went shopping so Sam could buy something to wear for that night. James was even fun to go shopping with. He picked out outfits for her and he didn't care if she showed off her body. In fact all the outfits he chose were pretty risqué. He goofed around trying on hats and fur coats and he made her laugh constantly. She had never been happier in her whole entire life.

CHAPTER 13

❀

They arrived at *HotShots* at 6:00 so they could eat dinner. James was in his usual black garb and Sam looked stunning in the tight leather pants, black lycra tee and black boots she had bought after lunch that day. All eyes were on her as they walked into the bar. It was packed as it always was. James was proud to be with her because everyone liked her and of course they looked great together.

Sam immediately went into the bathroom when they got there. She had to get her fix. She wasn't feeling very good and she figured that would help. She didn't want James to know because earlier she had gotten the hint that he didn't really want her using anymore. It definitely wasn't something you could build a relationship on. When she opened the bindle she realized she only had about enough for four more lines. She had a little more at home but she was going to have to stretch this out until she found someone who could hook her up. She wasn't going to ask James for any more for fear of disappointing him.

She came back to the table and James had already ordered for her.

"I ordered you a BLT and an iced tea."

"Thanks, but I really am still full from lunch."

"Bullshit," he said. "You need to eat something." She had only eaten half of her shrimp fettuccine at lunch and there hadn't even been that much on her plate.

"Okay," she smiled. She didn't want to argue with him. She was going to meet his band mates that night and she didn't want there to be any tension between them.

At 6:30, after attempting to eat half her sandwich and drinking all of her tea; Jason, Lance, and Kevin all walked in. They made up the rest of James' band, *Cruel*. They were introduced to Sam and she immediately liked all of them. Especially Jason, because there appeared to be an immediate connection between the two of them.

Sam saw Bob walk in alone and excused herself from the table to meet him. As she walked over to the door she saw a sign announcing who was on the bill. A name popped out at her, *Unkle Nasty*.

"Oh my God," she said aloud.

"What?" Bob asked, noticing the shocked look on her face.

"I went to school with those guys," she said pointing to the name on the list. She had been really close with two of the members. Justin, the bassist, had been a really good friend of hers during her sophomore year in high school. Matt, the drummer, had been her first love.

"Oh, in Timbuktu." Bob replied sarcastically. He always gave her shit because there were only 37 kids in her graduating class.

"No, smartass. The school I went to before that." She looked around to see if she could spot them, but the crowd was too large.

"Cool. Can we go sit down now?"

She grabbed his hand and they walked over to her table. "Do you know the guys?"

"Yep, hi everyone."

"Hey, Bob," they all said in unison.

They sat around for a while drinking and talking. Sam found herself involved in a conversation with Jason. She also found herself attracted to him. He had blonde hair with just a little bit of body and piercing blue eyes. He was shorter than James, but very well built. He had really strong forearms, which Sam had always found a major turn on. He also had a really nice ass tucked into a pair of stonewashed Levi's. They were talking about his life and what he did before he joined the band. He had actually been in another band and quit because there was too much animosity between him another member. Sam enjoyed listening to other people's stories about their lives. She found his particularly fascinating.

"Well boys, we better go." James stood up. The show started at 8:30 and they needed to set up. They were always first to play while the crowd was still strong. If the music wasn't good some people tended to leave. He bent over and gave Sam a lingering kiss on the mouth looking over at Jason as if to say, 'back off, she's mine'.

"You really like him don't you?" Bob asked as he watched Sam watch James walk off.

"Yeah, I really do."

They both sat at the table and ordered more drinks. After an hour Sam was feeling really good and a little drunk. She was surprised at how much she enjoyed James' music. He had such a powerful deep voice and he was incredible on the guitar. She loved watching his hands strum the guitar. He was so strong. Most of their stuff was a little too heavy for her taste but the crowd loved them. So did the groupie sluts hanging out by the front of the stage trying to get their attention. James never took his eyes off of Sam though, and that made her feel incredibly special.

Bob went to the bar to get to more drinks. When he was gone Sam heard someone call her name and she turned her head. It took a few seconds for her vision to clear but when it did, she immediately recognized the face. It was Matt. Her heart skipped a beat.

"Hey," he said. "Fancy meeting you here." Though they hadn't lived in the same town for a long time, he never really seemed shocked to see her whenever they ran into each other, which was quite often for two wandering souls. It just seemed like it was fate.

She looked especially pretty tonight and he couldn't take his eyes off her.

"Small world," she smiled. She wasn't surprised to see him either. She knew his aspirations and she knew he would've eventually landed in L.A. She had been in love with him for so long and every time she saw him he broke her heart all over again. But not tonight. She had James now.

She stood up and gave him a hug. They caught each other up with their lives. "You here with anyone tonight?" He asked, hoping they could hook up later. She had always been good for that.

"Yeah, James," she said, as she nodded toward the stage.

"He your boyfriend?" He stared at the lead singer of the band on stage.

"Yep."

"That's too bad." He looked down into her eyes, waiting to see the spark that had always been there. But they were different now. He could see the feelings that she once felt for him were gone. "I have to go backstage and get ready." He stopped for a moment and looked at her again. "If you ever need anything, call me." He wrote down a number for her on a napkin and walked away.

She looked at the napkin and the numbers on it. She looked up at James, who was just wrapping up his last song, and then put her glass on top of the napkin and watched the water smear the numbers into a mess of ink.

"Who was that?" James asked as he took a seat beside her at the bar.

"An old friend, nothing to worry about." She turned toward him and put her arms around his neck. "You were fabulous. I think you have quite a fan base here," she said as she looked at the group of girls that were standing by the stage.

"It's good to have fans, but you have nothing to worry about. I'm taken."

"I hope so."

They sat and watched *Unkle Nasty* set up. James watched Sam as she watched Matt up on stage. He could tell there had been something there once upon a time. He felt a tinge of jealousy spread through his body and he wanted to put it to rest. He reached out and lightly grabbed her chin and turned her face toward him. "Did he break your heart?"

Sam gave a half-hearted laugh at his question, "a few times. He never needed me like I wanted him to. But it's in the past and I'm over it. I never thought I'd be able to say that, but I am."

"Sam, I need you," the words had come out so loud that they startled her. She turned toward the stage and Matt was motioning for her to go up there. She looked at James and the displeasure on his face was evident. She looked back at Matt again and this time he said, "please."

She stood up, "I'll be right back. Let me see what this is all about." Before James could say anything, she was gone.

"What's going on?" Sam asked, as she stepped up onto the stage and followed Matt behind the curtain.

"Our singer didn't show up." Matt gave Justin a disapproving look and Justin just shrugged his shoulders. Apparently they hadn't been together for very long-"so I need you to play the drums while I sing. We'll have to do cover tunes tonight."

Sam looked at him as though he had told her to walk out on stage naked. "Are you crazy?" She looked at their song sheet. "I don't know any Metallica songs…"

"Yes you do."

"…and I haven't played in years. Not to mention the fact that James won't like this at all."

He gave her a bored look and then said, "Since when do you give a fuck what anyone thinks?"

Since forever, she thought.

"Look, you're a glory hound. I don't want to forfeit our chance. This could mean a regular gig for us here." He looked at her again with pleading eyes, "just do it for me this once."

"Like I've never done anything for you?" They stared each other down for a moment. "Oh, alright. But I need something before I can go on stage."

He knew exactly what she needed and delivered as if on cue. When she would go visit him in college she always asked if he'd had any—thanks to one of his best friends from school who had gotten her started on the stuff. She did a line behind the stage. There was nobody else back there, so there was nobody to hide it from.

They all walked on stage, Matt grabbed the microphone and spoke. "In order for the show to go on, we've had to recruit a good friend from the past."

"Good friend my ass," Sam muttered under her breath. "I did everything for you and you used me." Then she walked out on stage with her head held high and figured if this was stardom she could handle it. The guys went wild when they saw her. Most of them were regulars and knew Sam because she worked there.

When James saw her he about dropped his drink. "What the hell is she doing up there?" He yelled at Bob.

"I don't know man. That's Sam, though. She never ceases to amaze me."

"Fuck!" James said and sat down with the other guys. Jason had a hidden smile on his face because clearly this girl was going to be too much for James to handle.

Sam sat down and played and she was incredible. Even Lance looked a little worried about his job as drummer for *Cruel*. The did a few *Metallica* songs followed by a few from *Three Doors Down* and *Motley Crue*—an all-around favorite. Somehow she remembered everything and she only messed up once. Nobody noticed though. When they were done the crowd went wild but she hoped they wouldn't win over James' band.

When she got off stage, Sam walked over to James and sat on his lap straddling him with her legs. He stared at her and asked, "Is there something you want to tell me?"

"I can play the drums, baby. But my heart beats only for you." With that she kissed him passionately on the mouth, obviously not shy in front of the guys at the table.

"Get a room," Lance said. "Jesus Christ. Some of us are trying to watch a show."

"Want to go?" James asked.

"No, I want to stay and finish the show. Then I want to get really drunk and go home and fuck you like there's no tomorrow."

All of the guys stared at her, as if they had never heard a girl talk like that before. Then Bob said, "That's my Sam."

Cruel finished first, with *Unkle Nasty* coming in a close second. It was obvious that Sam's presence in the band had helped because all the guys gave a loud whistle.

They got home at around midnight and Sam did as promised earlier. After exhaustion won over ecstasy they both fell asleep on the living room floor.

Later that night, after moving Sam to the bed, James woke up and noticed the bathroom light on with the door closed. He could here a faint sob and started to go to the door but decided against it for fear of intruding on her space. He lay there and listened for a while, and then when she came back to bed he pretended to be asleep. She curled up to him burying her face into his chest, but for the rest of the night neither one of them slept.

CHAPTER 14

❀

"Oops I…did it again to your heart," Sam sang loudly. She was a big Britney Spears fan, and was dancing on the bed in her t-shirt and underwear, when James walked in.

"Don't give up your day job," he said after watching her from the doorway for a few minutes.

Startled, Sam turned to the door and fell on the bed out of breath. "I know, I can't sing," she said a little embarrassed, "but I'm practicing for the air band next Friday."

"Oh good," he said coming over and crawling on top of her. "Because I don't want to support another struggling musician. And believe me, baby, you would struggle for a long time. However, you can dance better than anyone I know."

"Maybe I should be a stripper," she laughed.

"Definitely not in my lifetime." He kissed her neck and she squirmed. He knew it tickled her so he did it again and she laughed.

"What did you bring for breakfast? I'm starving." She pushed him away before he tickled her more.

"Glazed donuts and coffee."

"Mmm. How about if you glaze and dip something else?"

He didn't have to be asked twice. He tore her clothes off and within minutes he was inside her again. She was so warm and soft, he could stay there forever. She was his salvation and she certainly seemed full of energy that morning. After round one, she brought him back up for round two.

She actually woke up with some energy that morning. She hadn't done any lines since the night before and she thought that maybe it wouldn't be that hard after all, to cleanse her system and get off the drugs. However, by noon she was drained and couldn't get off the couch.

He knew what was wrong but he decided not to feed into her desire anymore. He had gotten rid of his stash that morning when she was in the shower and decided it was time for him to quit as well. Maybe if he didn't do it, neither would she.

"C'mon let's go for a walk or something. It's a great day."

"I can't move. When I do, my head spins and I feel like shit. Let's do a line instead."

"Don't have any. C'mon, go into the bathroom and put some water on your face. You'll feel better then."

She went into the bathroom and locked the door. She knew he was probably just saying that because he wanted her to quit. And she so badly wanted to for him, but she knew she couldn't right now. She couldn't go without that high every day. It would kill her.

Luckily she had stashed some meth in the medicine cabinet when he was sleeping. She turned on the water in the sink so he wouldn't hear her and she poured some out onto the edge of the tub and snorted it with the straw she had hidden with it.

She came out after a few minutes. "Much better," she said. "Let's go do something fun."

They went and got lunch and decided to go to a baseball game. Sam had never had so much fun with anyone before. He was so wonderful that it made her feel guilty for lying to him, but when she remembered what she felt like without the drugs, the guilt quickly slipped away.

🍁   🍁   🍁

"I have been trying to get a hold of you for a week," he told her, the annoyance present in his voice.

"Well, I'm sorry that you finally did," she replied, recognizing his voice immediately. She was not happy to hear from him. She had wanted to get as far away from her family as possible but he seemed to always have a way of finding people. Especially the ones that didn't want to be found.

"Look sis, I know we parted on not so good terms, but it's time to bury the hatchet."

"Fuck you, and your whole family. I want nothing to do with you." She had tried so hard to block that part of her life out and just talking to him was like reliving it again.

"Some of that family is yours too and if you don't help me out, I will make you sorry."

"Sorry for what?"

"Sorry that you were ever born."

He still held a grudge against her. Him, his father, and his father's family—they had all hated her because she was a product of love. After years of physical and emotional abuse, their mom, Jillian, had fallen in love with someone else and had an affair. Veronica's father had been a wealthy businessman from New York and Jillian had worked for one of his West Coast finance companies. They had been having an affair for a year and he had promised to get Jillian out of her tumultuous relationship with Greg's father but he never got the chance. He was found murdered in his hotel room a week before Jillian was to go back to New York with him. She had been pregnant at the time and they had been planning to get married after her divorce was final. To Jillian's surprise he had left a huge sum of money to her in his will. At the time nobody else had known about the money Jillian had inherited. She had put some of it away for Veronica before she was born and it had grown to well over a million dollars which she was set to receive on her 30th birthday. For now though, Jillian sent her a monthly allowance, which along with her tips, was enough to keep her fat and happy. Jillian now lived happily in New York working for the same company but Veronica knew that Greg had connections through his father's family that were capable of destroying all of that.

"What do you want Greg?" She asked, the impatience rising in her voice. She knew he treated their mom like shit and she would do anything to make sure he didn't put her mom through hell.

"I am looking for someone and I need you to find her," he told her as he turned the mental image of her over and over in his mind.

Great, now I have to go on wild fucking goose chase in the city of L.A., Veronica thought, as she listened to the instructions from her brother.

CHAPTER 15

❀

The ride home was silent between James and Sam.

"What are you thinking about?" He asked her, putting his hand on her thigh and giving it an affectionate squeeze.

"You, me, us..., what happens after the record deal. What happens when you sleep with the first groupie..."

He almost ran off of the road. "Are you fucking crazy? I practically pour my heart out to you yesterday and you are thinking about me cheating on you. I really appreciate your confidence in us."

She could tell she hurt his feelings but she couldn't help it. She was so insecure. He could have anybody he wanted and soon that list would include models and actresses. She was nothing, maybe she wouldn't always be that, but for now she felt she had nothing to offer him.

"I'm sorry, I do trust you, it's just that we don't know very much about each other and this is all so great, but what happens when, as the saying goes, 'The Honeymoon's Over'?"

"Okay," he said pulling into the driveway, "what do you want to know?"

She turned in her seat to face him, "everything. Where you grew up, what you're parents are like. I don't even know if you have any brothers or sisters."

They walked through the house and onto the back patio. On his way out, James pulled a photo album from the bottom of his bookshelf and sat down next to her in one of the patio chairs.

"My mom made this for me when I graduated high school. She's kind of corny that way but sometimes I like to look at it." The truth was, he hadn't looked at it in about five years. He didn't like to talk about his family much. When he talked about them though he tended to make it sound a lot better than he had remembered it.

He explained about his older sister who was a lawyer in D.C. He showed her pictures of them growing up and they looked like they were really close. He showed her his first car, a '67 Mustang much like the one he drove now. She saw pictures of the vacations they took growing up and he showed her his first guitar. There were no more pictures after he had turned fifteen.

"Your parents must be really proud of your sister," Sam said.

"Yeah, she followed in my dad's footsteps. For me it was different. I got through school 'cause I knew I had to. Music was my life from the time I was 10. I knew the minute I picked up my first guitar, that that was what I wanted to do." He looked at her, "your turn."

"My life isn't very interesting. Dysfunctional at best. I never lived in one place for long and I was always tossed back and forth between my parents. Because of the lack of emotional support and stability I was really fucked up by the time I hit high school. I had no self-esteem so I thought the only way to get the attention I craved was by sleeping with whoever wanted me. I thought it was the only way to get them to like me. Now, of course, I realize that I was just setting myself up for heartbreak and that they were just using me over and over and over again."

He felt bad for her. He had been one of those guys in high school that used girls. *Take what you can*, had been his motto. After hearing her story though, he really felt like an asshole.

"I know that's what guys do at that age. The girl's hated me because they thought I was sleeping with their boyfriends, which I never did. Any way, that's part of the reason I want so badly to be famous. Kind of like a 'Fuck You' to everyone who ever treated me like shit." She looked at him trying to get some sort of feel for what he was thinking, but she couldn't, so she went on. "After high school, I went to college for a few years and couldn't figure out what I wanted to do with my life. After quitting school, I moved to Oklahoma to see what was out there. I have a cousin who lives there but she's about as useless as a hemorrhoid. I was there for over three months. After the first month I met this asshole who pretty much started stalking me. He was the only contact I had for drugs so I had to be nice to him, but when he didn't get what he wanted from me, he came after me and raped me. So, I left first chance I got."

James stared at her. She had said that last sentence with absolutely no emotion. It just came out of the blue. He was amazed at her strength. Most girls who get raped wouldn't get close to another man for years. She was so strong.

"I don't want you to feel sorry for me. It happened and I'm over it. He was an asshole and I am sure he will get what he deserves someday. Besides, the speed helps me forget about all that bad stuff."

Yeah, but what happens when that doesn't work anymore? He wanted so badly to ask that question, but he didn't.

Over the next few hours they talked about happier things. Favorite foods and colors and hobbies and places, and they laughed and they relaxed, and they had a great time. By the end of the evening, Sam felt as though she had known him for a lifetime.

CHAPTER 16

During the next week Sam had been able to lighten up her drug load enough to sleep at night and eat at least twice a day. James still heard her cry sometimes at night but he never let on that he knew. He just waited for her to come back to bed and then he held her close.

On Friday, Sam had decided to take her pictures into the city to some talent agencies. James gave her the keys to the car and let her go by herself.

"I'm working on a song and I want to go practice it with the guys before work."

"Don't you need the car?"

"No, I'll take the Jeep."

"The Jeep? Oh, that must be another thing you forgot to mention."

"It's in the garage, wanna check it out?"

Sure enough, in the garage was a shiny black Jeep. It was kept washed and waxed and free of dirt.

"I only bring it out in the summer," he told her and she could see why. It was absolutely beautiful. And of course it had an incredible sound system.

"Okay, well I guess I'll see you at work." She kissed him gently on the mouth and then walked out the door and into the start of her day.

※ ※ ※

"Put your name on the list and we'll call you." The fat receptionist behind the desk told Sam in what sounded to be a recorded voice. She looked to be about 45 with mousy brown hair pulled into a knot on top of her head. She wore cheap blue colored eye shadow, way too much mascara and a color of lipstick that must've been leftover from the neon days of the 80's.

Sam gave her a funny look. There were about twenty names ahead of her. "I'm just here to drop off my picture."

"You and everyone else. Now take a seat and we'll call you."

Sam took a seat in one of the metal folding chairs in the waiting room. The room was tiled with that same crap they used in classrooms and there was a dead Fig tree in the corner. She sat there for an hour before her name was called. She walked through a door and down a hallway into a back office and sat down in front of a small, unoccupied desk. The office was small with no windows and there was some sort of certificate hung crooked on the wall with a brown couch underneath it. She assumed that this was the infamous casting couch. She'd heard lots of stories about it. Sadly, that's how a lot of women were forced to break into Hollywood. Of course if the guy you had to fuck was decent, who cared? It was only sex; it didn't have to get personal. But what Sam watched walk through the door wasn't anyone she even wanted to be in the same room with.

"So you want to be an actress or a model?" The guy walked through the door and around to the other side of his desk. He was very heavy, what hair he had was very greasy and his face was offset by about three chins.

Sam almost fell to the ground in hysterics. This was an agent? She could tell this was not going to be a good situation. "Well I really don't care. Whatever gets me a job." Slip of the tongue. *Damn it, why did I say that?*

"Well then, you've come to the right place," he pulled a tablet out from one of the desk drawers. "First, we do a little screening to find out where your interests lie and then I do a little personal screening to see where your talents lie." He smiled at her with big, gross, yellow teeth. His breath reeked of alcohol and cigarettes. He questioned her about several things, taking notes as he went along. Then he motioned for her to sit on the couch with him.

"You know, maybe I made a mistake coming here." She was still standing in front of the desk, afraid any move she made would encourage him.

"No honey, you didn't make no mistake. This is Hollywood. This is what it's all about."

"Uhhh, I don't think so," she laughed. "If I can't get a part legitimately then I don't need one that bad."

"Suit yourself then. But don't bother leavin' a picture 'cause I won't be callin'. Too bad too, because you're so pretty."

All she could do was shake her head as she walked out of the office. She walked into the waiting room and noticed about twenty more girls in the small cramped space. "Unless you want to fuck a fat greasy bastard to get a part, you should probably leave while you still have your dignity." Then she added to the receptionist whose jaw had dropped about a foot at Sam's comment. "I was just curious…how do you look at yourself in the mirror without laughing?"

When she got back to the car she pulled out her little box with a bindle that she had managed to get without James' knowledge from a regular customer at the bar. She poured a line into the box and looked around to make sure she was alone and then she inhaled it all into her nostril. Eyes watering, she tilted her head back swallowing the grueling taste that had accumulated in her throat.

"How in the hell did I find this place?" She asked herself as she put a stick of gum in her mouth. Then she remembered it was called

Classy Cat Talent Agency. She had liked the name. She would've had better luck at *Whore's R Us*.

She had picked another one out of the phone book for today because it was right across the street. This one was simply called *Starz*. She was half tempted to not go in, but then figured it couldn't be as bad as the last one.

And she soon found it wasn't. This one had a nicely furnished and carpeted waiting room. The receptionist was very pretty and polite, and Sam only had to wait for 10 minutes.

"Samantha Steele," the man called from a doorway near the receptionist.

Sam looked up and into the face of a clean cut, well shaven, and well dressed man. She followed him into the office and there wasn't even a couch. She had scored! She didn't dare tell him where she had just been for fear of embarrassment.

"My name is Jonathan Fitch." Then he added, "no relation to Abercrombie and Fitch." He leaned back in his plush, leather chair and with his hands behind his head in an ever so relaxed position he said, "So Samantha, tell me about yourself."

"Please, call me Sam." She took a seat in a leather armchair across from him. "I'm here because I want to be an actress. My whole life that's all I've ever wanted. I want to make the kind of movies that make the viewer feel good when it's over. The kind of movies that you want to go out and buy and keep in your library to watch over and over again." She could've talked his ear off as wired and excited as she was.

"Well, it usually doesn't happen like that, but if you're willing to work at it then I don't see why it can't. You definitely have an all-American look to you, but it's different than most. I like the freckles and the hair. You may want to get a boob job though, but we can talk about that later."

She looked down at her chest and frowned. She had gone down to a B-cup since doing the meth but she didn't think they needed to be any bigger. In fact she liked them.

He laughed at her response. "Don't get discouraged, it's just a suggestion. Besides, you'll get all sorts of criticisms in this business so you'd better get used to it. Now tell me about your experience."

"I did some plays in high school and studied a little drama in college. I don't have anything to put on a resume."

"That's okay, because we can build one as we go along. I have some small parts on some primetime shows and a few commercials in the works presently. Would you be interested in those?" He looked at his calendar on his desk, "oh yeah, I also have a swimsuit calendar coming up. Have you ever modeled?"

"No, but there's a first time for everything."

"Great, then I will put you on the list for auditions. You need to be there a week from Monday at 10:00."

"No problem."

"Good, you'll need to bring a bathing suit. My recommendation would be a two piece that flatters your curves." He handed her a business card. "These people handle the wardrobe for most of these shoots in L.A. Go in and see if they can fit you with something."

"Thank you so much," she beamed.

"Call me when it's over and let me know how it went." He handed her his own business card this time. He had hoped maybe she would call him anyway. He'd like to get to know her on a more personal level.

※　　　※　　　※

She had to start looking for a guy named Bob who worked in a production studio. *Well that shouldn't be too hard,* she told herself. There must be at least 10,000 Bob's in L.A. not including the Roberts and Bobbys. She couldn't believe she had to do this. She hated her brother, but she loved her mother more and she knew if she didn't deliver something to him, her mother would pay the price. There was never a 'far enough away' when you were connected to the Fiori family. She scoured the Internet for commercial production studios and one by one began calling and asking for "Bob".

CHAPTER 17

❀

Sam walked into the bar at 2:15. "Sorry I'm late," she called kissing Lonnie on the cheek as she strode by in a black mini and a pastel blue, baby doll tee. She walked up to the bar and gave James a kiss on the mouth while giving his Levi's-clad behind a tight squeeze.

"Hi, baby," he said. "How'd it go?"

"Good, I have a swimsuit calendar audition a week from Monday."

"Swimsuits huh? Doesn't sound like acting to me." He had heard of a few of these so-called Swimsuit Calendar places and they turned out to be porn industry casting calls.

"You gotta start somewhere," she said as she whizzed by with her tray and order pad to table seven.

James followed her over to the table. "I want to go with you."

"I don't need a babysitter. Besides what's going to happen?"

"A lot of things can happen, Sam, this is L.A."

"He's right," interrupted the girl at the table. "I've seen a lot of crap go down in this town. And most of it isn't pretty."

"Well, I can handle my own," she said and James walked away before they got into an argument.

Sam found Jason sitting at the next table she went to. She smiled brightly as she recognized her friendly new acquaintance.

"How's it going?" She asked.

"Hey, Sam," he said happy that he had gotten one of her tables. "Can you sit down and have a drink with me?"

"No she can't," James walked up behind her. "She just got here."

"Since when did you become her boss?"

"Yeah, since when did you become my boss?" Sam repeated the same question Jason had asked. She didn't understand why he was being so difficult today. First, the calendar, and now this. It wasn't a secret that he and Jason were rivals though. She could tell that just from the other night. They played great together but it was just all a stage act. After the music there was nothing more they had in common.

Again James walked away. She was really trying his patience today. He was mostly angry because he knew she was high and they had made an agreement that she would stop doing it at work.

Sam decided to sit down and talk to Jason just to prove a point to James. He wasn't her boss. He didn't own her and she had a right to make her own decisions.

James stood behind the bar cracking his knuckles and watching the two of them together. They talked for about 10 minutes and when James saw her laughing with him it was all he could do not to go over there and slug Jason. Sam was his and Jason was treading on his territory.

Sam walked up to the bar to get some drinks for her tables. "What is wrong with you today? If you're going to act like this, maybe I should stay at Bob's for a while."

"Fine," he said knowing it wasn't what she expected to hear. "Take the car."

"Fine," she snapped back. That wasn't the response she had wanted from him. She had hoped to get an apology but apparently his stubborn ass wasn't going to give her one.

She decided to really piss James off and asked Jason to come have a drink with her after work. She was bound and determined to make her point to James.

❦   ❦   ❦

Amber found Sam at 7:30 and asked her if she was ready.
"Ready for what?"
"We have a performance in a half an hour, remember?"
"Oh shit! I totally forgot."
"I have our costumes in the car. Let's go get them." Amber told her.
"Yeah, we better get ready soon," Sam said, as she followed Amber behind the bar to get her purse. When she reached down to get it James grabbed her arm.
Knowing full well what she was grabbing her purse for, he shook his head at her. "Nope," he said, "remember our deal."
"Shit," she mumbled under her breath. What was she going to do now? She couldn't go on stage like this.
"FINE," she snapped at him. Then she walked outside to get her stuff from Amber's car. In the parking lot she saw a friendly face.
"Hi," Jason said. "What's wrong?"
"Nothing," she grumbled. "What are you doing here?"
"It's air band night. I never miss a chance to laugh at people."
Her self-confidence immediately shrunk. "Well, don't laugh at me. I'm performing first and last."
His eyes brightened. "Twice? Well, I promise I won't laugh if you tell me what's wrong." He could tell by the look on her face that she was a little mad about something.
"I need a line and James is guarding my purse like it's the fucking Arlington National Cemetery. I can't go on stage without one. I haven't had one since noon and I don't have the courage nor the energy to do this without one."

"C'mon," he said grabbing her hand. She looked back and saw James watching her as she went around the side of the building.

They went to his car and he pulled a stash out from his glove box.

"Hurry," she said. "James saw us come out here."

"Fuck James," he said pouring the stuff out onto a mirror.

She quickly inhaled it just as James walked up to her door. He opened it pulling her out of the car.

"What the fuck are you doing?" She yelled at him.

"I was wondering the same thing. You promised me, Sam," he said as his grip tightened on her arm.

"I didn't promise you anything," she told him, forcing herself to swallow the nasty taste in her throat. She could tell this was good stuff by the way her throat burned. True to the fact though, she hadn't said, *I promise I won't do drugs at work.*

"James, I have to get ready."

"Fine, we'll finish this conversation at home."

"We'll see," she said, pulling away from him.

He grabbed her arm again showing her the car keys he pulled out of her purse. "Now you have no choice sweetheart," he said giving her a cocky grin.

"Asshole," she mumbled as she walked away. She didn't need his car, she could get a ride home with anybody.

"Stay away from her, Jason. This is your warning."

"You don't own her, James. In case you haven't noticed, she is her own person and," he said adding fuel to the fire, "a damn hot one at that."

He took a deep breath and walked away before he punched Jason. He wasn't going to resort to violence like he used to. He had taken several anger management courses to get to where he was at today and he wasn't going to fuck it all up now. Besides the fact that he didn't want to piss Sam off even more.

CHAPTER 18

Sam and Amber got ready in the bathroom. They were wearing baggy jeans and flannels. Amber tied a blue bandana on Sam's head to hide her hair. The beginning of their act required them to look like boys.

"Geez, Sam, have you been losing weight?" Amber inquired, worried about her friend. Sam had a really nice body when she started working there but now she seemed awfully thin.

"Maybe a little," Sam said as she brushed another coat of mascara over her eyelashes.

"Well, try to put some more back on before you make the rest of us look bad."

"Are you ready?" Sam asked, ignoring her friend's comment.

"Let's go get the rest of the girls and go backstage." Amber grabbed her arm as they walked out of the bathroom. She immediately loosened her grip for fear that Sam's wrist might shatter.

When they walked by the bar, Amber looked at James as if to say, "What's going on?" All James could do was lower his eyes and shake his head. She could tell James was hurt. She and James were good friends and they had gone out on a date once. Realizing they had nothing in common though, they decided to stay friends. James had set her up with his band mate, Lance. They had a lot in common and a lot of fun together.

At 8:00, Lonnie walked on-stage and introduced the night's lineup. Everyone had picked a fictitious name for their band and Sam had come up with *Out of Sync* for their band. *Out of Sync* were first and Sam, Amber and the other three girls were the only ones performing that night who worked at the bar. Of course, none of them were new to this because during the week they all had to get up on the bar and dance. It was part of the atmosphere that attracted the customers. The lights went down and the curtain lifted revealing the girls. The music started. "Bye Bye Bye," they all lip-synched.

James watched from the other side of the bar as Sam soaked up the spotlight. *Too bad she can't sing,* he thought. *She could make a fortune.* He noticed Jason was sitting in the first row. He also noticed that he couldn't keep his eyes off of Sam.

By the second verse the girls had removed their flannels revealing rhinestone-studded bras. By the third verse they had removed their baggy jeans revealing very short spandex shorts that matched the bras. Sam had choreographed the whole song with moves she had picked up by watching MTV. When it was all over, she was so out of breath that she had to sit down backstage before she could come out into the audience. Her heart was beating so fast, between the speed and the dancing, that she thought it would explode.

"Are you alright, Sam?" Amber asked as she kneeled down beside her friend.

"Yeah, I'll be okay." She hesitated a moment. "Don't say anything to James," she said, her head still down.

Amber stood up figuring there was nothing she could do. "I'm gonna go sit with Lance until the end of the show. You sure you're okay?"

"Yes," she breathed. "I just need a minute." Her head was starting to spin and she thought she was going to throw up now.

Amber went out into the audience to find Lance. He was sitting next to Jason.

"Hey baby, you guys were awesome."

"Yeah?" she smiled kissing him on the cheek. All the other girls had come out but Sam.

"Where is Sam?" Jason asked.

"She's still backstage. I think there's something wrong with her. She's out of breath and she can't stand up-but she said she's fine. She made me promise not to tell James."

Hearing this, Jason got up and walked backstage. This time James didn't see him.

"What's wrong?" He asked, as he kneeled down by her side. She was hyperventilating and she kept lifting her head struggling for a breath. "Sam," he grabbed her face, "slow down. Deep breaths. Deep breaths."

She looked at him and tried to breathe slowly. After about five minutes she was back to normal breathing. But she was still shaking and her heart was still beating fast.

"Maybe you should call it quits tonight." He knew she still had one more performance to do. "You can save the next performance for next week."

"No, I'll be fine," she took a deep breath. "I just need to go get some cold water." She smiled at him. She didn't want James to find out he was back here with her. She knew he would blow his lid this time for sure.

She walked out into the audience and everything was a blur. It was almost like walking out into a dream. Her eyes hurt and her head was spinning. She just wanted to lie down. She tripped over something but caught herself on the table. She walked into the restroom and Amber went in after her.

"You okay, Sam?" She noticed Sam was shaking and she grabbed the paper towel that was in her hand. "Here let me help you with that." She wet the towel and wiped Sam's face with it.

As she sat down she said, "I must've eaten something that didn't agree with me."

"Sam, when was the last time you ate?"

She couldn't remember. She thought she had lunch the previous day but she didn't know. She had told James she had gotten something to eat before work, but that had been a lie.

"You go back out and watch the show. I'm feeling better now–I'll be out in a few minutes."

"Sam…"

"Just go," she half-smiled. "I'll be out in five minutes."

She sat in there for a little while longer trying to gather herself. When she walked up to the bar, she noticed that James had his head half way down some bar slut's shirt. She asked Ronnie for a shot of tequila with lime and salt as she sat at the other end of the bar—as far away from James as possible.

She licked the salt off her hand, threw the tequila back and stuck the lime in her mouth. She saw James whisper something to Ronnie and figured he was telling him not to give her anymore. That was okay, because she didn't want anymore. The shot hadn't settled well with her stomach.

"What's goin' on? Where have you been?" She asked, as Bob walked up to the bar and sat down on a stool.

"Sorry, I got tied up at work." He replied. "But I didn't miss your performance did I?"

"Not the best one."

※　　　　　※　　　　　※

When it was time for her next performance she heard Lonnie call her name but she couldn't make it to the stage this time. She motioned with her head to one of the people backstage to go out and cancel. When James saw the guy come out and talk to Lonnie, he knew something was wrong. He threw his rag down and ran backstage just in time to meet up with Jason.

"I can handle this," James told Jason, shoving him out of the way. "I helped her before."

"What are you talking about?"

"After her first performance, she was almost passed out."

"Well, maybe if you wouldn't have given her the drugs…never mind just get the fuck out of my way."

James went through the door with Jason behind him. But when they got backstage, Sam was not there.

CHAPTER 19

❀

She walked out the backstage exit figuring some fresh air would help. She was so weak that she had to grab a hold of the wall to make it out the door. She leaned against the side of the concrete building, inhaling the warm air. It was so hot inside that it felt about 20 degrees cooler outside, even though the difference was probably only minimal. She slid down the side of the building to sit down because her legs felt like rubber bands. She was so weak. Then everything went black.

James rushed out the backstage exit. He saw Sam lying on the ground. Jason was right behind him.

"Sam," he patted her cheek a little trying to get her to wake up.

"She needs a doctor," Jason told him.

"No, she needs to quit using drugs and start taking care of herself," James said still trying to get her to wake up.

Bob walked outside after he saw James rush from the bar. He saw Sam lying on the ground. "What's wrong?" He asked, panic rising in his voice. His best friend looked like she was dead.

"Didn't know your dear old friend here was a drug addict did ya, Bob?" James said sarcastically. He was mad at the world right now and he would take it out on whomever he could.

"What are you talking about?"

"I guess you wouldn't have noticed because you don't see her that much. But princess Sam here is a speed freak."

Oh shit. He never even had a clue. She didn't tell him. Why didn't she tell him? For fear of what he would think, he guessed.

"I suppose you have been contributing to it though, right?" he asked James.

"In the beginning…it's how we met."

"But I thought…" he was cut off as Jason came out with a glass of water.

"Here, pour this water on her face. It might wake her up." James looked at Jason as though it was the dumbest thing he had ever heard.

"Go get the Jeep so we can take her home," James tossed Jason the keys to the Jeep. He knew Sam was okay because she was breathing and her heart was still beating. She just needed to get home and get some rest.

※　　　※　　　※

When they got out onto the street Sam had come to. This had happened to her when she first started using. She knew that not sleeping and not eating contributed to her passing out.

"Where are we going?" She asked James, looking around her, wondering why they were in the Jeep.

"You overdosed and I'm taking you home to get some rest."

"No, I didn't overdose," she was afraid he knew how much she had done that day and it was better to deny it before he tried to make her quit completely.

She looked in the backseat and saw Bob, which made her even more upset. He was the one person she didn't want to find out about her nasty little habit.

Bob didn't know what to say except, "I wish you'd told me so I could've helped you."

"Told you what?"

"About your drug habit, Sam."

"It's not a drug habit! I only do it once in a while."

"Now you are just plain lying," James said.

"FUCK YOU! I am not lying. You are not my keeper. I suggest you back off." Irritation rose in her voice. The night was getting worse by the second.

"Or what, Sam?"

"Or maybe I'll just go home with Jason." She stared at him defiantly.

"Sam, you are only making matters worse." Jason told her. He didn't want to be used to get back at James although he had to admit he wouldn't say no to her.

When they got home Sam went into the bathroom to get her stash. She locked the door and took the drugs out of their hiding place. James was pounding on the door yelling at her and she had just poured out a line when he burst in. She tried to snort it but couldn't get her hands to her nose fast enough. He ran over and brushed it all away.

"Are you crazy?" she screamed.

"Maybe, but only because you made me that way!" He yelled at her.

She tried to hit him with her fists but he just grabbed her arms and pulled her to him. She started to cry and hit her head against his chest.

"Please, I just need one more line tonight," she cried.

"No. No more ever."

"No, I can't quit. I can't. I'll go crazy. I will. Please don't take it away. I'll do anything."

"That's so sad, Sam. Are you even listening to yourself?"

She was delirious and she was exhausted. It was so hard to be all of those things at once. He walked her out into the bedroom.

"You don't even care," she whispered, barely able to talk straight anymore.

"I do though, that's the problem. I care about you more than anything and all you care about is getting high."

He held her in his arms and she tried to push away but had lost all her strength. Finally, she gave in and he rocked her to sleep.

CHAPTER 20

❀

The next morning Sam was agitated when she woke. She walked out into the living room and saw Jason and Bob asleep on the couches. It was only six and she didn't know why she was up so early. She figured if Jason was there then his car must be, so she went outside to see if she could find his stash. She saw only the Jeep and vaguely remembered riding home in it. She went back into the bedroom and decided to try to go back to sleep. Within minutes she was.

🍁   🍁   🍁

"I thought we were having a few drinks, not a fucking party," James said when he answered the doorbell. Sam was still asleep from that morning.

Lance and Amber, Kevin and his girlfriend Alicia, and Jason all walked in. James found it odd that nobody was with Jason. He had been seeing some girl named Amy and he wondered where she was.

"Where's Amy?" James asked.

"We broke up," Jason said.

"When?" James asked, knowing full well what the answer would be. The moment he met Sam.

"Few weeks ago," he murmured, mixing himself a drink in the kitchen. "I have to use the jon," he said, as James put some music on.

"Just be quiet, Sam's still asleep."

He walked into the bedroom quietly and saw the sheets lumped in the bed. He walked into the bathroom and saw her in the shower. She had her back facing him and she had the nicest ass he had ever seen in his life.

"Baby, can you hand me my conditioner," she turned around, "oh my God," she yelped, "I thought you were James." Sam was not modest by any means so she stood there with no attempt to cover up any part of her body. "Can you hand me the conditioner?" She smiled at him seductively.

He grabbed the bottle off of the sink and took it over to her and she opened the shower door. Her body was about two inches from his. Immediately he was hard. She was like a goddess. She had the most perfect body he had ever seen. Her skin was creamy white and her breasts were full and firm. Her legs were long and sleek. She had water droplets on her eyelashes and they sparkled in the light.

The bathroom door opened and James walked in.

"What the fuck?" He yelled at Jason.

"She needed the conditioner." Jason grinned as he walked out the door, unable to do what he had come in there to do.

"You're an asshole," James called after him.

"Wanna join me, baby?" She asked, as stood at the open shower door. She was feeling better after over 15 hours of sleep.

As mad as he was, he couldn't resist her and before long they were making love in the shower.

CHAPTER 21

❈

Veronica had been searching for Bob for two days now. She had only made a few calls a day because that was all the time she had. She worked five nights a week at *Baby Dolls*—an upper class men's club on the strip. So far she had found two Bob's. Neither had panned out.

It was Saturday and she was going out with the girls. She had the night off and they were going to a place she had never heard of, called *HotShots*. They had dancing and that night they had live bands. She was excited. She loved bands. She had especially loved James' band but she hadn't seen him perform in a long time. She had hoped his band wouldn't be there because she had finally gotten over him and didn't want to flare up another spark if she happened to run into him.

❦   ❦   ❦

"Are you ready yet?" He asked her.

"Almost," she called through the bathroom door. She was looking for her stash. By now she had forgotten all about the incident of the previous night and couldn't wait to get another line up her nose. *Fuck quitting*, she thought. It made her feel too damn good.

"Looking for something?" James asked standing at the door. She hadn't even heard him open it.

Startled, she jumped up and looked at him, "yeah my chapstick, have you seen it?" She asked, as she walked past him through the door and into the bedroom.

"What chapstick?" He had never even seen any damn chapstick. But he knew what she was looking for. He had gotten rid of everything he had found, including what had been in her purse.

"Well, you know," she cleared her throat, "anyway are you ready?"

"Yeah, let's go," he said, following her out of the bedroom.

She figured she would mix a drink for the road. Since she couldn't get wired, she may as well get drunk. She found the biggest cup James had and mixed orange juice and vodka together.

"Let's go everyone," she called from the kitchen.

❦   ❦   ❦

Bob was driving down Sunset when he noticed a red, Chevy Neon on the side of the road with a flat tire. He also noticed the four girls inside of it. He turned his truck around and pulled up behind them.

"You girls need some help?" He asked, walking over to the car.

"Can you change a flat tire?" Veronica looked out her window and took her sunglasses off. She had big brown eyes and her skin was a light mocha color. Her hair was long and jet black and it shimmered in the sun like a freshly waxed Harley.

"Do you have a spare?"

"I think so," she answered. She didn't know much about cars and she had never needed it before.

"Can you pop the trunk?"

"That I can do," she smiled a bright white smile behind the red lip-gloss that glazed her lips.

Within minutes he had the flat changed and the tire put back in her trunk.

"You'll need to take that in and get it fixed."

"Do you have any suggestions?" She asked.

"Any tire center will do," he told her. He couldn't stand dumb women. But maybe she was just playing him. You never knew these days. Women were so complex.

She thought he was cute and she didn't just want to say goodbye. "Can I buy you a drink?"

"Sure, where ya goin'?" He didn't have anything else planned and he knew Sam was with James at *HotShots*.

"*HotShots*. Want to follow us?"

"Sure." It was going to be a better evening than he thought.

❦   ❦   ❦

Sam and the rest of the gang walked into *HotShots* at 7:00. She and the girls got a table and the guys went up to the bar to get drinks.

While they were at the bar she started looking through her purse. Her box was gone! She couldn't believe that James had gone through her purse. *Damn him!* She looked up just as he was walking up to the table.

"Still trying to find that chapstick?" He looked at her in a way that let her know that he knew what was going on.

"Yeah," she said, closing her purse. She picked up the drink and took a big swallow.

"Hey guys." Bob walked up and gave a Sam a kiss on the cheek.

"What's goin' on?" James asked, before he took a swallow of the cold beer on the table.

"Just picked myself up some women on the side of the road and figured I'd come have a drink with them." He pointed to four ladies at a table across the room. Veronica happened to be sitting with her back to them and James wasn't able to recognize her.

"Want to join us?" Sam asked.

"No way! I don't get an opportunity to hang with four girls by myself very often. I'll catch up with you later." Then he added, "are you feeling better, Sam?"

"Yeah, and I've got to tell you about my talent agent scout out yesterday. But we can talk about that later. Go have fun stud!"

As Bob walked away she noticed Matt standing up at the bar. "Excuse me a minute," Sam said, as she got up and walked over to him.

"Hi. You guys performing tonight?" She asked.

"Yeah," he grabbed his bear from the bar, "our singer showed up tonight. We probably won't be as good as your boyfriend's band but we're here more for exposure than winning." He took a swallow of beer. "By the way, you kicked ass last week. I was happy to see you remembered all that stuff."

"Yeah, well," she gave him a coy smile, "I've practiced on and off over the years."

"Heard you got sick last night after the performance. Feeling better tonight?"

"I didn't know you were here last night." She turned her head, "I'm fine now, I just hadn't eaten very much and I haven't been sleeping well."

"Maybe you're hitting the meth a little too hard..."

She cut him off before he could say another word. "Well, I just wanted to say hi. I'll see you later."

❦   ❦   ❦

At 8:00 the guys walked through the bar and behind the stage. They walked right by Bob's table but James didn't see Veronica sitting there. She noticed him though. And Jason noticed her but he didn't say anything to James. He figured the night would get interesting if she got drunk.

"So Bob, what do you do?" One of the girls at the table asked.

"I'm a production assistant at Sterling Studios," he replied. Veronica never even heard him because she was still starting after James.

CHAPTER 22

❀

"You know what, I'm not feeling very well, Sera," Veronica looked at her roommate. "I'll let you have the car and I'll call a cab. I think I need to go home and lie down."

"Veronica, we haven't been out in ages," Sera said, her cherry red lips in a pout.

"I know I just have a headache and I don't want to listen to all this hard shit tonight."

"Why don't I take you home so you don't have to get a cab." Bob told her. Of the four girls, he had taken interest in Veronica. She turned out to not be as dumb as he had suspected.

"That would be great Bob, thanks."

🍁 🍁 🍁

"We're going to do something a little different tonight. We have a new song that we'd like to play for you tonight," James told the audience. "It's a melody called *Alone* and we hope you like it."

They started playing the song and Sam was sitting at the table with Amber and Alicia. She didn't really pay attention to the song until she heard the chorus.

When the wind does blow
And she's all alone
Can't you hear your baby crying?

She looked up at James on the stage and he was looking right at her. She knew the song was about her. He heard her cry at night when she thought he was sleeping. He had never even come to comfort her and now he was writing a fucking song about it. Tears welled up in her eyes and she quickly walked outside. James saw her leave and it took all he had to not run after her.

She sat outside and went to the car and cried. She hadn't cried this hard in a long time. All the emotions that she had locked away for the last six months had come out. The breakup, the rape, and the fear she constantly felt inside from doing drugs. And then there was James. She knew she loved him. She loved him more than anything. But what if it didn't work out? What was she going to do then? Her heart had been broken so many times in the past she didn't think she could survive another loss.

🍁 🍁 🍁

"Wanna go get some coffee?" Veronica asked, as they got into his pickup.

"Sure, but I thought you had a headache."

"Well, it's better now. I know a nice little coffee house up the street from where I live."

They talked for more than two hours over coffee that night. Veronica had told him about her job and about her previous relationship with James (although she didn't mention him by name). She told him a little bit about her family and that she had grown up in Oklahoma.

"Really?" Bob asked. "My best friend Sam just came from a small town in Oklahoma." He mentioned the name of the town and Veronica almost dropped her cup.

"Something wrong?" He asked her, a little concerned.

"No," she laughed uneasily, "the damn thing just slipped from my hands." Bob could see she was shaking.

This couldn't have been any easier, she thought. However, I didn't think I would actually like the guy. *But families come first right?* she tried to convince herself as she swallowed the lump in her throat.

🍁 🍁 🍁

She wished so badly that she could get a line. She knew she could ask Matt but James would see her, besides he already tried to lecture her about it. She couldn't bear anymore of this emotion. So she went back inside and did the next best thing, got drunk.

Matt was still sitting at the bar when she walked back in.

"Can I buy you a shot?" She asked him.

"You know what happens when we get drunk together," he said, in answer to her question.

"Let's not go there," she said as she attracted the bartender's attention. "Jack, can I get two flaming Dr. Pepper's?"

"Getting fancy, huh. I thought we were just going to do the tequila and lime thing."

The bartender fixed the drinks and Sam downed hers.

"Have you been crying?" He asked, seeing how bright her eyes were. He'd known that look all too well.

"No, it's allergies," she lied. "Jack, can we get a couple of Cuervos with lime and salt?"

By the time James was off stage she had downed three more shots and was working on her second fuzzy naval. Matt had already gone to the back of the stage, so she sat at the bar alone.

"Seat taken?" He asked her, as he sat down anyway.

"Was, but now it's not." She looked at him. She was really quite drunk now.

"Havin' a party all by yourself?"

"No, I was havin a party with an old friend."

"Where did she go?"

"**He** is up on stage now," she told him blinking her eyes so she could focus on him.

"Oh, the heartbreaker. Nothing like stirring up old feelings. Maybe we should go."

"Nope I promised Jason I would dance with him tonight after the show. Besides, you need to be here to claim your prize."

"No, I don't." He picked up her hands and held them. "I think you should stay away from Jason. You are my girlfriend and I don't want you hanging all over other guys," he was trying to be calm about it.

"I've got to keep my options open you know, I may not always be your girlfriend. Besides the fact that you don't own me and I don't hang all over other guys." It took her a long time to get that out. "Jack," she called, "can I get another naval?"

Jack looked at James for approval and James shook his head. He ran his hand over his face in disbelief at what she had just said.

"Did you hear the song I wrote for you?"

"You wrote it for me? I thought it was for your adoring fans." *Go ahead, Sam, push as hard as you can.* She couldn't help it.

"So is this what I get to look forward to? Are you gonna drink now instead of snort lines? Sam," he grabbed her with both arms and pulled her right into his face, "you are going to have to learn to feel things again. You cannot go through life like this."

"I feel it when you fuck me, James." Another cold hearted stab. She didn't know why she was doing this. She wasn't intentionally trying to hurt him.

At that point he pushed her away. He didn't want to be near her. "Have fun with Jason tonight," he said as he walked away.

She got up to go after him just as Jason came up behind her. "Let him go, he's just jealous."

After the bands were done and *Cruel* had won again, the DJ came out and turned the pit back into a dance floor. Jason and Sam were first out to the dance floor. They made quite a pair. Jason really liked the fact that Sam liked to get close when she was dancing and she was rubbing and grinding herself up against him. He had the urge to pick her up, take her outside and make love to her in the middle of the parking lot. His desire quickly faded when he saw James walk up to him. Before he could even defend himself, James fist was in front of his face.

"James, NO!" Sam screamed, bending down to help Jason up, but James picked her up and dragged her out the side door.

He threw her in the front seat of the Mustang and took off. She was so angry with him for punching Jason and making a fool out of her that she tried to slap him once but he caught her wrist in midair and twisted it away from him. At the first stoplight they came to, she jumped out of the car and ran.

"Fuck! SAM!" He yelled after her, pulling the car to the curb. Why was he going to all this trouble over this girl? *Because I love her. Because I've never felt this way about anyone before.* He caught up with her quickly since she was too drunk to run very fast. He ran up behind her and grabbed her arm, swinging her around.

"Why are you doing this to me?" He asked. "What did I do to deserve this?"

Then she threw up.

CHAPTER 23

❈

James held her as she let all of the alcohol go. After the alcohol it was all bile because she hadn't eaten anything again that day. She couldn't even stand up anymore. He picked her up and carried her back to the car. By the time they got home she was fast asleep. Once again, he picked her up and took her inside the house and tucked her into bed.

🍁   🍁   🍁

The next morning Sam woke up with the worst headache ever. She couldn't even lift her head, because every time she moved, it felt like someone was hitting her with a bag of rocks. James brought her some food, but just the smell of it made her run into the bathroom and vomit.

"Close the curtains and leave me to die," Sam said as she slowly crawled back into bed.

"We need to talk, Sam," James told her taking a seat next to her.

"I need to sleep more." She looked up at him, "please. I promise we'll talk later."

The next time she opened her eyes she saw a shadow lurking in the hallway. When she sat up, Greg came into the room. She tried to scream but she couldn't. He came over to her and held her down and he wouldn't get off of her. Then she saw the knife. He brought it to her face and sliced her cheek ever so subtly, whispering that this was just the beginning. She was finally able to scream.

"Get off of me!" She screamed. When she opened her eyes she realized that James had her in his arms and was yelling at her to wake up.

"Wha....?" Startled, she twisted away from him. She was sweaty and breathing hard. He brushed her hair back from her face.

"Whatever it is, you need to deal with this, Sam, so it doesn't haunt you for the rest of your life. You are gonna have to deal with a lot of things in this town because you won't make it if you don't." She saw so much love in his eyes that it brought tears to her own.

"I know, James, but I am scared. I am so scared," she cried.

CHAPTER 24

Sam stayed home from work for three days. She was agitated and anxious. She cried most of the time and hardly even saw James because she was asleep before he got home and when he left for practice. She picked up the phone to call Jason a few times but decided against it. She tried to take the car out to go find some meth but James had taken the keys so she couldn't leave. She was living in her own private hell. When James came home at night the stereo was up loud and she was curled up on the couch on her hands and knees. He always carried her to bed. He felt bad for her but he didn't know what else to do. He knew her drug use was more than recreational, for her it was a way of life and she didn't want to live without it. It would've been easier to just let her go, but he couldn't. He didn't want to lose her. Most of the time she made him feel incredible, like he was the only person in the world. He would do whatever it took to keep her safe.

By Thursday, Sam was ready to go back to work.

"I'm going crazy here. I need to get out and start living a normal life again. You can't keep me holed up in here like some kind of prisoner." She was also very grumpy.

"Okay then, get ready, but don't try to pull anything over on me. I mean it, Sam, 'cause I will be watching you."

"Yeah, yeah," she said as she went to get ready. "Maybe I should stay at Bob's for a few days," she said, announcing her train of thought to James. "I should take my head shots to a few more talent scouts and start looking for my own place."

"Why do you need your own place? You have two places as it is."

"Because I am an independent woman and I don't expect you to support my dying ass while I'm here."

"What do you mean, while you're here? Are you planning on leaving L.A.?" He was confused now. God she confused him!

"No, that's not what I meant." She was getting more frustrated by the minute. "Ughh," she grunted, "just leave me alone."

"You won't make very many tips with that attitude darlin'. I think I know what you need though," he said as he grabbed her and threw her onto the bed.

"I need you and Mr. Rosy Palm to go take care of yourself while I get ready," she answered as she rolled out from under him and went to the bathroom and locked the door.

James fell back onto the bed in more confusion.

🍁　　　🍁　　　🍁

She couldn't decide if she should call Greg and lie to him about Sam or not. She had gone out with Bob that afternoon and decided she really liked him. On the other hand, she had found out Sam was dating James and she was jealous of that. But she didn't know Sam and she didn't want to judge her. After all, she had dumped James three years ago when she found him in bed with another woman. That other woman wasn't Sam, so she really had no reason to dislike her. Plus, the way Bob had gone on and on about her, you would've thought she was a queen.

The phone rang twice and Greg answered it on the third ring.

"Hello."

"Hi, Greg. It's me."

"Did you get the information?"

"Yeah, I found Bob."

"Well, what about Sam?"

She hesitated for a moment before continuing, "apparently she didn't come out here, Greg." She was shaking from fear that he would know she was lying.

"Okay then, thanks for trying."

"I'm sorry, Greg."

"No problem, have a nice life." And with that he hung up the phone.

That was so typical. I don't need you anymore so that's it—goodbye. It was probably better that way. In fact she was glad, she didn't want any contact with her crazy brother. She decided to call the phone company and have her phone number changed. She would call her mother at work and give her the new number with explicit instructions to keep it to herself.

🍁 🍁 🍁

Damn it! He had to find that fucking bitch. She had ruined his life. Now he had lost his job because of her. Or actually because of the anger that he had inside from what she had done to him. He punched another employee during work hours. But the guy deserved it because he had made some snide remark and about taking what nobody would give you. Maybe she hadn't gone to Bob. Maybe Veronica didn't find the right one. Or maybe Veronica was lying. He needed some time to think about it. He was going to have to go to L.A.

CHAPTER 25

On Monday morning Sam went to her swimsuit audition. She and James had an incredible weekend. They watched movies, ordered in and made love all weekend. They didn't go out of the house once. There was no Battle on Saturday night because the last Saturday of the month was comedy night. Sam was starting to feel better. She had even gotten a membership to the gym James belonged to and they worked out Friday before work. She was still struggling a little though, but she was determined to do it on her own. She didn't want to be in a drug rehab with a bunch of junkies. She was beyond that. Her nightmares had come back though, and James had to wake her up more than once to calm her down.

She had found the address of the studio easily. James had wanted to go with her but she had insisted he not. She walked into the brightly painted reception area and gave her name and headshot, which was promptly handed back to her. There were about 15 other girls in there. Most of them were kind of trampy looking. There weren't any really gorgeous girls there. She had thought Jonathan had told her it was a modeling event. Maybe these were just long lost hopefuls.

At 10:30 Sam was called back into an office. She had her swimsuit on underneath her clothes. She had picked out an indigo two-piece

Rio cut with a padded halter-top, hoping to enhance her small bosom.

"What do you do?" A bored guy, behind a poorly made black desk, asked her. He was smoking a cigarette and looked like he had just crawled out from under a rock.

"Excuse me?" Sam asked.

"Rachel and Jeanine, could you come in here please?"

Sam turned around and two naked girls appeared through an adjacent doorway.

"I need you to remove your clothing and pose with the girls," he told Sam in a monotone voice.

Sam stripped down to her bikini and folded her clothes and put them on the chair in the office.

Rock man sighed. "No sweetheart. Take off **all** of your clothes and make these girls happy to be here."

Sam's eyes almost popped out of her head. "Hang on a minute. I thought this was a swimsuit calendar shoot."

"Sure, there will be some swimsuits in there hanging on trees and lying in the sand but this is a *Fantasy Girls* calendar. All the girls in it will be nude and doing nasty things." His smile sent chills up Sam's spine.

Fantasy Girls was a men's publication similar to Hustler but with less class.

"I'm sorry, I must've misunderstood the agency," she started to pick up her clothes.

"Look honey, I have been interviewing girls all day. I have seen no one as pretty as you. Help me out and I'll help you out." He smiled a big toothy smile. His dirty blonde hair kept falling on his forehead and he kept pushing it out of the way with his hand.

"This would ruin the career I am trying to establish," she told him.

"Okay then, what about drugs. Everyone in L.A. uses. Will that change your mind?" He pulled a tray out from under his desk.

"Meth, coke, heroin, pills? What's your pleasure?"

She stared at the bag of meth for a long time. She was tempted to take it. It had been too long since she'd had a good high. She wanted it so badly she could taste it. She didn't know what to do.

❦   ❦   ❦

Jason walked out of the office with the packages. He worked as a courier for a film company. He'd been doing it for several years now. The hours were flexible and the pay wasn't too bad, plus he didn't have to sit in an office or do manual labor for a living. It worked for him while he waited for his music career to take off. He saw the black Mustang parked across the street. He wondered what James was doing over there. He knew that's where *Fantasy Girls* held all of their photo shoots. They had kind of sleazed out the neighborhood. Then he remembered that Sam had a swimsuit audition that morning. He had heard from other girls that this magazine would call casting agents under an alias to recruit fresh meat.

"Shit, that girl just can't seem to keep out of trouble," he mumbled, crossing the street.

"Is Samantha Steele here?" He asked the strung out receptionist as he approached her desk.

"I'm sorry sir, I don't know." She smiled her best smile, blatantly flirting with him as she pushed her cleavage into his face.

"About 5'7, reddish-brown curls with blonde highlights, great body." He looked around. "Certainly you would've noticed," he added.

She just shrugged her shoulders and Jason decided to check it out for himself. He walked into the back offices as the receptionist chased after him.

"Sir, you can't go back there," she called after him.

He opened four doors before he came to the room she was in. She had a straw in her nose and was about to snort a line.

"Sam!" He yelled. She jumped so fast she knocked the tray over with all the drugs on it.

"Baby, what are you doing?" He asked, seeing the fear in her eyes.

"I uh…" She looked at him as tears welled up in her eyes.

"You stupid bitch. You knocked over my tray." The greasy man behind the desk yelled at her. "Get out of here, I don't have room for stupid people."

"Listen asshole," Jason walked over to the greaseball and got in his face, "you are the idiot luring innocent girls with drugs to tramp around in your magazine. You are the stupid one. I am almost positive there are laws against that."

He grabbed Sam and her clothes and led her out of the building. When they got outside she sat down on the curb trying to absorb what had just happened.

"Was I really going to compromise my morals for a line?" She asked more of herself than Jason.

"You were just scared, Sam. You were in a bad situation."

"No, I am an idiot. I can't do this, Jason." She looked at him as he sat down next to her and held her hand. "I was ready to do anything for that high. I won't ever be able to quit. It's going to haunt me forever." She put her head in her hands.

"You aren't an idiot. You are young and this is a fast scene, you need to be careful. I am just glad I happened to be here today."

"Yeah, me too," she smiled at him. "Thank you," she said as she kissed him lightly on the lips. "I have some business to take care of before I go to work. Will you be there tonight?" She asked, referring to *HotShots*.

"Do pigs roll in mud?"

"See ya," she said as she got into the drivers seat and took off.

❦   ❦   ❦

She stormed into Jonathan's office. "You fucking prick!" She screamed, spitting on his wire framed glasses. "Do you realize what I just had to go through for that swimsuit audition?"

"I'll call you back," he said into the phone. "Hi, Sam. Do we have an appointment?" He asked, clearly annoyed by her behavior.

"Do you realize that you just sent me on a shoot for a porno magazine calendar? I was humiliated in front of a bunch of scumballs. Why would you do that?" She asked, her anger seething.

He hadn't researched the shoot. It was only his second month there and he kept forgetting that he had to do that. The porn industry preyed on everyone.

"Sam, I apologize. It was my fault."

"Damn right it was your fault. Maybe I should take my headshot elsewhere, Jonathan. Clearly this office isn't any more professional than the roach motel across the street."

"You've been to Ernie's?" He asked. If she thought he was a prick, he wondered what she had thought of Ernie.

"It doesn't matter where I've been. It only matters where I am going. I came to you and I thought you would help me succeed. Clearly I was wrong." With that said, she stormed out of the office.

He knew she would bring him revenue. He also knew that she would make it someday and that notoriety would help his business take off. He had to get her back. He picked up the phone and dialed the receptionist. "Ann, get me an address for Samantha Steele. Home and work." He was going *to have* to kiss ass on this one.

CHAPTER 26

❀

Sam was so mad she was shaking when she got back in the car. She couldn't believe how close she came to snorting that line. Then what? What would have happened to her then? Would she have been forced to have sex with those girls? Her stomach turned at the thought. It was one thing to have sex with good looking guys who may be able to get you somewhere, but girls—no way. She had nothing against those choosing to participate in that kind of behavior, but it wasn't for her.

She sat in the car, taking deep breaths before she started it. What if Jason hadn't shown up? She owed him big time for that. She still had two hours before work and she knew just what to do for him.

🍁 🍁 🍁

Jason was sitting on his worn out, plaid couch reading a sci-fi thriller when he heard the doorbell ring. He opened the door and saw Veronica standing there. She was the last person he expected to ever be standing on his doorstep. After James had dumped her, she had turned to him. He didn't want anymore from her than the one night they had shared and that had made her crazy. He knew she just used him to try and get back at James. He wasn't into that.

"What do you want?" He asked, looking at her as though she were more boring than watching dust settle.

"Good to see you too, Jason." She walked through the door inviting herself in. She didn't like Jason anymore than he liked her, but she figured he was the only one who could help her.

"Who invited you in?" He asked, staring at her.

"I did. I need to find James."

"So, here we go again, huh? Got to find James because you saw him the other night and it sparked a fire in you again."

"You saw me at *HotShots*?"

"Yep. But I didn't tell James. See the funny thing is, Veronica, that James has moved on to bigger and better things. You won't get him back because this time it's the real thing."

"I am not interested in that, Jason. James and I are through. But, his girlfriend is in trouble."

"Get out, Veronica. I know your sick and twisted games, and they aren't going to work this time." He grabbed her and pushed her toward the door.

"But, Jason, please listen to me…"

"Good bye." He slammed the door in her face.

He didn't really know why he threw her out. He could've cared less about protecting James from her. In fact, if he'd been thinking straight, he probably should've been nicer to her, gotten her back into the swing of things. With her in the picture, James and Sam would surely split up and then Sam would be free to be with him. Another missed opportunity. But he wasn't about to give up so quickly. After all, he'd had plans from the beginning.

꧁ ꧁ ꧁

Veronica stalked off to her car, opening the door and shoving the keys into the ignition. She needed to find James to warn him about Sam. However much it would hurt her to encounter him again, she needed to do it. She knew what her brother was capable of, or maybe she didn't, and that was what frightened her the most. If she went to Bob about it, she would have to give him the whole story and even though she hadn't done anything wrong, she still felt guilty inside. It was better to get to Sam another way. No matter how hard it would be.

❧ ❧ ❧

When Sam got to work she stayed busy so she wouldn't have to explain her day to James. Finally, at 7:00 they both took a dinner break together. She decided to tell the story, purposely leaving out Jason's appearance.

"I think I got a scary taste of Hollywood today and I am not sure if it's for me," she told him as she sat down with her hamburger.

"What happened?" He asked, worried that she had gotten into some kind of trouble.

"First, promise me you won't say, 'I told you so'."

"Okay." Now he knew it wasn't good.

"That calendar shoot turned out to be a *Fantasy Girls* shoot, although, it wasn't so fantastic. I was humiliated by the photographer and coerced with meth." Tears welled up in her eyes. It wasn't an experience you wanted to have, especially when you pictured it all so differently.

"I'm sorry, baby," he sympathized, pulling her toward his chest.

She pulled her head up, "but I did go and scream at the talent agent after that," she laughed. "I don't know if this is for me, James. There seem to be more corrupt and crooked people here, than there are honest and good ones." She started crying again. "This isn't how it was supposed to be. I was supposed to come here and get discovered for my talent and my looks, not because someone wanted me to fuck another girl on the beach." She slammed her fist down on the table outside in frustration.

"Sam, don't give up. We'll get through it. I know you don't want to hear it, but that's what this town is about. It takes the fresh dreams of the young and turns them into smut and filth. Nobody is safe here alone. This town will eat you alive if you let it, but, on the other hand, it can help you grow and make you stand on your own two feet. In another year you'll be able to overlook the bad and focus on what you came here for." He looked into her eyes for a few seconds and then remembering what he wanted to tell her, he said, "on a happier note, how do you feel about going to Las Vegas next weekend?"

Her eyes brightened and her smile was like a gift from God, "Do you mean it?"

"You bet I do. Since we are signing our record deal next week, we've been asked to do a concert with other bands to benefit a charity. We will be playing with *Metallica, Kid Rock, Red Hot Chili Peppers*, and a few other bands."

She pulled herself onto his lap, throwing her arms around his neck. "As long as when it's over, I get to come backstage," she said, putting on her best groupie bit.

"I'll make sure you get a pass," he smiled, kissing her on the lips.

❦   ❦   ❦

Sam pulled into the driveway and saw the living room light on. She pulled out her package and walked up to the door, knocking gently in case he was asleep. Jason pulled open the door and smiled at her as if she had just made lemons sweet.

"Hey," she said as she walked in. "I missed you tonight."

"Yeah, sorry. I got tied up with work."

"Did James call you and tell you the good news?"

"About Vegas? Yeah, I'm stoked," he said, eyeing the large package in her hand.

"I can't wait," she said as she handed him the present. "Here, I got this for you because I heard you talking to James about it the other night and well, I owe you for today."

"Sam…"

"Shhhh, just open it!" She was so excited. She loved giving gifts.

He opened the package and inside was a cherry red, four string, *Music Man* bass guitar.

"Oh my God! Sam, I've been eyeing this guitar forever." He knew it cost a lot of money and he had told her just that.

"Don't worry about the money. It was dirty money gone clean." She watched him pick at the strings and begin to tune it. "So, do you like it?" She asked, hoping he did.

"I love it, Sam." He grabbed her and kissed her on the mouth. Then, silence. As he pulled away they looked at each other. He was just a few inches taller than she was. He leaned closer to her face again, this time slowly, and grabbing the back of her neck, he pulled her mouth toward his. This time the kiss was like fresh drops of rain on his tongue. She put her hands on his face and returned the sweetness he had been craving from her. She glided her tongue around his in a soft, yet firm motion. He pulled her shirt over her head and undid her bra with one hand. He cupped her breasts in his hands while he kissed her neck. She kept telling herself to stop, but she couldn't. She always did this. She got caught up in the moment and had to live with the regrets later but right now she didn't care, it felt good and it felt right. After all, she wasn't married to James.

She unbuttoned his shirt, slowly kissing his chest after every button. He picked her up and carried her to the bedroom, laying her down gently on the bed. He couldn't believe how soft her body was. It was like kissing a feather. And she tasted so good, like vanilla. He couldn't contain himself any longer. He delved into her, like a kid with a chocolate bunny on Easter. She wrapped her legs around him and he thrust into her, causing her to gasp for breath.

Afterwards, the regret came with lightening force. As she pulled her clothes on she begged him not to tell James. "I'm sorry," she said. "This shouldn't have happened." She felt a little delirious as she rattled on to him. "I love James you know. I don't know what I was thinking. Fuck!! Why do I always do shit like this? Damn it!" She yelled as she tried to get her bra on.

He grabbed her and held her. "I won't tell. I'm sorry, it was my fault. I know how vulnerable you are and I just got caught up in the moment. Maybe I read you wrong, Sam. I thought there was a connection between us."

She looked at him. "There is…I just…I've got to go," she said as she ran out the door. She was interested in him wasn't she? She wanted both of them. But you just couldn't go around having your cake and eating it too.

On the way home she cried and laughed and yelled at herself. The memories of the love they had made caused her to smile. She did feel good. He had made her feel good. She relished on the memories of his strong body overcoming hers and taking over her soul as she exploded with ecstasy. But she loved James, didn't she? Did she love Jason too? Or was it just lust? She wasn't sure, and now she had to live with the guilt and hope that James wouldn't find out.

CHAPTER 27

✥

"Where's your stuff?" He asked, when she walked into the living room. He was sitting on the couch flipping through the channels on the t.v.

"What stuff?" She asked, her mind elsewhere.

"You said you were going to pick up some stuff at Bob's."

"Oh shit," she said trying to act as though she forgot, "I must've left it on the chair in the living room. I'll go get it tomorrow." She walked over and kissed him on the mouth. "Do you mind if I go to bed? I'm exhausted," she said, making an excuse to not make love with him. At least she had that much decency.

"You want me to tuck you in?" He asked, holding her hand. He had his song notebook on his lap.

"No, sweetie. You just write. I'll be fine. See you in the morning."

She got into bed and cried herself to sleep. Outside, in the living room, James listened with concern and dread.

🍁   🍁   🍁

Bob went and watched Veronica dance that night. She was really good. He had never actually been in a strip club before, and he was shocked at the class of people this place held. There were a lot of well dressed men there and he could tell by the expensive cars in the parking lot that it wasn't one of those cheap dives. There was a $15 cover charge at the door and a two-drink minimum. He could also tell from the tips being given out, that Veronica made a lot of money dancing. No wonder she didn't want to quit.

She had seen him come in and when she went out on stage she did her favorite routine. He was so cute sitting there with his friends. He tucked a twenty in her g-string. She smiled at him, but she wasn't allowed to show preference to anyone in order to not discourage the customers from requesting private jobs. Stripping had been a good way for her to get over James after they broke up. Her self-esteem blossomed 100%. She was a favorite at the club, and therefore was requested quite a bit for private jobs. The men she escorted treated her like royalty. She used the material things they gave her to un-break her heart.

She had decided right now that she wouldn't pursue Sam. After all, Greg wasn't crazy enough to come to L.A. and stalk her. Besides, he didn't even know she was here. She had hoped he had believed their conversation but she couldn't be sure. As long as he stayed put, there was no reason to alarm Sam.

※　　　　※　　　　※

The next morning Jason woke up in bed alone. Had he dreamed about making love to Sam? Then he smelled her scent on the pillow and saw the guitar sitting in the corner.

She was an incredible lover. He wanted her so badly. He promised himself a long time ago that he would never let a girl break up their band, but she was different. She wasn't just any girl. She was the girl he wanted to be with. He knew that James would never let her go, though. So, he would try to do as she asked and enjoy the memory that he had.

❧ ❧ ❧

"Good morning, sleepy head," she kissed his forehead as she held a hot cup of coffee in her hands.

"Mmmmm, something smells good and it's not the coffee." He put the coffee cup on the nightstand and pulled her back into bed with him. "Showered without me huh?" He asked, burying his head into her neck.

"Sorry," she smiled up at him. "But, at least I didn't get dressed," she said as held him in her hands bringing his erection to full stature.

He made love to her so passionately that it brought tears to her eyes. Because he noticed the tears he asked, "Is there something you want to tell me? Or are you still upset about what happened yesterday?"

She had forgotten about the porn incident. *Thanks for reminding me*, she thought. "It's just that things are harder than I planned," no lie there. That was definitely the truth. *I'm in love with two guys, and I just slept with the other one last night, before I came home to you. Do you mind playing second fiddle once in a while?* That was the other part of the truth that she didn't happen to mention on this lovely morning.

"How about you get up, and we go to the gym. After all, I have to be in perfect shape to fight off those women that are going to be all over you this weekend." She pushed him up and out of bed.

"I suppose we have to go shopping again too," he groaned, turning on the shower.

"What do you think?" She asked him as she made the bed.

"I need to find you some girlfriends," he said as he pulled open the shower door and stepped into the steam.

Jason was at the gym when they got there. Sam didn't know whether to ignore him or keep him away from James. She decided to act natural, after all this might be her biggest part yet. She said hi, put her headphones on, and cranked up the stair climber for 25 minutes. After five minutes, Jason joined her.

"How's it going?" She asked, pulling her headphones down around her neck.

"Good, and you?"

"Just fine. You didn't say anything to James did you?"

"About what?" He asked, as if he didn't have a clue what she was talking about.

"Good," she smiled and put her headphones back on.

Sam worked out harder that day than she had in a long time. She wasn't sure if she had just started getting her energy back or if she was trying to sweat the guilt she felt out of her system.

CHAPTER 28

❀

Jonathan walked into *HotShots* at 3:00 that afternoon. He had been trying to track Sam down all day but with no luck. Finally, he had gotten a hold of Lonnie who told him she started work at 2:00. He sat down at the bar and ordered a martini.

"What are you doing here?" She asked, stomping over to where he was sitting.

"Well, I came to apologize about the other day and I want to make it up to you."

"Yeah? How? Send me to a porn film audition? I don't know what kind of sleazy business you are trying to run and cover up, but I am not interested," she glared at him with eyes that could cut through ice.

"Look, I made a mistake the other day. I didn't check out the client before hand and I'm sorry. I've only been here two months, Sam. This is a beginning for me as well."

"Well, that's just great. A novice is not what I need, Jonathan. You should've told me that before you wasted my time." She pulled her tray off of the bar and started to walk away.

"Another prima donna trying to make her way in the world. And to think, I thought you were different."

She flipped her body around. "Excuse me, Jonathan, but I didn't send you out to be humiliated. I came here for a reason and if you can't aid in that, then I don't need you."

"You know, sweetie, you better get used to wasting your time, because you will waste a lot of it in this Hollywood game. You aren't just going to get the perfect movie role by walking down the street shaking your pretty little ass. I've got news for you, Sam-this business is hard work. It's going to every audition, even if you don't want to, just for the experience. It's busting your ass to make them notice you, when they just want to go on to the next one. I was going to bend the rules for you and get you an audition tomorrow with Jacob Byrnes for his new film. Now, I see, I've wasted my time."

"Wait," she held up her hand. "An actual audition?" She sat down next to him. "Okay you have my attention now."

"He only wants girls with experience, but I figure with your looks and your sassy attitude you can get his attention. Be there Thursday, with your headshot, at this address." He handed her a card with the information on it. "Do just what you did to me yesterday and I bet you get the part."

"Thank you, Jonathan." She kissed him on the cheek. He didn't need an apology for her earlier actions, that kiss was enough to send him to cloud nine for a week.

"Kissing the customers now?" James asked, clearly a little jealous.

"Only the ones who can get me where I want to go," she said and walked over to one of her tables.

      🍁   🍁   🍁

Bob came over to the bar after work, and Sam had dinner with him.

"I met a fabulous girl," he told her, as he put a dollop of ketchup on his burger.

"Really?" She was surprised at the pang of jealousy she felt.

"Yeah, she's a dancer and she's so incredible, Sam. We spent the night together last night, and I mean, she's incredible."

Sam smiled. "You slept in my bed?"

"Your bed? It was my bed first, remember? Besides you haven't slept there in weeks."

"I know. I need to find my own place. I should come get the rest of my stuff soon. I'm sorry."

"No hurry, Sam. Mi casa es su casa," he said toasting her with his beer.

James walked over and sat down overhearing part of the conversation. "I thought you got your stuff last night?"

"Last night..." Bob started to say that she hadn't been there, but Sam stopped him.

"Yeah, remember I came by and we talked and I left my bag there," she said, giving him the 'go along with me or I'll have your balls in a bag' look.

"Of course. I was going to bring your bag today but I forgot it this morning."

"So dude, what's been going on?" James inquired. "Haven't seen you since Saturday."

"I met this incredible girl." He told James about Veronica with a little more detail than he told Sam.

"Well, you'll have to bring her in so I can give my approval." Sam told him, sounding almost motherly. "What's her name anyway?"

"Veronica." Bob said smiling as the name rolled off his lips.

Sam and James both spit out their drinks at the same time. James knew by the description that it was his ex-girlfriend and Sam knew because that wasn't a common enough name for it to be coincidence.

"Something I said?" Bob asked, dumbfounded at his friend's actions.

"No," James replied immediately. "Sam, I forgot I needed to ask you something in private." He got up and pulled her away just as she was about to say something.

"Don't say anything about Veronica and me, to Bob."

"Why not? What's the big deal? You aren't jealous are you?"

"No, I am not jealous. It just might make things a little weird that's all." He didn't want Bob to find out, because he knew Veronica would tell him why she and James had broken up, and he didn't want Sam to know. Sam would never trust him again.

"Okay, whatever," she said and walked back to the table, while James went back inside.

"We're going to Vegas this weekend. Wanna come?" Sam asked Bob as she picked up her drink and took a sip.

"No, Veronica and I are going to San Diego for the weekend."

"Moving kind of fast aren't we?" She gritted her teeth against the comment, but she couldn't help it. She didn't want anyone taking her place.

"You should talk, sweetheart. And what's this stuff about last night?"

"Just cover for me, its no big deal."

"What's no big deal?" Jason asked, as he walked up to the table and helped himself to Sam's fries.

"Nothing." She could tell he was wired and that pissed her off because she really wanted some. Between the talk of Veronica and last night she was getting more annoyed by the minute.

"I have to go back to work now. You two enjoy the rest of my dinner, just don't tell any secrets," she said.

❦ ❦ ❦

His bus pulled into the station, not long after dark. He wasn't sure if he would find Sam or Veronica but he knew one thing for sure—L.A. was the place to be for drugs and sex. Two things he required to keep his psychosis at bay. Plus, he didn't have a reputation here like he did back home. Nothing to uphold, and nothing to ruin if the going got tough. He knew it wouldn't though. This was L.A. Everything goes in L.A.

CHAPTER 29

Sam walked into the building with her headshot in hand. She was one of the first to arrive, and that had been hours earlier. She wanted to be ready and she wanted to be first. She had picked up the script from Jonathan and she played it a thousand different ways. James had helped her until 3 o'clock that morning.

At twenty after ten she was escorted into a room. She was the fifth one and by now there must've been 100 other girls in there, not counting the ones standing outside of the building. She walked in, handing her headshot to Jacob Byrnes.

"Good afternoon, Mr. Byrnes. It's a pleasure to meet you."

"You haven't met me yet, Ms. Steele. May I see your resume?"

"Well sir, I don't have an actual resume. You see…"

"Ms. Steele, you are wasting my time and so is your casting agent. I explicitly asked for experience here so I wouldn't have to deal with the Midwest farmer's daughter trying to make it big in Hollywood." He called to the escort; "please see Ms. Steele out, her audition is finished."

Sam turned, lowered her head and took a deep breath. Rejection. It was so hard to take. She'd felt the hand of rejection most of her life but now she decided was the time to change that. She turned around and looked Jacob Byrnes in the eye. "No, wait a minute," she said, pointing her finger at him. She was flabbergasted by the harshness and rudeness he had displayed toward her. "You know sir, just because I don't have a resume doesn't mean I can't act. What right do you have to put me down like that before you even see what I can do? Why don't you come down to earth for a moment and pull your head out of your ass and treat people with a little more respect? You might get better talent that way, unless of course you want all of your movies to get poor ratings like *Jasper's Ghost* did." She knew that had been a low blow, but what good was knowledge if you couldn't use it for leverage. Before he could get a word in edgewise, she added, "I came here to audition and that is precisely what I am going to do." She had shocked her own self by her bluntness.

"Get her out of…." he was cut off this time by the casting director.

"No, wait. Let's see what she's got. She certainly has the attitude for the part, not to mention the looks. Let her read the lines and see where she takes this." She was just happy to have someone put Jacob in his place. He was an honest, hard-working man who demanded a lot of respect and professionalism from people. He had a good heart, but sometimes he could be a real pain in the ass.

Jacob gave Sam the green light and when it was over, he knew she was the one. She gave the character the passion and feeling he was looking for. She knew her lines perfectly and had put a different angle on the part. Something they hadn't thought about doing before. He hated to admit to being wrong, but this time he definitely had made a mistake telling her to leave.

"Thank you," Jacob stood up and shook her hand. "We'll be in touch."

"No, thank you, Mr. Byrnes. I know we'll be in touch." She knew she had nailed the part. She could tell by the look on Jacob's face when she fell to her knees and cried. She could cry in an instant. She supposed it came from having so much pain in her life. But that's what made her good. That, and her desire to succeed. She ran out of the building and into Bob's arms. He had come with her for support because James needed to practice for Vegas.

"I got it, Bob. You should've seen the look on their faces. Let's go celebrate." She gave her best friend a hug and walked arm and arm with him to the car, filling him in on her experience along the way.

Bob took her to lunch and they drank three bottles of champagne. By the time they left, Sam was too drunk to go to work. When they got to *HotShots*, he left her in the car while he ran inside to get James. He came back out with James and Jason.

"Hi, baby," she grabbed his face and kissed him sweetly on the mouth. "I did it, they loved me."

"I'm so proud of you," he said before he returned her kiss. "You had a little head start on the celebrating, huh?" He helped her out of the car and took her over to his. "Jason is going to take you home because Bob has to get back to work and I can't leave. I told Lonnie your audition might take all day so Amber is covering for you. I'll see you tonight." He kissed her again as he left her in the passenger seat of the Jeep.

He threw Jason the keys. "No funny stuff, huh?"

"Get real bro," Jason shrugged him off as he climbed into the driver's seat.

"I am," James glared at him.

On the way home Sam put her head in Jason's lap and fell asleep. When they got back to the house he brought her inside and into the bedroom. She put her arms around his neck and whispered in his ear, "make love to me."

"Sam, you're drunk. Just go back to sleep," he ran his fingers through her hair.

She pulled his face toward her own and kissed him. It was a long, sweet kiss and he gave into it.

"I want you now. Please make love to me," she repeated her earlier request, this time with an urgent need.

No matter how hard he tried, he couldn't resist her. She was the girl of his dreams. To make matters worse, she removed all of her clothes and lay there naked knowing he wouldn't say no to her. She was right. He buried his face into her sweet womanhood as she grabbed the headboard for support. She came so hard she shuddered and didn't stop shaking until he entered her. He thrust harder and harder until her back was completely up against the wall. On his knees, he wrapped her legs around him and made pleasure wash through her body. When he came, the sensation was so great that he knew for sure this was it. She was the one and he had to be with her. He brought them both back down to reality and she curled up against him and fell asleep.

The phone rang and he knew it would be James. If he answered it, James would be questioning him as to why he was still there. He held Sam in his arms while the answering machine picked up.

"Sam, it's just me. I hope Jason got you home okay and you're not answering the phone because you're asleep and not because you're in bed with him. Ha Ha. We'll celebrate your success when I get home. I love you, baby."

Jason had never heard James use the L word in the whole time he'd known him. He was treading in dangerous territory and knew better, but he couldn't help himself. Sam was irresistible. He knew he could keep doing this with her forever and that scared him. What kind of life would that leave him? Waiting for the next chance when they could sneak away and be alone again. That wasn't what he wanted, but he knew he would never tell her no.

He quietly got dressed, careful not to leave any signs of his presence behind.

❦   ❦   ❦

The late afternoon sun poured heat in the bedroom like a waterfall, and woke Sam up. She had a horrible headache, so she went to the bathroom to get something for the pain. When she dumped the contents of the Advil bottle into her hand, a bindle of meth fell out. She had completely forgotten that she had hidden one in the bottle. She knew it would be safe there because James never took Advil. He obviously hadn't thought to look there when he purged her stash. Deciding she'd given into enough temptations that day already, she put it back in case she needed it another time.

When she walked back into the bedroom she vaguely remembered the intimacy she had shared with Jason that afternoon. The memory stirred something up inside of her. The feeling was pure excitement—like being asked out on your first date. It was so fresh and so innocent—yet she knew what was happening, wasn't. Once again, like so many times before, she was torn between two guys and at the risk of hurting either one of them she would destroy her whole being.

CHAPTER 30

❀

He decided to check out some of the strip clubs on the Sunset Blvd. He had heard this was the best place to party if you liked to party hard. He had nothing but time now. The first strip joint he went to was called *Bangers*. It was pretty seedy and most of the girls looked as though they were underage. He stayed to have a few beers hoping he could at least get a blowjob. He remembered the first time he made Ronnie give him a blowjob. Just the thought of it gave him a hard-on. She'd been his favorite sex toy for a long time. He missed those days. Hopefully he'd meet up with her while he was here and have a little reunion.

🍁   🍁   🍁

James came home at 11:00 with roses in hand and Chinese take-out. He was hoping Sam would be waiting for him so they could have a late celebratory dinner together. But that thought quickly faded when he opened the door and heard her screaming. He dropped everything in the entry way and ran into the bedroom. She was lying on her back struggling as though she were fighting with someone. She was swinging her fists at the imaginary intruder. Her sobs were racking, leaving her almost breathless. He sat on the edge of the bed and grabbing her with both arms, shook her into consciousness.

She sat up fast, regaining her senses. "Oh my God, what happened?"

"You tell me. I came into the house and you were screaming."

"It was so real. It was so fucking real," she pulled her knees up to her chest. "He was there—on top of me-holding a knife to my throat and raping me all over again." She got up out of bed. "It's almost like I sense him. Like he's here looking for me. I can feel his evil."

"That's ridiculous. He would be a fool to come looking for you here. L.A. is not the place to go when you are trying to find someone."

She thought about it for a moment. "Yeah, I suppose you're right."

"Now, let's salvage what's left of the Chinese and champagne and celebrate your success," he said, grabbing her hand and pulling her into his arms. God, he loved her so much.

She never felt safer than when she was in his arms. The world could end and she wouldn't care, she loved him that much.

※　　　　※　　　　※

She woke up screaming. She looked like she was trying to push someone away from her. She kept yelling at the invisible perpetrator to get off of her. After shaking her for almost five minutes, Bob was finally able to wake her up.

"Are you okay?" He asked, the terror evident in his voice as he held her in his arms.

"I think so." She pulled herself back from him. "I'm sorry—it was just a really bad nightmare. I haven't had one in a long time."

"What was it about?"

She looked at him with wonder in her eyes, "I can't remember. It's gone." She lay back down on the pillow and curled herself in his arms. She had remembered the nightmare. She remembered every little detail. She'd had it so many times it was hard not to. This time the ending was different. This time the intent to kill lingered over her.

※ ※ ※

Jason poured the line out onto the table and pushed it together with the card. It was 2:30 in the morning and he couldn't stop thinking about Sam. In fact, she was all he ever thought about anymore and without the drugs, he wasn't able to focus on anything else. With them he could write music and jam all night long, never giving her another thought.

※ ※ ※

He walked with the girl back to his hotel. She looked kind of like Sam, although her hair was blonde and her body less voluptuous. He had bought the girl a few drinks, more than she probably needed, and she was stumbling along as she held onto his arm. She wasn't old enough to drink, but apparently the management didn't care as long as the money was coming in and the cops were staying out. He had to pay her $50 for sex and a blowjob. She had told him it would be another $20 if he wanted anal sex. *Only in L.A.*, he thought.

Back at his hotel room he sat on the bed pushing her between his legs. She unzipped him and started at it. She wasn't very good but she had gotten the job done. He pulled her clothes off and threw her back on the bed taking her with such massive force that she screamed as he slammed her head into the wall.

He was really rough and she was starting to wish she hadn't taken his money. He kept crying out the name Sam and what a bitch she was. She tried to tell him her name was Lora but she couldn't speak, for his hands were wrapped tightly around her slender neck. Some of the girls talked about men who liked to pretend to kill them while they were having sex with them—but this was going too far. She felt life slipping from her as she tried to pry his hands away. He was too strong for her. She thought of the life she had before she had gotten involved in stripping. Maybe it wasn't so bad having rules and curfews, good meals and a warm bed. Maybe she shouldn't have been so hard on her mom, helped her out more. Maybe she should've given more to her family. Maybe it could've been different, maybe…

🍁   🍁   🍁

He had never killed anyone before. He felt so powerful. People had always told him he was a narcissist. Even the school counselor had told him that when he was in high school. She had tried to get him to take medication, but he was too smart for that. He wasn't going to be some zombie walking around for the world to laugh at. Calm, rational, no feeling, nope, it wasn't for him. He needed to be in control, have people need him, want him, worship him. Today he felt like God. Now that he actually had the thrill of the kill—he didn't think he could stop himself from doing it again. Now that he knew he could do it-he would do it to Sam. That fucking cunt, Sam. Too high and mighty for him, using him to get what she needed, then dropping him like a bad habit. She brought all this hate and rage on. She killed this hooker tonight. It would be her own fault that she was going to die as well.

CHAPTER 31

❁

On Friday morning Sam got up early and packed for the weekend. She had bought several new outfits, and unable to decide which ones to take, she took them all.

She packed for James also, which wasn't hard because his wardrobe consisted only of black shirts and black jeans. She danced around the bedroom in excitement for their trip. She had never been gambling before and she couldn't wait.

She jumped on the scale in the bathroom, unhappy to see that she had gained seven pounds. James had noticed as well, only he was thrilled about it. Said it looked good on her.

"Hey, sexy girl," he said walking into the bathroom. "Checking your weight again I see." She did it about three times a day.

"Can we workout before we leave?"

"I'll work you out right here," he said as he grabbed her and threw her over his shoulder.

She laughed and told him to put her down. "No, I mean it."

"So do I," he threw her down onto the bed and ravaged her body for the second time that morning before she could protest his actions.

He had been up all night trying to figure out what he was going to do with the body. When he heard the maid in the hall that morning, he got an idea. After inspecting what she was missing on her cart, he asked her if she could go get him some extra garbage bags. She tried to give him the brush off, explaining in broken English that she was too busy, but he came back at her in perfect Spanish handing her a $20 bill. She took the money and headed to the elevator. He grabbed some latex gloves off the cart and went back into his room. He grabbed the girl and quickly inspected the hall for other guests. He ran across the hall and into the room the maid had just started cleaning. He dumped the strangled girl into the bathtub and slit her wrists, making it look as though her death had been a suicide. He knew it was a poorly concocted scheme but it would buy him enough time to check out and find another hotel.

At 11:00 Friday morning, Jason pulled into the driveway and threw his stuff into the back of the Jeep. He was riding with James, Sam and Kevin; Lance and Amber were going in Lance's pickup with all the equipment. Kevin's girlfriend, Alicia, hadn't been able to get the weekend off.

"Hey, beautiful," he said to Sam, kissing her on the cheek as he walked into the kitchen.

"Hey, yourself," she smiled at him. "Turkey, ham or roast beef?"

"Sandwiches? You **are** the best. Roast beef sounds great. Do you have Swiss cheese too?"

"Yep, get it out of the fridge for me." She called to James who was in the bathroom primping his goatee, "honey, what kind of sandwich do you want?"

"Whatever is fine, baby."

She turned to Jason again, "did you bring your new guitar?"

"Absolutely, it's my favorite."

"It better be," she smiled at him in a way that melted his heart, even though thirty seconds before it had turned to stone when she called James, honey.

"Will you put ice in the cooler for me?"

"Anything for you, sweet girl." He put his arms around her waist and kissed her on the top of her head.

He was so sweet to her that it made Sam want to cry. He was different than James, but she knew she was falling in love with him too, and their stolen moments together only made it worse. How could she be in love with two guys at once? Was it really possible? She knew she would eventually have to choose one of them. If she didn't, she'd go mad.

After the Jeep was packed they hit the road to pick up Kevin. In four hours they would be in Las Vegas.

CHAPTER 32

Cruel's management put them up at the *Mirage*. They were all on the same floor. Lance, Amber, James and Sam had adjoining rooms and Jason and Kevin were across the hall. After they settled into their rooms, the band had to take their equipment and go practice for the next day. Sam and Amber decided to go to the pool. The band was in Sam's room when she walked out in a very black, very string bikini.

"You aren't going out there like that are you?" James asked, as Jason choked on his drink.

"Why not? Do I look bad?" She asked him, raising her left eyebrow for emphasis.

"No, but you're missing half your bathing suit." He got up to grab a towel and throw it around her. He didn't want the other guys in the room getting hard-ons over his girl.

"No darlin'—this is it," she moved away from him as Amber walked into the room. "See, it's called trendy," she said as she pointed to Amber's red bikini.

"Shall I send a guard with you to keep the men at bay?"

"I think I can hold my own. Besides it's so much fun to be untouchable."

"Oh, is that what you are now? Untouchable?"

"I will be someday. Just you wait." With that said, she grabbed her sunglass, slipped her sandals on and the two girls walked out of the room.

He yelled at her from the doorway as she walked down the hall. "You aren't even going to put something on over that while you walk through the casino?" She threw her hand over her shoulder and waved.

"Calm down, James," Jason said, shifting his pants. "She'll be fine."

"She's my girlfriend. I don't want every guy in the world to see what belongs to me."

"Jeez man, you talk about her as if she's a trophy. Quit being so overprotective or you'll lose her for certain."

"Fuck you. You just want her and it kills you that she's with me."

"Whatever. I'm not fighting with you this weekend so get off your high horse, asshole." James had hit a nerve and they both knew it. He did want her. **He** wanted to be the one to tuck her in at night and **he** wanted to be the one who was there when she got scared and **he** wanted to be the one to brush away her tears. **He** wanted to be the one to share her laughter and wake up to her smiling face.

❦ ❦ ❦

"James is so possessive, Sam. How do you stand that?" Amber asked as they walked toward the elevators. Even though she was good friends with James, she was starting to see another side of him that she hadn't known existed.

"He's not usually like that. I don't know what the deal is. Who cares though? Let's go have fun and get drunk." She knew full well what his deal was. They both had seen the look Jason gave her when she walked out in her bikini.

"I'm with you, girlfriend."

As they walked out to the pool, people stared. Guys gawked at them while their girlfriends and wives pulled them away. Sam enjoyed every minute of it too. Someday they would look at her like that because she was famous, not just because she was pretty and had a great body, but because she was going to be someone. Someone untouchable. She held her head up high and gave everyone she passed a seductive glance.

At the pool, Sam and Amber got margaritas and sat in the sun. They swam for a while, then got out to reapply their sun block. While Sam was rubbing lotion on Amber's back, two guys came over and offered to buy them drinks.

"Absolutely," Sam looked at them over the rim of her sunglasses. "We're drinking margaritas." One of the guys went to get the drinks while the other one finished the sun block applications on both girls.

"Were gonna be in big trouble, Sam," Amber giggled. Then she whispered in Sam's ear, "do you realize how hot these guys are?"

"I'm not blind, sweetheart."

When the other guy came back, they went to a table to drink their margaritas. They talked all afternoon. Several hours later, both girls were so drunk that the guys thought for certain they were going to get lucky that night, at least until Jason showed up and put a damper on their plans.

He walked up to the table, "sorry guys these belong to me."

"You lucky dog," said one of the guys, clearly believing him.

Just to screw with the guys a little bit, Sam gave Jason a full open-mouthed kiss as she stood up.

"Sorry boys, but thanks for the drinks." She winked at them as she walked away with Jason and Amber.

"You girls are shit-faced and sunburned," Jason said poking Sam's skin with his finger and watching it turn from red to white. "I'm glad I came down here instead of Lance and James. They wouldn't have been very happy. In fact there probably would have been some fist throwing."

"Oh come on, silly, we were just having a little fun."

"Making a guy sit with a hard-on all afternoon is torture, baby, not fun."

"I bet we made their day though," Amber said as they stumbled into the casino.

Jason caught her before she fell flat on her face. "Amber, I didn't expect this kind of behavior from you."

"Sam's rubbing off on me."

"Yeah, apparently she's rubbing off on everyone," he muttered under his breath as he guided them to the elevators. "Everyone's ready for dinner, so you're going to have to get ready fast."

By the time they got to the room, Jason was holding both girls up so they wouldn't fall down.

"Found 'em," he said, practically dragging them into the room.

"Looks like you did a swell job of handling yourself," James said.

"We were just having fun," Sam slurred. "We better get ready for dinner."

"I don't think you'll make it to dinner, sweetheart. Besides if you put any clothes on you'll die from that sunburn. I'm going to get you some aloe downstairs."

"Some in my bag," Sam said as she started to remove her swimsuit in front of everyone else in the room.

James quickly pushed her into the bathroom. "Stay here, I'll get the aloe."

She grabbed him before he could leave and unbuttoned his pants. "Let's make love right here in the bathroom."

Never able to resist Sam's advances, he picked her up and set her on the counter. She wrapped her arms and legs around him as he slid into her. They had been more than ready for each other, as they both came fast and hard, and he had to cover her mouth with his own so she wouldn't alert the rest of the hotel guests as to how good she felt. Then he helped her into the shower and rubbed aloe all over her body when she got out. She put on a white halter-top and black leather pants. She pulled her hair up into a twist and applied some makeup. She felt better now after having sex and she was ready to go eat.

They ate seafood at *Kokomo's* and then drove down to *Club Rio* for dancing. Sam and Amber immediately hit the dance floor, joined later by Jason and Lance. Sam knew that James didn't like to dance, but she was hurt that he wouldn't dance with her at one of the best nightclubs in Vegas. She also knew that James didn't like it when she danced with Jason, so maybe that was a surefire way to get his butt to the dance floor. Her plan worked, just not in her favor.

She saw two girls walk up to the table and noticed that James had encouraged the girls to join them. She felt a twinge of jealousy move through her when she saw James laughing with them. James looked up at her to see if she was watching him and she bit Jason's ear seductively as if to say to him, "Don't fuck with me".

James took one of the girls out onto the dance floor. Sam couldn't believe he was dancing with some stranger but he wouldn't even dance with her. She was even more shocked when she discovered that James actually could dance, and this girl had moves even Sam hadn't seen before. Sam decided to crank up her act a little more. She turned her back against Jason, placed her hands on his hips and rubbed her body up against him. Then she whispered something in his ear and they left the dance floor.

They sat at the table and ordered shots. When the shots arrived at the table with the lime and the salt, Sam unbuttoned Jason's shirt, squeezing the lime onto his chest and pouring salt on him. She licked the salt from his body and drank her shot, shoving the rest of the lime into her mouth.

"Sam, you're playing with fire."

"No, I'm having fun," she said as she pulled her halter top up to right under breasts and squeezed lime on her naval. Jason poured salt on the lime and bent down to lick it off her body. As she tilted her head back, she saw James walking toward them. She put her boot up on the back of the chair Jason was sitting in just as James walked up.

"What the fuck is your problem?" She asked him, blocking Jason's face with her leg. "Jealous? I didn't even know you could dance," she flipped around and put her finger in his face. "Don't even say one fucking word to me. I am having fun. Go get your little friend and go back out on the dance floor and shake your ass all night long."

He grabbed Sam's arm. "Let's go."

※　　　　　※　　　　　※

After a silent ride back to the hotel, James finally let Sam have it when they got to their room.

"What the hell is the matter with you? Why do you act like a little slut every time we go out? Do you think Jason likes being used by you? How do you think that makes him feel?"

She came back at him, "why are you so jealous of everything I do. Fuck! You didn't want to dance with me so you danced with someone else. Your choice, not mine. You had better back off because I can't stand to be smothered and that's what you are doing."

She walked out of the room as he grabbed her arm. "I love you, Sam. Don't do this to us."

"Maybe you better take a minute to think about what love is, James."

This time she made it out of the room and walked downstairs to one of the bars and sat down.

Jason saw her and sat down next to her. "You okay?" He asked.

"Are you following me?" She asked, clearly annoyed at the whole situation.

"No, but I would like to say I told you so."

"And I would like to say that I need to get high. Do you have anything?"

"I thought you quit."

"I did, last week. This week appears to be different," she looked at him again, raising her eyebrows. "Well?"

"Yeah, let's go," he said and grabbed her hand.

They got to his room without being spotted by anyone. He poured two lines out on the table.

"Where's yours?" She asked.

"Oh, we're going for an all-nighter huh?"

They each snorted two lines and Sam enjoyed the feeling that she had suffered without for the last week.

"Let's go out."

"Now? It's almost one."

"This is Vegas darlin', the night is just beginning."

They took a cab back to the *Rio* and went upstairs to the *Voodoo Lounge* and enjoyed the view of the strip. They ordered martinis, which Sam soon discovered she couldn't stomach, and chatted idly about their lives. Sam decided there was a lot more to Jason than good looks and a hard body. They enjoyed a lot of the same things—reading, volleyball, the beach, and of course music. He didn't open up much about his family and Sam didn't ask. She was too wired to really care if he talked to her or not. Deciding she'd had enough sitting around she suggested they go downstairs and play some video poker.

By 8:00, Jason was worn out, "we'd better go. I have a big day ahead of me."

"Oh yeah, I forgot. I'm sorry. Are you going to be okay?"

"Done it many times," he grabbed her hand. "Let's go get breakfast."

They went back to the Mirage and had breakfast at the coffee shop. Sam got back to her room at 9:30 and James was waiting for her with Lance and Amber and Kevin.

"Where were you last night? With Jason?" He asked, following her into the bathroom.

"Out and no." She said, starting the shower. She smelled like cigarette smoke and she hated that.

James sent everyone out of the room and he walked back into the bathroom. He watched her undress, then went over to her and looked into her eyes.

"Wired again, huh?"

"No, I'm not. I am extremely exhausted and have been drinking coffee for the last 8 hours so I wouldn't fall asleep downstairs because I didn't want to come back up here and go to bed angry."

He bought it. Didn't even question her twice. "I'm sorry. Take a shower and get some sleep. The concert starts at 6:00 tonight. Do you want me to get you something to eat?"

"I already ate," she lied. Jason had eaten, she had just had a cup of coffee.

He left her alone and she hoped Jason wouldn't say anything. Although, Kevin probably knew he hadn't come back last night. Hopefully, he wouldn't say anything either.

She was starting to see things in her field of vision and hallucinate a little bit from the comedown. She hoped she could go to sleep after the shower or she wouldn't make it without another line.

❧   ❧   ❧

He checked out of the hotel the previous day, before the cops started swarming the place. Luckily the club was dark and nobody could've gotten a good description of him. Plus, he didn't think anyone really kept track of the girls there. He checked into another hotel with one of his fake I.D.'s that he had prepared himself with before his trip. *Anthony Steele*, it said on the Driver's License. He was hoping to disguise himself as Sam's long lost brother, if he got that far. He didn't know if she had one or not, but probably nobody there did either. He wanted to find his sister as well, but she wasn't as important as finding Sam. Nothing meant more to him now than making that bitch pay for ruining his life.

CHAPTER 33

❀

Amber came in and woke Sam up at 4:00.

"C'mon sleepy head," she said bouncing on the bed, "we've got to get ready."

Sam opened her eyes, not sure where she was at first. Then she remembered. "Where's James?" She asked, sitting up in bed and giving a hearty yawn.

"All the guys have already gone. The show starts at 6:00, and there will be a limo here to pick us up at 5:15."

"Did James seem mad about anything?" Sam asked quizzically, not sure if Amber knew where she had been last night.

"You mean because you spent the whole night with Jason? Yeah, he's a little pissed. I think Jason smoothed it over a little though."

"How'd he find out?"

"Someone from the hotel saw you two together last night and asked Jason where his girlfriend, meaning you, was. It sparked a nasty little conversation between James and Jason but he's forgiven him enough to play with him. You, on the other hand, may have some major ass-kissing to do."

"Nothing happened, I swear. Please believe me."

"Look, even if it did, I'm not your guardian, I'm your friend, and whatever you decide to do, or not do, I will stand by you. I will tell you this though, I've been friends with James for a long time and I've never seen him so head over heels before. You have got that boy's heart in knots. Just be gentle with him is all I ask. I know he's a bit possessive but he means well."

Sam smiled at Amber's little speech. It was the first time anyone had told her how James felt from an outsider's view and she was giddy with excitement. She couldn't wait to see him later.

By 5:00, both girls were dressed. They were both wearing daisy dukes and halter-tops and anyone seeing them would have thought they were models. Amber wore her long black hair straight and Sam wore her hair curly as usual. They were definitely going to have to fight men off of them tonight.

On the way to the concert, they passed another limo. One of the passengers rolled the window down for a minute and when Amber saw his face she started screaming.

"Oh my god. OH MY GOD! Sam, do you know who that was?" Amber was waving her arms up and down with excitement. "That was Jeremy Todd of *Felony*! Oh my God, I am so in love with him. I have to get his autograph." She pressed the intercom button, "driver, can you get that limo to pull over, please?"

The driver tried persistently to get the other limo driver's attention, but it was no use. Finally, Sam told him to pull in back of it and stay on their tail honking the horn. She opened the sunroof and stood through it, while the driver did as she had asked. Then, in a brave and bold move, she removed her top. That was it. The limo pulled into the next parking lot.

Jeremy Todd got out of the limo. Amber flung open the door and ran over to him.

"You little girls are going to cause an accident out there with stunts like that," he scolded them.

"Well, I do more dangerous acts after midnight," Sam said, still sitting in the limo. She had lost her shirt somewhere on Tropicana Ave.

"Give me a call sometime, I would like to see them," he said; only half-joking. He signed Amber's shirt and then asked, "You girls going to the concert?"

"As a matter of fact, our boyfriends are playing there. You may have heard of their band, *Cruel*."

"New guys, huh?" He asked, climbing back into the limo, clearly uninterested now that they weren't available. Then the limo took off, just as fast as it had pulled into the lot.

"I can't believe I touched him. Oh, Sam, this is the best night of my life. Thank you so much!" She exclaimed as she sat down in the limo looking at the autograph on her shirt.

"No problem. I, on the other hand, do have a problem. I'm shirtless and we don't have time to shop."

"I'm sure you'll blend in just fine," the limo driver said, staring at Sam's creamy white breasts.

"Thanks," she smirked, covering herself with her arms.

🍁   🍁   🍁

"Did you fuck my girlfriend, Jason?" James asked as he was warming up his vocals.

Jason didn't have time to answer because a very famous man walked through the door, nearly throwing him into shock.

"Which one of you belongs to the fiery, golden haired beauty with freckles?" He asked.

"That would be me," James said, barely able to keep his composure. He had never met anyone that famous before and he was one of the biggest *Felony* fans on earth. Jeremy Todd was God to him. Now, here he was, standing in front of him talking about his girlfriend.

"She's something else, man. You are one lucky dude," then, Jeremy Todd walked out of the room.

"Holy shit!" Jason yelled.

"Yeah, holy shit," James said. "How does he know my girlfriend?"

"Maybe she fucked him too," Kevin said, tuning his guitar.

Jason turned around and glared at him.

"Too? Do you know something I don't?" James addressed Kevin as if he were a fifth grade schoolboy.

"Nah. Just making conversation."

Kevin was a strange one to the say the least. He was really quiet most of the time and then he would just pop off and say something totally bizarre. Like the remark he had just made. He had no clue what was going on between Sam and Jason or even if there was anything, because Jason never told Kevin anything. Nobody did. The guy was a freakin' space case but he could play the guitar and that was why he was there. It was a wonder he even had a girlfriend but, she was a few chords short of a tune herself.

"So, did you fuck my girlfriend?" James asked. His voice was like the calm before a storm and Jason knew he would blow at any second.

"Trust her," was all he said and then he walked out of the room.

※ ※ ※

Sam and Amber were escorted backstage. On the way in, they passed several other bands and performers scheduled for the big show. They all noticed Sam and one of the wardrobe girls came up to her and asked if she could get her something to wear.

"I don't have anything feminine," she told Sam. "But I could find something decent."

"That's okay, if you can get me something that I can maybe tie in a knot around my midsection, that would work."

She went looking and five minutes later she had a white silk button up shirt from *Kid Rock's* collection.

"Thank you!" Sam hugged the girl. She saw Jason in the hallway and when he saw her, his eyes almost bulged out of his head.

"Where are the rest of your clothes?" He asked, a little jealous from all the guys that were staring at her.

"It's a long story." She was just finishing tying up the shirt when she saw James. She was about to walk his way when he glared at her and turned the other way.

"I guess it's going to be a long night." She was disappointed in James' behavior, but she also understood.

"I'm going to see Lance," Amber said. "Meet me over there in fifteen minutes," she pointed to an area next to a huge table filled with all kinds of food and drinks.

"Hungry?" Jason asked.

"For a line? Yes. I'm going to go do one in the bathroom. Care to join me?"

"No. Are you sure you need one? You got pretty wired last night."

"You my guardian now?" She asked, walking into the bathroom, not waiting for a response.

"In my dreams, sweet girl, only in my dreams," he mumbled to himself and walked back to the rest of his band.

※ ※ ※

Sam and Amber were in the very front of row of the amphitheater. Everyone around them was standing around drinking beer and smoking pot. When *Kid Rock* came on stage the whole crowd went wild. People started shoving each other and moshing. *Cruel* came on next and since the crowd was already rowdy, it got extremely worse.

There were girls taking off their shirts and throwing their bras onstage. Even a few pair of panties went flying up to James. He caught them and stuffed them in his pocket, which really pissed Sam off. The girls were crazy about him. Sam found herself getting extremely jealous and the drugs only intensified that feeling. At about the third song, Sam had gotten separated from Amber and the crowd started moshing like crazy. She tried to hold onto the guardrails at the edge of the stage but the crowd was shoving so hard that she couldn't hang. She had almost gone down when a hand reached down and pulled her up on stage.

Jason couldn't believe how well the crowd was responding to their music. Of course, it didn't hurt that they had followed *Kid Rock*. The women were going absolutely nuts over them. Shirts and bras and panties were flying everywhere. He noticed that Sam was kind of in shock about the whole ordeal. He also noticed that she was about to get trampled on by about six drunken college kids and that's when he reached down and pulled her out of the crowd.

James was so excited at the response to their music that he wasn't even mad at Sam anymore. He knew she wouldn't be happy about the panties in his pocket but he figured he was going to fight fire with fire this time. He didn't even know where she was in the crowd; all he saw were tits everywhere. Then he saw her up on the stage out of the corner of his eye.

The crowd had gone out of control when Sam was pulled onstage. They had thought it was just a random thing, they didn't know Jason pulled her up there to save her. They started pulling the guardrails down and rushing the stage. Security came in from all directions and *Cruel* and Sam were ushered off the stage.

When they got backstage however, things were just as crazy. There were girls everywhere, and they shoved Sam out of the way to get to the guys. One girl jumped into James' arms and stuck her tongue in his mouth. Sam couldn't get so much as near them. She held back to go find Amber as the band walked into one of the rooms backstage with the flock of girls.

CHAPTER 34

❀

"Let's get out of here," Sam said when she found Amber on the side of the stage.

"What the hell happened?" Amber looked a little disoriented.

"It's crazy here, that's what happened, and our men are backstage with about 50 girls," Sam said, pulling Amber out of the crowd. "Let's go back to the strip and gamble and drink, have dinner and then go dancing." They found a taxi out front and headed toward the *Bellagio*.

❦   ❦   ❦

James couldn't get the women off of him. They were ripping at his clothes, trying to kiss him, one offered him a blowjob and a few others offered him sex. He saw Kevin and Lance were having the same problems he was, but he couldn't see Jason anywhere. He wondered if he had gone after Sam and that thought had pushed him over the edge. With enough alcohol in his system to make him regret it in the morning, he grabbed one of the girls and kissed her hard on the mouth. He saw Jason come in and pick up his guitar pushing the girls out of his way. He wondered what his problem was. After all, they were famous now and they might as well enjoy it. Besides, how would Sam find out what he was doing unless Jason told her? And he knew he wouldn't do that, guys didn't work that way.

Jason left the maddening scene of rock star heaven. He wasn't into that. That wasn't why he got into the music business. He loved music, it was his life. He had been playing guitar since he was seven. His mom and dad had bought him one for Christmas that year. He hadn't even cared about any of the other presents under the tree. He took lessons every week and he would play concerts for his parents. His mom had been so proud of him. Then when he was ten she had gotten sick. He would play a song every night for her at bedtime. Before she died she had asked him to always think of her when he played, and she had told him she hoped the music stayed with him for the rest of his life. Well, this was his way of making her dreams come true. He had loved his mom more than anything in the world and never thought he would ever find another woman to love again. Now he had, only now she was involved with someone, who by the looks of things backstage, could give a shit less about her. He hailed a taxi, and headed back to the hotel, hoping to find the woman of his dreams.

Sam and Amber were having a great time at the craps table. Sam was on a roll and had won several thousand already. She had no idea what she was doing and that was what made it so much fun. The pit boss had already comp'd them both dinner and if she kept winning he was going to offer her a suite for the night. Amber had done well at blackjack, raking in about a grand, which she planned to go shopping with on Sunday. At the end of her evening at the table, Sam had won about a year's salary for the average American and a suite for the night. She had the casino hold the money for her so she and Amber could go clubbing. Sam decided to call back to the room first to see if any of the guys were there. Nobody had answered her or Amber's phone, so she tried Jason's.

Jason could hear the phone ring as the hot spray of the shower sluiced over his body. He didn't feel like answering it. He figured it was a wrong number anyway. He knew Sam and Amber weren't around and nobody else would be calling him.

"Well, the guys must be having a great time tonight," Sam said, after nobody answered any of the phones.

"I'm gonna go back and wait for Lance," Amber said. "I'm too tired to go dancing and I want to take a nice hot bath." It was already 11:00 p.m.

Sam rolled her eyes. It figured that just as the night got hopping, Amber would ditch her. "You don't want to stay in my suite with me?"

"Yeah, but I bet you'd have more fun with James," she smiled at her friend as they walked away from the phones.

"Okay let's go back to the hotel," Sam moaned.

They entered the hotel lobby at the *Mirage* and neither girl noticed the man following behind them. When they got to their floor they got out of the elevator but the man stayed in, so as not to be suspicious. When they were around the corner he stepped out and followed them. He didn't know the money Sam had won that night was still at the *Bellagio* waiting for her.

Sam heard footsteps behind her, so she turned around and saw the man from the elevator. She had thought it strange that he had stayed behind while they got off and was now following them down the hall.

"Can I help you?" Sam turned around and asked as she neared her room. She didn't want the creep to know which room she was in.

"Yes, maam. I'm sorry to bother you but I'm from the *Bellagio* and we forgot to have you sign a form when you collected your money," he spoke with a bad southern drawl and smiled at her with a crooked grin. The one people had when they were lying. It wasn't in the eyes, it was always in the smile.

"Who are you, really?" Sam asked, while Amber stood near her with her hand on the mace in her purse.

"I told you maam…"

"Don't maam me. I'm not your mother. If you were really from the *Bellagio* you would know that I don't have the money yet, asshole."

The guy freaked and lunged toward Sam. She wasn't carrying a purse so all of her money was in her small pocket billfold. She thought that carrying a purse was just asking for someone to mug you. When she went out, she carried her I.D. and money in her front pocket.

Amber tried to spray him with her mace but he smacked her out of the way and she hit the floor hard. He was reaching into Sam's pockets but she kneed him in the groin to make him move. He flew back against Jason's door with a loud thud. Before he could lunge for her Jason opened the door and the guy fell backwards.

"He's trying to steal my money," Sam yelled as the mugger got up to run away. She ran into Jason's room to call security when she saw James and Kevin with a bunch of women. One of the girls was sitting on James' lap. She glared at him and picked up the phone and dialed for security, then left the room.

James had run out after Sam but she warned him to back off. Jason and Lance held the guy down while waiting for security and Sam tended to Amber. She had a bump on the back of her head but other than a headache, she was fine.

After security had taken the guy away, Sam let James have it.

"I have a suite at the *Bellagio* because I won a whole hell of a lot of money at the craps table. I had wanted to spend a romantic evening with you but I see you have other plans. I thought you loved me James. I didn't know the fame was going to go to your head and your dick." Tears rolled down her cheeks as she confronted him in front of her friends and the groupie whores that were there. She went into their room and grabbed her stuff. "Don't wait for me tomorrow. I'm flying home."

"Sam, please listen to me. It's not what it looks like," James tried to explain but he could see his efforts were wasted.

"Really? Maybe you could pull this over on a stupid person, James, but I am not that dumb. I know what I saw. You are an asshole. I just wish I would have seen that before I fell in love with you." Here she was lecturing him for doing something harmless when she was the one who had cheated on him. She was angrier about that, than about the girls. She was angry with herself because she was the dishonest one. She didn't deserve him. But that was different. She needed to be loved by more than one person. She craved it, it made her feel complete. With her suitcase in hand, she walked down the hall.

🍁 🍁 🍁

About an hour later he decided he was going out. He knew exactly where he was going, but he told the guys another story.

At 12:30 there was a faint knock on the door. She had been sitting on the bed stirring her ice cream sundae that had been delivered by room service. She hadn't even taken a bite of it yet. She was only wearing a cotton tank and shorts when she opened the door.

"Hi," she said, shocked to see him. She'd had a chance to settle down by now.

"Can I come in?"

"I'm sorry," she stepped back from the door. "Of course." Seeing him gave her butterflies in her stomach.

"Nice room." He looked around. It was three times as big as his room at the *Mirage*. The bathtub alone could fit six people.

"Not much fun to have when you're all alone," she said, reclaiming her spot on the bed.

"This yours?" He pointed to the sundae on the table.

"No, it belongs to the man I have hidden in the closet."

He took a bite. "Chocolate-marshmallow, my favorite."

"No it's not," she smiled at him, happy he'd come to see her. "You have whipped cream…here." She licked the whipped cream off the side of his lip. Taking that as a cue, he put his arms around her and kissed her. His tongue explored her mouth looking for answers. She responded willingly, giving him the answers he was looking for.

He pulled her shirt off and, grabbing a handful of ice cream, rubbed it all over her breasts. Her nipples grew hard at the extreme temperature change they had just encountered. With his mouth searching for more territory to devour, he licked and sucked, removing the ice cream that had turned into a melted mess from the heat. Hungry, searching for more sweetness, he removed her shorts pushing her up onto the king size bed. He buried his face between her legs and kissed her gently, sucking the sweet juices from her body. Not able to handle anymore, she pushed him away and walked out onto the balcony.

He found her out on the balcony sitting in one of the lounge chairs. She motioned for him to take a seat and when he did, she climbed on top of him. She rode him hard and fast against the lights of Las Vegas giving him an incredible memory of the strip.

CHAPTER 35

When Sam got back to L.A. she had taken a cab from the airport to James' house. She had packed all her stuff and had gone back to Bob's before James got home.

Sam explained all about her weekend to Bob. Everything that is, up until the point when Jason came to her room the previous night. She decided she needed something to take her mind off the situation she was avoiding, so she took Bob to dinner at *Spago*. She had been dying to go there ever since she arrived in L.A.

"So why are you really looking for a place?" Bob asked between the appetizer and the main course.

"Well, I need my own space. I need to feel independent again."

"You know you can stay with me for as long as you want," he told her, a little sad to think of her leaving, even though she hadn't really been there.

"I know, but I need a place of my own. Plus, you have Veronica now and I would just be in the way. Besides, I need to start going out on more auditions and get this acting thing going."

That reminded Bob of something he had forgotten to tell her. "Jonathon called you and left a message. That Byrnes guy wants you to do a screen test with the male lead."

Sam almost fell out of her chair. "Omigod! Are you serious? Why didn't you tell me? Shit! What am I gonna do? I need to call Jonathon!"

"Hold on a minute, cowgirl. It's Sunday, remember? The office is closed and he said for you to call him first thing MONDAY morning. So relax and take a deep breath. You'll be fine. Do you want me to go with you?"

"Would you? That would be so wonderful, Bob. Thank you." She grabbed his hand from across the table.

"You know I would do anything for you, Sam," he responded with a smile.

"Let's order another bottle of champagne, we have so much to celebrate."

༺ ༺ ༺

He walked into the strip club on Sunday night. There was a hefty cover charge at the door but he didn't mind paying it because the place looked really classy. It was called *Baby Dolls* and from what he had already seen, these girls were definitely dolls. He took a seat up near one of the stages and stayed put for the rest of the evening. At the end of the night, he tried to get a date to take back to the hotel but it was a lot harder than it had been before. You pretty much had to be a regular customer and well known by the owner. That was okay with him because he would definitely be back.

༺ ༺ ༺

When Veronica came back from her trip she had spilled everything to her roommate.

"We had such a great time, Sera. He is so much fun to be with and he is so funny! I have never been with anyone like him before. He could be the one."

"Yeah that's what you said about James and Bill and Nick and…"

"Okay, okay, point taken but this time it's different. He treats me like a human, not a possession. I've never felt this way with anyone before." She sat reveling in her memories of the weekend while Sera got ready for work.

"You workin' tonight?" Sera asked her, snapping her fingers to bring Veronica back to reality.

"Huh? Um no. I have tonight off. I'm gonna go call Bob and see if he wants to do something."

"Don't smother him, honey. You know what happens."

"Yeah, I know, I won't," she said picking up the phone and dialing the number.

※ ※ ※

James couldn't believe Sam had taken all of her stuff and left. She hadn't even left a note and he couldn't get a hold of her anywhere. He was so upset, he was sick to his stomach. He hadn't really cheated on her. Kissing another girl really didn't count, did it? He didn't know, but he told himself it didn't. At least it shouldn't. Besides, he was drunk, so it really didn't count. He had wanted to go after her last night but he knew she needed her space. He didn't sleep at all and the ride home with Jason and Kevin was dreadfully long and silent, even though Jason seemed to be in good spirits.

He needed to get her back. He wanted her there with him when he woke up and when he went to bed. He already missed her. He had already planned on spending the rest of his life with her. He had to find her. He knew she had gone back to Bob's so he would go over there and wait for her.

※ ※ ※

Bob hadn't answered his phone so Veronica decided to go over to his house and wait for him. She knew wherever he was, he wouldn't be long.

After two bottles of champagne and a wonderful dinner Sam and Bob decided to call it an evening. They were both tired from their weekends. When they pulled up into the driveway, James and Veronica were yelling at each other on the front step.

"What's going on?" Sam asked. "Why is James yelling at that girl?"

"That girl is Veronica, and I'm wondering the same thing," Bob replied angrily.

"What's going on here?" Bob asked after he stepped out of his truck. James and Veronica both stopped talking instantaneously.

"Nothing," James said.

"Nothing," Veronica mimicked.

"You two know each other?" Bob asked.

"No," said James.

"Unfortunately," said Veronica. "We used to be together."

"No, you used to be a pain in my ass," James said, angry that she had ruined his already crappy evening.

"What do you mean you used to be together?" Bob was confused. People were keeping things from him left and right.

"James is my ex-boyfriend. The one I told you about."

"The one that cheated on you?" Bob asked.

The mention of those words sent Sam into shock. She couldn't breathe for a minute. She looked at James, "you lied to me."

"He probably told you I was some psycho who ruined his life, right?" Veronica asked, feeling so sorry for Sam.

"Something like that," she ran her fingers through her hair. "Can I borrow your truck, Bob?"

"Keys are in it," he answered still dumbfounded.

"Where are you going? Don't walk out on me again!" James yelled, walking over to her.

"You get in that truck and keep going, girlfriend. He is not worth it," Veronica cheered her on.

"Shut up, you stupid bitch," James looked at his ex over his shoulder.

"Hey," Bob said. "That's enough."

Sam got into the truck and James got in on the passenger's side.

"Get out," she said. "This is a one person trip."

"Sam, wait," he pleaded. "Let me explain."

"No, I don't want to hear it. Please get out James. I need time to think."

"Don't do this, baby," he said. Tears were welling in his eyes and he tried to blink them back. "I love you so much. I love you so much." He repeated for emphasis.

"If you love me, let me go," she cried. "I don't want to get hurt and I know you are just the guy who's going to break my heart again."

"No, I won't, Sam. I need you. You are like the air that I breathe."

"Then you better get an oxygen tank," she looked him right in the eyes. "I love you more than anything, James. That scares me. You scare me. Your fame scares me. The women scare me. Everything scares me when I'm not high and that scares me. I need some time now."

For lack of anything more to say, he got out of the truck and let her go. He knew it was the hardest thing he would ever do and it may be the biggest regret of his life.

※   ※   ※

"Why didn't you tell me James was your ex?" Bob asked Veronica inside the house.

"Because, I knew you were friends and it wasn't really important. He was dating Sam and I didn't want anything I said to have a negative effect on their relationship."

He was so amazed that she cared that much to salvage James' reputation at the risk of Sam's happiness. She didn't even know Sam.

"Besides," she said, "it wasn't all his fault. I was young and extremely jealous of everything he did without me. We didn't have a healthy relationship." Veronica completely opened up for the first time about her relationship with James. Bob was very understanding and listened to her every word. He could see she had grown so much since then, that he wasn't worried about their relationship in the least. Hearing her talk about her relationship with James made him sad. She seemed to have let go of her past though. She had moved on and wanted to start a brand new life with Bob and she told him as much. Hearing that made him feel really good inside because he felt the same way. Sometimes love came and smacked you upside the head and if you didn't grab it, it might not come around again. He felt very lucky to have her in his life.

She drove around for a long time and finally ended up on the strip in some bar across the street from a classy strip club. It was really crowded inside the dark and smoky building and she walked over to the bar and sat down on a padded barstool at the end. She ordered a Tequila Sunrise, hoping it would get her drunk fast. She had a nice long conversation with the bartender, who came into *HotShots* on occasion, about the chaos in her life. It was nice to unload on someone who was unbiased. After four more drinks she could barely speak so he asked if he could call someone for her. She told him to call Jason. She never saw the guy at the other end of the bar staring at her.

He couldn't believe his luck. Almost a month out here and he already found her, and all by chance. He had left *Baby Dolls* after a few hours and went to get drunk where the beer was cheaper. He couldn't approach her here. There were too many people and he wasn't going to cause a scene. He couldn't follow her because somebody was picking her up and he didn't have a car. But it appeared that the bartender knew her from the greeting she got when she came in. He could probably get some information out of him.

❦ ❦ ❦

Jason came in and helped Sam out to the car. He was surprised, to say the least, to receive the phone call so late at night but he hadn't been asleep. In fact he had been thinking about Sam and their last night in Vegas together. She was something else. He took her back to his house and tucked her into bed. He curled up beside her and wrapped his arms around her.

❦ ❦ ❦

Greg asked the bartender about Sam. He made up some story about seeing her before, but not being able to recognize her. The bartender told him she worked at *HotShots*. Greg pretended as though he had been there before, and that was how he got his information. He was good at playing people. It was probably his best quality. He figured he had enough information to put his plan in motion.

CHAPTER 36

❦

James had let Sam use his Mustang for work, even though she was staying at Bob's house. He figured if she had something of his it meant she was still in his life, even though she wouldn't talk to him for more than a few minutes a day. He tried to get her alone several times, but couldn't.

On Tuesday, Sam walked outside to get some fresh air. She had been feeling a bit queasy that day and blamed it on the drugs and no food. She had called Jonathan on Monday and went in for a screen test. She had gotten the part right then and there, but he wanted her to lose 10 pounds in two weeks. So she was using most of the time to keep the weight off. She had a few contacts from the bar. It was easy to find drugs in L.A.

It was early evening, and the after work crowd was just starting to come in. She waved at some of the customers who frequented the place as they walked into the bar. She saw a man walk around the back of the building and she thought it weird that anyone would go back there. There were a lot of weird people in L.A. though, so she decided to follow him in case he had a gun and was going to shoot up the place. Sometimes she felt brave enough to do things like that.

She walked around the corner but there was no one there, instead she found a Barbie doll with it's eyes gouged out and piece of paper wrapped around it lying on the ground. She removed the rubber bands and opened the article. It was an article about the stripper who had been killed a few weeks ago. Above the headline someone wrote in black ink, *your fate is sealed Sam*. She dropped the doll and looked around her. She swore she heard someone whispering her name. She wondered who would do something this sick. Who would want to hurt her? She didn't have any enemies in L.A. as far as she knew. She ran back into the restaurant losing her desire to be a hero.

🍁   🍁   🍁

On Wednesday, Sam was carrying a tray of drinks to a table near the front of the restaurant when she bumped into someone. She looked up and could have sworn it was Greg. She dropped the tray but before she could say anything he walked out the door. James immediately came over to help her pick everything up.

"What's going on? Are you okay?" He was concerned about her.

"Yeah, I uh…nevermind." She didn't want to sound like a nut so she didn't say anything.

"You don't look well. You look like you've seen a ghost."

"I haven't been feeling well."

"Maybe if you quit snorting, you'll feel better," He said quietly so no one would hear him.

She was annoyed with his little comment and she shot him a look that told him just that.

"Mind your own business," she snapped at him.

"I've made you my business."

"Well don't," she said and picked up the tray to go get more drinks.

🍁   🍁   🍁

On Thursday, James walked her out to the car after work. He did every night, against her wishes, but he wanted to make sure she was safe. When she got to the car there were a dozen roses on the windshield.

"Did you do this?" She asked James, picking them up. But when she did, she realized they were dead and they were infested with nasty little bugs. She screamed, dropping them and frantically wiping her arms and legs with her hands.

"What the hell?" James asked, looking around.

"I don't know. There has been weird stuff going on all week."

"Like what?" He questioned her, wondering why she was keeping him in the dark.

She told him about the doll and about seeing Greg the night before. She also could have sworn someone was following her yesterday when she walked down to the store from Bob's house.

"Did you tell this Greg guy you were coming to L.A.?" James asked.

"I told him I wanted to be an actress and that I had a friend who lived in L.A."

"Well, I think it's a little far-fetched that he would put that together and track you here. However, there's obviously something going on and I don't want you staying at Bob's alone. Especially, if someone is following you. Please come home with me."

"No, I'll be fine, really. Besides I still need time."

"Time for what," he asked, annoyed at her for dragging this stupid bullshit out.

"Never mind," she got into the car and took off.

🍁   🍁   🍁

He was standing on the other side of the shrubs that lined the parking lot. He had spooked her and the best part was, that she actually thought it was him. His plan was working. Plus she was still trying to play the strong part. She was going to be an easier target than he thought.

CHAPTER 37

Friday was Sam's last day at *HotShots*. James had pretty much made her quit. He told her that if she didn't quit, he would have Lonnie fire her because he felt she was in danger. After reluctantly agreeing, she decided maybe it was best after all. That would give her time to move into the apartment she had leased over on Melrose and then take some time off before she started shooting the film.

She had been apartment-hunting most of the week before work. She found a nice second floor apartment overlooking a garden and pool area. It was like something out of an Aaron Spelling show. She paid the guy for six months in advance and planned to move in the following Monday. There were a lot of windows and it was very open. She was looking forward to going shopping for furniture on Saturday.

By Monday night, she was all moved in and the furniture store had delivered her furniture. She had cable and her phone was even hooked up. Sometimes paying more for things had its advantages. She hadn't seen James since Friday night and she hadn't seen Jason in over a week. He hadn't been in to *HotShots* at all. She didn't give either one of them her new phone number or address, even though James had called her all weekend at Bob's. The only two people privy to that information were Bob and Amber.

She had met a few people who lived around the apartment complex and found them all to be very interesting. She knew she would like it here. Maybe by the end of the month she would have some new friends and find someone to take her mind off of James.

      🍁   🍁   🍁

On Tuesday night, Sam awoke with a start. She could have sworn somebody was hovering above her, breathing on her. She quickly reached over and turned on her lamp. She looked around the whitewashed room. There was nobody there but she still had a feeling of violation. She was afraid to go back to sleep. She wanted to call Bob, but it was 2 a.m. and she didn't want to wake him. So instead, she did a couple of lines, turned on the TV and played solitaire until dawn. She never even had a clue that somebody was in her closet watching her through the cracks in the door.

      🍁   🍁   🍁

She had quit her job at *HotShots* and apparently had moved out of her friend's house. She had a bad habit of disappearing. He was going to have to work his magic to find her again.

      🍁   🍁   🍁

On Saturday, Bob had talked her into going out to *HotShots*. She knew everyone would be there and since she hadn't seen James for a week and Jason for longer, she decided to get really wired and then she would be able to face them both. She would have to keep using anyway until the movie finished shooting. It was really the only way to maintain her weight at this point. She wasn't going to risk this big break for her health.

🍁   🍁   🍁

Veronica got ready to go to work. She had felt funny all day, like something was about to go down. She had hoped it wouldn't have anything to do with Bob because they were getting closer every day and she figured by the end of the summer they would be living together. She proceeded to get ready with a bottle of vodka in front of her to ease the nerves. It was her only escape from her past.

🍁   🍁   🍁

James had begged and pleaded with Bob all week to bring Sam in on Saturday night since he wouldn't give James her phone number. They were doing their last Battle of the Bands and he wanted Sam to be there. He was going to sing her song that night and he hoped it might change her mind about things.

🍁   🍁   🍁

Bob picked Sam up at seven. She looked incredible. She was wearing a black lace tee with a pair of jeans and boots. He also noticed she was wired, but he decided not to say anything about it. He figured it was because she was nervous about seeing James and he could understand that. He also noticed something else about her.

"You've lost weight." He told her as they left the apartment. He hadn't seen her since she moved into the apartment.

"Yeah, I have to lose 10 pounds for the part. Only three more to go," she said, as she locked the door behind them.

"That's a lot of weight to lose in a week."

"Well I'm eating healthy and taking some diet pills," she lied afraid of telling him the truth. "I'll be okay," What would she say? *I do a line for breakfast, one for lunch and two for dinner. Occasionally I have some yogurt-covered pretzels.* That wouldn't go over well.

They got to *HotShots* and Jason, James, Kurt, Lance, Amber and Alicia were all sitting at a table. They had two seats left open for Bob and Sam. Before Sam sat down she excused herself to go to the bathroom.

"She's high as a kite. What's up with that?" James asked Bob when she walked away.

"She's just nervous. I'm sure she's not using again."

"She's using now and she's lost a lot of weight."

"Only seven pounds, she had to do it for the part." Bob didn't know why he was sticking up for Sam. He totally agreed with James.

They ordered drinks and started talking about other things. Jason got up and walked over to the women's restroom. He waited until someone came out and asked if anyone else was in there.

"Just one girl in a stall," the girl said, walking away.

He opened the door quietly and heard Sam in the stall snorting a line. He waited until she came out before he said anything.

"I've been trying to get a hold of you," he said.

She jumped at the sound of his voice. She turned around and looked at him. He could see that her pupils were overwhelming her irises. She was so far gone he wasn't sure if she was capable of having a conversation.

"I moved," she said, washing her hands.

"I figured that out. Don't you have a phone?"

"Yeah." She turned around and looked at him again. "I'm sorry. It's been a busy time for me. I've been getting my apartment set up and signing contracts and, we'll, I've been busy."

"Looks like you've had time to find some good drugs."

She pushed past him to the door. "I don't need the third degree from you. I'm not using again."

He grabbed her arm and pulled her around in front of him. "You've lost a lot of weight and if you do another line tonight your eyes will be completely black."

"I had to lose weight for the movie. I'm taking diet pills." She lied again. Why she just didn't tell him that she couldn't quit again even if she wanted to was beyond her. Her first night back from Vegas she had a nightmare so real that it took Bob almost twenty minutes to wake her and another half hour to settle her down. When she didn't sleep she didn't have nightmares.

"Unless you want to have sex right here on the floor, I'm going to go back to the table," she said, a little annoyed with his heroics.

"Let's do it," he said unbuttoning his shirt. "That's all it is to you, Sam. A quick romp in the hay and you can go on your merry way. Did you ever think it might be more than that to me? That you mean more than that to me? Did you ever think I just might have fallen in love with you?" He crossed the line now. He told himself he would never tell her how he felt because he didn't want to lose her, but it was too late now.

She pulled away from him. "I will only hurt you, Jason. And I know you will do the same to me. Casual sex is great. No strings attached and you're always there when I need you."

"What about when I need you?" He asked, pain filling his eyes as he absorbed what she had just said.

"I'm always there for you, too."

"How can you be when I have no idea where you live, let alone your phone number?"

She needed to get out of there before she told him how she really felt. That she loved both him and James and she was torn between them. She wanted to fall into his arms so badly she couldn't stand it. She wanted him to hold her like he'd done so many times before, but now wasn't the time nor the place. She was afraid of losing him, so it was best not to say anything at all.

"I will give you my number tonight and you can come see me whenever." Then she walked out the door leaving him staring after her.

❦ ❦ ❦

He showed up to *Baby Dolls* at seven. He picked an empty seat at the front of stage three. He hadn't sat at this stage before so he thought tonight would be a good night to try it. He ordered a vodka tonic and sat back to watch the show.

❦ ❦ ❦

Veronica's show started at 7:15. She was on stage two tonight. They all danced to the same music, they just had different routines. There were three separate stages. She was a little buzzed and tried to keep her concentration on her dancing. She never even saw the man who was over at stage three, watching her.

❦ ❦ ❦

Sam came back to the table and immediately struck up a conversation with Amber, so James wouldn't speak to her. She managed to avoid both him and Jason until they went on stage. The last song they played was her song and even with the drugs and the alcohol she couldn't take it, she had to go outside. She found James' car and went over to it and sat in it. He had a picture of her from the day they went to the baseball game taped to the dash. The scent of him filled the car and she was taken aback by how comforted she felt. She grabbed a t-shirt, he had stashed in the back, and held it up to her face. It was so much like being in his arms. She couldn't stop the tears once they started. They fell down her cheeks like a glass that was overflowing with water. She wanted another line but she was so tired at this point she didn't know if she even had the strength to pull the box out. She hadn't slept in three days. She knew she needed rest before Monday, but paranoia always set in at night and she couldn't go to sleep.

🍁   🍁   🍁

At the end of her shift, Veronica walked out back, to her car. This day she had worked from three until 8:30. Sometimes she worked the late shift but this Saturday she didn't have to. She traded with another girl who had something planned that afternoon. Her plans were to meet Bob at *HotShots*. Veronica didn't see the man step out of the shadows and she certainly wasn't prepared for him to get into her car.

"I'm just a lucky guy. I've found all the people I was looking for within the short amount of time that I've been here." He grabbed her wrist so she couldn't pull the mace out of her purse.

"Greg! What in the hell are you doing here?" Her voice trembled as she spoke his name.

"What's the matter, Ronnie? You look like you've just seen the big bad wolf." Ronnie was his nickname for her. He was the only one who called her that.

"Just shocked I guess." She tried to hide the fear in hear voice. "What brings you to L.A.?"

"Just a little investigation. I found Sam. Funny thing, Ronnie—did ya know she lives with your boyfriend?"

She almost threw up. He knew and he was going to make her pay for lying to him.

"By the way, you dance really well."

"You watched me dance?"

"Yeah, I came in here last week and I liked it so much I thought I'd come back. Guess it was my lucky night."

"How do you know about me and Bob?" There was no point trying to deny it, he knew and she knew that he knew.

"I've been following him and Sam around. I decided it was easier to follow people behind the wheel, so I rented a car. I followed him to your house last night. Sam seems to be gone on vacation or something because I can't find her anywhere." He decided to test her again.

"She's gone back home." She hoped it wasn't too late to save her now.

"Wrong, Ronnie!" He screamed her name shaking his head in her face. He was definitely getting more agitated now. He was bi-polar and his medicine had run out a week ago. When he drank, his condition became worse. "She's moved into another place, only I can't find her and now you are gonna help me."

She didn't say anything else. Everything was a game to him and she was caught up in the middle of it now. She had a funny feeling that the rest of her life was about to change tonight and it would probably be for the worse.

"The point I'm here to discuss right now, is the fact that you lied to me and you are still lying to me," he said, getting in her face.

"No, no I didn't lie at first, Greg. I actually met Bob after our last conversation."

"I don't think that's true but if it were, why didn't you call me."

"Because I didn't want you out here."

"Why not, Ronnie? Didn't you miss your big brother?" He put his hands up her skirt and she pulled herself as far back as she could.

"What's the matter? Don't you miss the good times with me?"

"I don't miss anything about you, Greg. You're sick and you make me sick." She turned her head away from him.

He grabbed her face with his free hand squeezing her cheeks together. "Listen to me, you little bitch. You treat me with respect, you hear me?" He noticed people out in the parking lot. "Get this piece of shit started so we can go."

"I have a date and if I don't show up, he'll know something is wrong."

"Do you think I really give a shit, Ronnie?"

"Please, Greg."

"Don't please me. You lied to me. Did you think I'd really let you get away with it?" He told her to start the car.

She didn't know what he would do to her, but he had that crazed look in his eyes. The same look he had when he had killed her dog, Pugs, warning her he'd do the same to her if she ever told anyone what he was doing to her.

"Where are we going?"

"Let's go meet Bob," he said joyfully.

"Let's just go back to my place. You can do whatever you want to me, there." She didn't want Bob getting involved. She hadn't told him about Greg for fear of what he would think. She certainly couldn't spring Greg on him like this, especially when he was in this state.

"Oh yeah, I will do whatever I want to you, but first I want to meet the guy who gets the luxury of everything I taught you." He lit up a cigarette and she pulled out of the parking lot, hoping she would die in a car accident on the way to the bar.

❦ ❦ ❦

James, Jason and Bob searched all over for Sam for about twenty minutes. Finally, James walked by his car and noticed Sam curled up in the passenger's seat asleep.

"Found her," he yelled across the parking lot to the other two. Bob and Jason came over to the car.

"I'm going to take her home," James announced to his two friends.

"You don't even know where she lives." Jason said angrily.

"I'm taking her to my place, Jason." He glared at this guy he dare call his friend. "That's her home." He jumped into the car and drove off barely missing the red Neon as it pulled into the parking lot.

Jason walked over to his car deciding he'd had enough fun for one night. Bob had gone back inside the bar. He had a few other friends that he could sit with until Veronica showed up. He didn't even notice her walk into the bar with the other man.

Veronica and Greg sat down at a table in the back of the restaurant.

"Where is your friend?" Greg asked. He hadn't gotten that good of a look at Bob before so he didn't know which one he was.

She noticed Bob sitting over at another table near the bar when she walked in. She was thankful he hadn't seen her. She remembered that Sam was supposed to be there as well. She prayed that Sam wasn't around.

"He's not here yet. Why don't I go get us a couple of drinks while we wait for him," she said, getting up from the table.

"Get me a Heineken with a frosted glass," he told her, anxiously awaiting his new acquaintance.

She walked to the other side of the bar, out of Greg's eyesight. He seemed to be pretty interested in the atmosphere and the music from the band. Maybe that would take his mind off of her for a few minutes. He was incapable of focusing on more than one thing at once. Too much chaos, and he went crazy. Veronica asked the bartender to get Bob in five minutes and ask him to get in his truck, call her from his cell phone, and drive to her place. She walked to the kitchen and went out the back door. From there she ran to her car, got in, locked the doors and took off around the back way so Greg wouldn't see her. Lucky for her, he was still engrossed in the music and it was 10 o'clock before he even realized she was gone.

CHAPTER 38

❀

"Veronica?" He asked, as she answered the phone.

"Yeah, I'm here. Are you being followed?"

"Why would I?"

"Go down a few different streets to make sure you aren't," she instructed him. "Please."

"Okay. What's going on?"

"It's a long story. Meet me at my house."

"Okay, bye." He hung up the phone and did as she asked, making sure he wasn't followed.

Veronica knew that Greg knew where Bob lived, but he didn't have any idea where she lived. She didn't hang out at *HotShots*, so nobody there could give him the information either. However, he could find out where Sam lived, but she needed to wait for Bob before she could go over there. As reluctant as she was to do this, she was going to have to get Bob involved.

There was a knock on her door. With her butcher knife in hand she walked over to the door and looked out the peephole. It was only Bob.

She opened the door and grabbed his shirt pulling him inside.

"What's going on?" Bob asked, staring at the knife in her hand.

"Did Sam ever mention that anyone from Oklahoma might have a grudge against her?"

"I don't think so," he said, trying to remember. "She didn't say much about her life there. I assumed it wasn't that exciting. Why?"

She let out a sigh, sitting down on the floral covered couch that brightened her living room. "Apparently, she had befriended my brother, Greg. He still lives in Oklahoma. He is actually my half brother, we have different fathers." She told him about her father and what had happened to him. "Greg is a manic-depressive. Bi-polar to be exact. Actually, more like psychotic. Anyway, he's here looking for Sam."

He interrupted her before she could say another word. He already had so many questions. "What does he want with Sam?"

She took a deep breath and exhaled. "I don't know, but I think he wants to kill her."

"That's absurd. What in the hell are you talking about? This is real life Veronica, not a fuckin' Stephen King movie. People don't just fly 1,000 miles to kill someone."

"I know it sounds crazy, but you have to believe me." The only way he was going to do that of course was if she told him about her past. "I've never told anyone this in my whole life and you'll understand why after I tell you. I am risking our whole relationship on this so you will believe me and help me save your friend." She hesitated, daring herself to go on. "My brother, Greg, the one that's here, started sexually abusing me when I was thirteen. When I threatened to turn him in he threatened to kill my dog, Pugs. I'd had that dog since I was four. Pugs was my best friend in the whole world, not to mention the only friend I had. He took that away from me anyway in the end. He is going to take Sam away from you if we don't stop him."

Bob put his head in his hands and rubbed his forehead. This was a little too much to bear right now. Before he could say anything, she went on.

"I left Oklahoma when I was eighteen, I didn't even finish high school. I needed to get away from him. He was fucking up my life completely and I needed a fresh start somewhere else. I don't know how he found me, but he called me three days before you and I met, asking me to track you down so he could find Sam. I hadn't spoken to him since I left. Apparently he knew some vague information about you. I called a few studios and tried to track you down. Not because I knew what was going on or anything, but out of fear of my brother. I only called a few places and then I met you. I called him the day after that and told him I found you but Sam had not come out here."

"Why protect Sam? You didn't even know her?"

"Because you talked so highly of her and I really liked you. I figured she didn't deserve the wrath of my brother if she meant that much to you. Nobody deserves to get tangled up with him."

"So meeting me was all a hoax? You played me for a fool?" He asked, getting up of the couch.

She grabbed him before he could go to the door. With tears in her eyes she begged him, "please don't go. It wasn't a hoax, I swear. There was nothing premeditated about our meeting. I didn't put anything together until after I got to your house and you told me about her. I would've told you later, but I thought Sam was out of danger and I really liked you. I didn't want to jeopardize what we had going for us." She tightened her grip on his arms. "You can hate me all you want, I deserve it, but let's find Sam and get to her before he does."

※　　　　※　　　　※

James carried Sam into the house. He undressed her and put her into his bed. The moonlight shone on her, illuminating her face. She was so beautiful. Why did she have to be so complex? Sometimes he just didn't understand her.

He went through her purse once again and found what he was looking for. He had to find a way to get her clean.

He opened his dresser drawer and pulled out a small box. He opened it, looking at the 3-carat diamond engagement ring he had bought for her last week. He had just enough in savings to cover it. Of course, he knew he couldn't ask her to marry him under these circumstances, but he figured this would be the surefire way back into her heart. He got into bed with her and she turned toward him burying her face into his chest just like old times.

        🍁   🍁   🍁

Jason drove around for a long time that night. Sam was all he could ever think about anymore. It was almost making him crazy. Their last night in Vegas had been incredible. But it wasn't just about the sex, it was about her. She was like this magical person out of a fairy tale. She could light up a room with her smile, make people laugh in an instant, bring men to their knees, and put the most beautiful of women on guard. He didn't want to be without her and he needed to find a way to get through to her. No girl had ever made him feel that way and he knew without a doubt that he wanted to spend the rest of his life with her.

CHAPTER 39

Sam woke up at seven in the morning. It took her a few minutes to realize where she was, but she got her senses immediately when she saw James lying next to her. She got out of bed and put her pants on.

She found her purse in the living room. She needed a line. She felt like hell. He had cleaned her out again. She wasn't going to risk waking him, besides she had a lot more at home. She grabbed his keys and quietly walked out the door.

Bob had stayed with Veronica at her place since Greg knew where he lived. He was still angry with her the next morning, but they got up early and went to his place to get his gun before going over to Sam's house. He had never been a big fan of guns but he kept it for protection. A lot of things happened in this city and he didn't want to fall victim to an intruder, unprotected.

He pulled into the driveway and made Veronica stay in the truck while he ran inside. He had checked the street and didn't see any strange vehicles. He looked around the property and didn't see anyone lurking in the bushes. When he came out of the house with his unloaded pistol, Veronica was being pulled away with a gun to her head.

Greg turned and looked at Bob, "no funny stuff, Mr. Bob, or we'll have a big mess." He started walking away with Veronica when he turned around on a second thought, "don't call the cops either or you'll be burying your lover and your best friend." He laughed as he pulled Veronica to his car.

Bob knew Sam had to have gotten semi-close to this bastard for him to know her pet name for him. He wondered why she always attracted the freaks and losers. He knew the answer to that one though, but he didn't have time to analyze it again. He needed to get help.

❦   ❦   ❦

She parked the Mustang under her covered parking space. She walked through the wrought iron gated entrance and noticed the roses in bloom. It was going to be a nice day. Later she would come down to the pool, get some sun and maybe swim a few laps. She could use the exercise. She climbed the concrete stairs to her apartment. She put her key in the lock and struggled with it a little to get it to turn. She hadn't had that problem before, but made a mental note to talk to the manager later. She opened the door and closed it behind her without switching on the light. She turned the deadbolt and replaced the chain and threw her purse on the couch. Instead of just landing on the couch softly it had made a noise like it hit something. She switched on the lamp and, like walking out of her worst nightmare, she found Greg sitting on her couch with a woman between his knees.

"Ah, Sam, you're home. You've met my sister haven't you?" He pulled Veronica up by the back of her head and turned her face toward Sam.

"Oh my God," she gasped.

CHAPTER 40

Bob drove over to James' house in a panic hoping Sam was still there. After three tries on the doorbell, James came to the door.

"Where is Sam?" Bob asked.

"In bed, why?" He answered and questioned wondering why in the hell Bob was there so early in the morning.

"Where's your Mustang?" He noticed it hadn't been in the driveway.

"In the drive…" he looked out the door and saw the car was gone. "Shit!" He walked back to the bedroom and noticed Sam was gone as well.

"She's gone," he yelled from the bedroom.

"She's in danger," Bob said, coming into the house.

"What are you talking about?" James asked, throwing on a shirt.

"It's a long story, but we need to get to her apartment. Do you have a gun?" Bob asked.

"Yeah, why?"

"Just get it, I'll explain on the way."

James grabbed his gun and they headed out the door, unsure of what they were about to face that day.

❦ ❦ ❦

Jason couldn't stand it any longer. He drove by James' house. He needed to talk to Sam. He hadn't slept all night and he couldn't do it any longer. He didn't care anymore about James or the band. He had to tell her how he felt. But when he got there nobody answered the door and he noticed the Mustang was gone. He didn't know where else to go. He called Bob from the cell phone but nobody answered there either. Of course, he might be at Veronica's but he didn't know her number. As a last ditch effort, he called Lance to find Amber. He knew Amber would know where Sam lived. They were really good friends. He hadn't asked her before because he didn't want her to get suspicious about why he was looking for her. Now he didn't care though. He dialed the number.

"Lance, it's Jas."

"Dude, do you know what time it is?"

"Yeah, sorry buddy. Is Amber there?"

"Yeah, why?"

"I need Sam's address. It's sort of an emergency. Don't ask any questions, I'll explain later."

He could hear Lance talking to Amber. Then he got back on the phone and gave him the street.

"Thanks bud, I owe you."

"You owe me a lot," Lance said. He had been keeping Jason's secret for a while now. He hadn't even told Amber anything.

❦ ❦ ❦

"What are you doing here?" Sam asked, trying not to be afraid, but she was so scared that she thought she might wet her pants.

"Come on, Sam. Did you think I would let you get away with what you did to me? You ruined my life. First you teased me and led me on, pretending to like me so I would hook you up. You used me and then you stole all of my money and ruined my reputation. I'm from an Italian family, Sam. It would dishonor my ancestors if I let you get away with it." He was acting very calm. A little too calm for her.

"First of all, I never pretended to like you. Second, I didn't lead you on and you didn't want any money for the drugs, so I didn't use you for anything. Didn't I already explain this? Third, you deserved to have your reputation ruined. You raped me, you FUCKING ASSHOLE!" Sam screamed the last two words. She was on the brink of losing control. He had been haunting her for months now and she was tired of being afraid of everything. Even if he killed her, she was not going to be afraid anymore.

"RAPED YOU? Are you smoking crack now, Sam?" He jumped up and grabbed her, shoving her back into the wall. She screamed and he yelled at her to shut up. He hated listening to women scream. He hated women period. They were all stupid whores. Every woman he had ever known was like that. He glared at her as he pushed her up against the wall with one hand around her neck. He was easily 70 pounds heavier than she was and six inches taller. "You shut up. I'm going to make you pay for everything you've done to me. Do you hear me, Sam? It's not going to be fun and you are going to suffer so badly that you are gonna wish I would just kill you. You and your baby."

Oh God, Sam thought. She had done the test yesterday and forgot to look at it before she left. It had been sitting on the counter in the bathroom. She was pregnant and she didn't even know whose baby it was. Once she had time to think she might be able to pinpoint it. Most likely it was James' baby. She didn't know what to do. If he would want to keep it, or demand she have an abortion. It was a moot point now though, because they were both going to die at the hands of this maniac. She looked into his eyes trying to plead with him somehow, but it was useless.

"STOP IT," Veronica ran up behind Greg but he swung his free arm throwing her across the room like a rag doll. Her head slammed into the wall and she fell to the ground in a whimper. Adrenaline was a funny thing. When people got crazy or scared, it seemed to pump through them at supersonic speeds making them stronger than Superman.

He pushed Sam down on the floor and repeated what had been done to her in Oklahoma. "You wanna accuse me of rape, you stupid bitch, go ahead." Something seemed different about him this time though. The way he approached her, the hatred in his eyes, the way he moved. She hadn't realized how big he was compared to her. But maybe it was because she felt about two inches tall now. He just kept going and never seemed to be near completion. She wondered if he'd taken a bottle of Viagra or something. She tried to keep her mind in a far away place, remove herself from the incident at hand, but she was in too much pain. By the time he was done, she was bleeding and raw, and so sick to her stomach she thought she would throw up. She didn't want to cry though. She hadn't before and she wasn't going to do it now. Something inside of her gave her the strength to not do that.

She wished now that she hadn't been in such a hurry to get out of James' house. What was she so afraid of? That somebody could make her happy for a lifetime? No, it was more like she was torn between two lovers and didn't know whom to choose.

She heard someone banging on her front door. She prayed it was someone who could help her.

Greg heard the banging as well, and after slamming his hand over her mouth, he told her she'd better be quiet or he would kill both her and Veronica right then. He got up and went to the door, leaving Sam on the floor. The banging was so loud it was driving him nuts. This person was going to wake up the whole damn complex and he didn't want that. He looked through the peephole and saw some guy standing there. He thought it must be Sam's boyfriend. Out of the corner of his eye he watched Sam run for the gun he had foolishly left on the table, but he was able to step back and push her out of the way before she got to it. She hit the edge of the end table on her temple cutting it open. Then he smacked her across the face giving her a fat lip.

"Stupid bitch!" He yelled at her.

"Sam? What's going on in there?" Jason could here a lot of noise and what sounded like another man's voice.

"Jason!" Sam screamed his name, recognizing his voice. "Help me!" She screamed as loud as she could.

"SHUT UP!" Greg walked over to her putting his hand over her mouth and the gun to her head.

Veronica started to stir in the other corner of the room. She pulled herself to her hands and knees and struggled to get to her feet. Greg was at a loss as to what to do. He hadn't planned on having them both together at the same time. He was losing control of the situation and he needed to be in control at all times. Needed things to be orderly and well planned. It wasn't going that way anymore. He was confused and didn't know how to regain control. So he pulled the trigger.

🍁 🍁 🍁

Jason heard the shot just as Bob and James started up the stairs.

"What the hell?" James yelled, catching the stairs two at a time.

"What's going on?" Bob asked.

"I just got here. There's a lot of noise in there and a man's voice. Sam called out to me to help her but I can't get the door open. Then I heard a shot." Jason had never been this scared in his whole life. He just knew something bad had happened to Sam.

Bob filled Jason in on the story.

"What?!" Jason asked, as James pounded on the door, screaming Sam's name.

"Fuck! This must be why Veronica came to me last month." Jason said.

"What do you mean?" James quit his effort on the door and turned around to look at Jason.

"She told me Sam was in danger. I thought it was a ploy to get you back. I didn't know she was seeing Bob and I blew her off."

James couldn't blame him. He would have done the same thing. But instead of agreeing with him he said, "do you feel better now knowing **you** put her in danger?"

🍁   🍁   🍁

The shot made both the girls quiet and he could think again. But it sounded like more people were gathering outside the apartment and that was making him more nervous. Veronica started to cry and he told her to shut up before he used the gun on her this time. He was starting to lose his train of thought again. He was shaking and sweating now, wishing he hadn't used so much crank with his medication. He'd had it all mapped out, everything he was going to do to them both. Now he couldn't remember his plans.

🍁   🍁   🍁

Sam had cramps in her stomach and they hurt like hell. She was curled up in the fetal position and she watched as blood spilled from her body onto the white carpet. *Who puts white carpet in an apartment?* she wondered. She could hear James and Jason both outside the door. *My heroes*, she thought. She knew Greg was going to kill her and Veronica both, but the pain in her belly was so excruciating that she didn't care anymore.

🍁   🍁   🍁

"I'm calling the cops." Jason said, dialing 9-1-1 on his cell phone. James was trying to kick the door in.

"There's no point in doing that," Bob told him. "It'll make matters worse. The cops aren't going to be able to do anything and as soon as he hears the sirens he'll panic and kill them both."

Jason turned off his cell phone before the call had gone through. They descended the stairs in despair. They had no choice but to sit and wait.

🍁　　　🍁　　　🍁

Greg moved both girls back into the bedroom so he could be out of earshot from the outside. The noise was making him anxious.

Sam was angry now. Her pain had turned into a hatred she had never known before. "You are the filth of the earth. You are a maggot. I knew that the first time I laid eyes on you. You are a fucking piece of shit. I can't even believe you thought my deceitful flirting was sincere." She regretted it the moment it came out of her mouth but it had made her feel better to say it.

"Is that right? It really doesn't matter what you think because you are a fucking slut." Bam! He hit her across the right side of the face. "All women are whores." He hit her across the left side of the face. "Women are only good for one thing." He punched her in the stomach. "And you're not even good at that." He punched her in the chest.

She screamed so loudly from the blow to the stomach that the noise echoed through the grounds. When he hit her in the chest she fell to the floor, the wind knocked out of her.

"Greg, please stop." Veronica begged him. "If you let us go now, you won't get in that much trouble. We won't even say anything. I promise. The cops aren't here and you can walk away, scott free."

"Ronnie, this isn't a movie." He laughed at her naiveté. "You're not ever going anywhere again. You lied to me, remember? Remember what used to happen when you lied to me?" He narrowed his eyes, "imagine it a hundred times worse."

❧ ❧ ❧

On the outside they could hear Sam scream.

"What are you doing?" Bob asked, as Jason headed for the stairs again. "You're going to get them both killed."

"I'm not letting that bastard lay another hand on her."

This time James grabbed Jason. His strong hand crushing Jason's shoulder. "Bob's right. Don't go trying to play hero."

❧ ❧ ❧

When Sam came to, Greg was doing the unspeakable to Veronica. Tears silently flowed down her face and she appeared to be in a lot of pain. Sam couldn't imagine someone doing that to another person, let alone his own sister. Greg was a lot more fucked up than she thought.

She spoke to him through the seers of pain that washed through her abdomen. "What kind of a pansy ass had to fuck his own sister? Couldn't find anyone who would touch you, huh? So, you have to force your sick and twisted pleasures onto your sister." She didn't care what he did to her now. She turned away from the gruesome scene in front of her, not wanting to be a spectator. "Come on, asshole. Be a macho man and beat me up some more. Me, the inferior woman."

He came at her, "you are a fucking cunt, Sam." He hit her on the side of the head with the butt of the pistol knocking her out again.

❧ ❧ ❧

It had been almost two hours and they were still holed up in the apartment. Jason was getting apprehensive and James was going crazy. Bob was still trying to comprehend what the hell was going on. A few people had gathered around, curious as to what was going on.

"Do you know what Sam did to this guy?" He asked James, still looking for answers.

"She stole all of his money and put him in jail."

"Why?"

James didn't mind putting this asshole Greg in his place. "He raped her." Jason looked away.

"Jesus." Bob said. "I wonder why she never told me?"

"It's not really the thing you make public." James said, a little ticked off that Bob felt privy to that information.

They were all on edge now, angry that there was nothing they could do. The people they loved were in the hands of a madman and it was all up to God now to save them.

🍁   🍁   🍁

While Sam lay unconscious in the bedroom, Greg was shooting heroin into Veronica's veins in the living room. Veronica had been clean for five years and this was her worst nightmare. He had gotten her hooked on it when she was sixteen. When she was high she could deal with the abuse he imposed on her. This time though, she begged him not to do it. He lit up a cigarette, touching it to her skin every time she spoke. He was starting to feel comfortable now that he had Veronica under control and Sam was unconscious in the bedroom.

🍁   🍁   🍁

She came to and she was alone in the room. She could hear Greg and Veronica out in the living room. She hoped she wasn't about to walk in on another gruesome scene. Gritting her teeth against the pain that had overcome her, she crawled over to her bed and reached under the mattress. She pulled out a bag of meth and her mouth watered at the thought of a line going up her nose; the freedom she would feel as the crank filled her body with numbness. She put the bag back and reached farther to the right and grabbed the gun. She pulled the drawer out of the maple nightstand that sat next to her bed and carefully grabbed the clip. She was glad she had put this obvious necessity on her shopping list last week. She was also glad she had opted for the more expensive furniture set, now realizing it's value, as the drawer slid easily and silently into place.

Giving herself a mental pep talk, she pulled herself up using the bed as a crutch. Her ankle was twisted and it hurt badly. But she bore the pain and walked out to the living room as if nothing of the past two hours had affected her.

Sam walked up behind them, watching as he put a burn mark on Veronica's chest. "Leave her alone," Sam said and before he could turn around she pulled the trigger. One, two, three, four shots in the back.

🍁   🍁   🍁

By now a resident of the complex had called the cops. They had just walked up when the four shots rang out. They ran up the stairs followed by Jason, Bob, and James and kicked the door in.

Sam stood there in shock as the door was kicked in. Jason ran over to her and pulled the gun from her hands. James and Bob stood in the doorway stunned at the scene before them.

"Drop the gun and stand back!" One of the cops yelled at him.

"I'm just trying to help her," Jason replied angrily.

"Stand back!" The cop yelled at Jason again, this time pointing his gun at him.

"FUCK! She's hurt!" Jason yelled as he held his hands up and moved away from her.

Veronica sat in shock as she looked at her dead brother slumped over the coffee table, his face buried in it. She was still high from the heroin but coherent enough to realize what had just happened.

When Jason and James were allowed to, they both went over to Sam. She tried to walk over to a chair to sit down but now her ankle wouldn't allow her the ability. She was only half aware of what was going on. Still in shock that she had killed somebody. It was as if her body had given her enough to fight back but now it had no more to give. Jason went into the bathroom to get a cold cloth to put on her head. When he came out he looked at the cop, who had given him a hard time, in the eye and said, "get an ambulance, she's pregnant." Sam passed out.

CHAPTER 41

Veronica and Sam were transported to the hospital in the ambulance. The guys followed in their vehicles.

James chose to ride with Jason. "So tell me, Jas. Why were you at Sam's house this morning anyway?" He was trying to be nice, but underneath he was madder than hell.

Shit! How was he going to get out of this one? "It's a secret."

"Bullshit. She's my girlfriend and anything that has to do with her, has to do with me."

"That's kind of a fucked up theory, don't ya think? I mean she is her own person. Besides she isn't really your girlfriend anymore. She broke up with you."

"Why were you over there." James asked again in his 'quit fucking with me' voice.

"Fine. I wanted to talk to her about throwing you a surprise birthday party."

"My birthday's not until the end of July. That's like six weeks away."

"I know, but I had this great idea and I wanted to get her help."

"At seven thirty in the morning?"

"Look, don't dig any deeper." Jason warned. "Did you know she was pregnant?" He asked, changing the subject.

"No. No, she didn't fucking tell me she was pregnant." He looked out the window as he clenched his fists. He thought she was on the pill. A baby was really going to throw things out of whack.

They all three got to the hospital and sat on opposite sides of the waiting room. It seemed like they had been there forever, when finally, after about four hours, they were allowed to visit the girls.

"Hi," he said to Sam as he walked into her room. It was late afternoon now and the sun filled her room with bright yellow rays.

"Hi," her voice was hoarse from being choked. The bruises made her look paler and more fragile than she actually was. "I guess I better call Mr. Byrnes. He'll have to find somebody else for the part."

He couldn't believe that was the first thing on her mind. But he had already taken care of that for her, giving him something to do while he waited to see her. "Nope. I've already spoken to him. He says he'll hold off until you are ready. He has other scenes he can shoot without you. He wants you, Sam, not anyone else."

She looked at Jason. He was such a good friend to her. She needed to quit leading him on, but she was afraid she'd lose him forever if she cut him out of her love life.

"Thank you," she said, as tears rolled down her cheeks.

"Now don't do that. No more crying. You are alive and you are going to be okay and you never have to worry about that bastard again."

"I lost the baby," she whispered, looking out the window.

"I know. I'm sorry, baby. Do you know…" He let the words drop. It was a silly question to ask her. It didn't matter now.

"I was two weeks late. I don't know whose it was." She rolled over and started crying. "I'm such a horrible person. I've led you and James on because I want you both. Because I'm not secure enough to be with just one person. I need to always have someone else on standby. There is so much missing from me as a person and I use you and James to fill that void." Guilt racked her body with sobs.

He pulled the bed rail down and sat down next to her on the bed and held her hand. "It's okay, Sam. There are a lot of things missing from a lot of people." He was certainly an expert on that. "No one is whole on their own. Everybody needs somebody. I should have stayed away from you. I brought a lot of this on as well, but I couldn't help it. When I look at you my day gets brighter, when I hear your voice all my sorrows seem to float away. I'm sorry, Sam." He was about to tell her he was in love with her, but James walked into the room.

"Can I have some time alone with her now?" He asked bitterly. Jason had snuck in while he was on the phone with Lance.

"Absolutely," he squeezed Sam's hand and walked out of the room.

"Hi, sweet girl," he said, pulling up a seat by her bed so he could look into her face.

"Hi," she said, as tears fell down her cheeks.

"I'm going to pick up your things and bring them back to the house. I will take care of everything at the apartment and talk to the manager. I know you are bound and determined to be this stubborn, independent woman, but you can't live there anymore. You can stay with me and I will take care of you until you get better. Then we'll go from there."

"No, James, I can't ask you to do that."

She was still determined to frustrate him even though she'd just been through hell. "You aren't asking, I'm offering. Besides, you are still my girlfriend, Sam. We never officially broke up," he mused, hoping she wouldn't try to say otherwise. "I know about our baby. I just want you to know for the record—I would've wanted to keep it." He'd thought about it as he sat in the waiting room. He could handle a little one running around. Besides, it would've been a part of him and Sam and if nothing else they would be bound together forever.

That made her cry more. She didn't even know if it was his or not. What if she would have had it and it had been Jason's, and James' thought it was his? What would she have done then? He would know what kind of person she was, and he would hate her. She couldn't bear to have him hate her.

"It's going to be okay. We'll pull through this." He was trying so hard to comfort her, but she was pushing him away.

She wanted to be alone now and bury herself in her misery. She didn't want to see anyone else. She wanted to die. She felt so bad inside and she didn't think the pain would ever go away.

James got the hint and kissed her lightly on the forehead. He was going to head over to the apartment to retrieve her belongings and talk to the manager about breaking her lease. As he walked through the hospital room door, he turned around and peered at her through the window. She looked so frail and so alone and tears spilled out of his blue eyes as the realization hit him that he had almost lost her.

Bob put a hand on James' shoulder as he walked up to talk to his best friend. No words were spoken, but the look they exchanged said it all—fear and relief had consumed them that morning. Probably the most horrible fear either one would ever face and the most gratifying relief either one would ever feel.

James held the door for Bob as he entered Sam's room. He sat down on the side of her bed and relived the events leading up to that morning for her. He told her about Greg contacting Veronica to find her and he also told her about what Greg had done to Veronica since she was a young teen.

"My God." Sam said, shaking her head in disbelief. "How can people go through that much pain and still come out singing like a bird?"

"She feels bad about all of this and she blames herself. She also wanted me to thank you for saving her life."

"It's not her fault, I brought all of this on. If I hadn't been so hot to get revenge on him he would have never followed me here."

"James told me what happened."

"I figured he would."

"Why didn't you tell me?"

"Because I didn't want your sympathy. I want you to always think of me the way you did in college. We had so much fun back then, didn't we?" Sam looked into his face remembering the trips to *Baskin Robbins* and the late night parties.

"Yeah, we sure did," he said, memories whipping through his head like a movie trailer. "We still have fun together though. You will always be my best friend. Nobody is going to take that title away from you."

Tears welled up in her eyes. "You are the greatest man I've ever known, Mr. Bob. I truly love you with all my heart."

"Ditto," he said, brushing the hair off of her forehead. "I'm sorry about the baby."

"Yeah," she said, thinking back to the day she and Bob had taken Taylor to get an abortion. She'd been so angry with Taylor and she never really knew why. When they had gotten back to their dorm room, she had abandoned her friend and left her alone all night. She'd pretty much ignored Taylor for a whole week. What a terrible friend Sam had been to her in her time of need. The only good thing that had come out of it was Sam's friendship with Bob. And now she knew exactly how Taylor had felt that day because there was no way in hell she was ready to have a baby. Funny how ironic life was.

CHAPTER 42

❀

Sam was released from the hospital on Wednesday. The doctor told her no sex for three weeks so she would have time to recover. Her bruises were starting to turn yellow, a sign that they were healing. She didn't have a fat lip anymore and besides the bruise above her left eye, her face looked normal. She still had finger marks around her neck though.

James picked her up at 8:00 in the morning, as he was anxious to get her home as soon as possible. He was able to clean her whole apartment out and they put most of her furniture in Jason's basement. Her couch had been ruined and he figured she wouldn't want anything else from her living room. She was lucky the cops hadn't arrested for all the meth he found in her apartment. When they got home he made her comfortable and then went to the store to buy her favorite foods.

🍁　　　🍁　　　🍁

All of her stuff was put away in her dresser. James had moved it into his room. His house was spotless and he had fresh flowers on the kitchen table, that fragranced the house like a garden. She figured he had found most of the drugs, but she looked inside her sneakers for the bag she kept there. She also kept some in a pocket in a pair of her jeans. He hadn't found those ones. Most of her stuff had been hidden under her mattress but she kept a few small bags hidden elsewhere just in case.

❦   ❦   ❦

On Thursday, Jason was going over some music with James when the cops came by to ask Sam some questions. They had found an I.D. on Greg that showed him having the same last name as Sam. Sam cringed when she saw his picture on the card. She explained that it must've been a fake I.D.; that his last name was Fiori, and he was Veronica's brother and they could get more information from her.

Jason's' eyes almost bulged out of his head when he saw the picture. He couldn't believe it.

❦   ❦   ❦

By Sunday, James had caught on to Sam. He was on a rampage. He went through the medicine chest in the bathroom and through all of her clothes. He tore the bed apart, ripping off the comforter and the sheets. Then he moved to the living room and pulled out all the CD's and movies from the entertainment center.

"Where the fuck is it, Sam? I thought I had found it all, but I guess not. You thought you could hide it from me. Well, you'll have to do a better acting job than that. You haven't slept since you've been home and you've hardly eaten. You are wasting away into nothing. I can't help you if you won't be willing to help yourself first." He grabbed her by both of her arms. "WHERE THE FUCK IS IT?" He hadn't been this angry in a long time. He was mostly upset because he pampered her day and night and she refused to open up to him. He was mad because he hadn't been able to protect her from Greg. He was mad because no matter how hard he tried, he could not stop her from using drugs. He was mad because he wanted her to get better so they could get on with their lives. He was mad because he knew if she were still pregnant she would not have stopped using.

"I can't be here right now," he said, letting her go. "I need some time alone before I end up physically hurting you." Even when he grabbed her, she showed no response. It was like she was dead to the world. "I'll be at Lance's for a while." He threw some things in a bag and left.

※ ※ ※

The guys practiced that evening and James opened up a little to his friends. He felt better but he needed some time away from her. He hoped that would straighten her out.

Jason couldn't believe James was so heartless to leave Sam alone. She had been through hell and all he could think about was himself. He made a mental note to go check on her after practice.

※ ※ ※

Once it was dark Sam was completely freaked out. She left all the doors open so if he came to get her, she would have a way out. She didn't really believe he was dead. He was a monster and monsters didn't die. She had all of the lights on in the house and she was sitting on the kitchen floor next to the door of the pantry with James' gun in her hand. There was a mirror, a razor blade, a dollar, and a bag of her nasty habit sitting next to her. When she felt like she was coming down she would do another line. She had done so many lines since James had left that she had lost count.

At ten o'clock he came through the door. She held the gun up in front of her.

"Don't shoot," he spoke quietly from the hallway. He knew if he yelled that might spook her. He cautiously walked over to her and pulled the gun from her shaking hands. He didn't know if her shaking was caused from fear or having too many drugs in her system.

She had big black circles underneath her eyes and there was meth all over the mirror that sat next to her on the floor.

"Sam, it's me, Jason." He knelt down in front of her coming to her eyelevel. "What's going on?" He asked.

She broke down. "I'm sorry. I thought you were him. I thought he would come back for me. I'm so scared, Jason. I can't stop. I can't quit using the drugs, because I'm so afraid. He's in my nightmares, I see him on the street. Sometimes he's in bed with me. I'll never be able to stop. I am going to die a drug addict. My movie career is finished before it even started." She was talking so fast and shaking so badly that Jason was afraid she would go into shock. He wiped the tears from her cheeks. Her teeth rattled as if she was freezing but it had to have been at least 80 degrees in the house.

He cleaned up the mess on the floor, washing any evidence of the drugs down the drain. He unloaded the gun and put it away in the closet. He put some of her clothes together, closed up the house, picked her up and took her to the car. He sat up with her all night trying to get her to at least drink something. She couldn't though. She smoked a whole pack of cigarettes and they stayed up until well past dawn. By seven o'clock he was able to put her into bed. They both slept until late that afternoon.

CHAPTER 43

On Wednesday Jason received a phone call asking if he knew where Sam was.

"She's with me." He didn't feel the need to lie. "I picked her up Sunday night. She was sitting on the kitchen floor with a gun in her hand scared out of her mind. She was so wired, she was delirious. Every light was on in the house and all the doors were open. Nice way to leave your girlfriend, James."

"We'll, I'm coming to get her."

"No, you're not. She's fine here. Leave her alone for awhile, after all you're good at that."

"Fuck you, Jason. You can come in and act like the hero all you want, but I'm the one who will always be there and I'm the one she'll always want to be with."

"Don't count your chickens, pal." Jason said and hung up the receiver.

"Who was that?" Sam asked. She was on the back deck relaxing in the sun on a chaise lounge sipping a glass of ice water.

"Sales call." He said, pulling the glass from her hands and crawling on top of her to kiss her neck. She still wasn't able to have sex yet and he was making it very difficult to resist. But she did kiss him back on the mouth. He had taken care of her for the last three days, taking time off of work for the whole week. She hadn't done any drugs and he made her feel safe. He had been able to get her to come out of her shell and today she felt stronger than she had in a long time. Her body was still recovering from all the damage it had endured but her mind was healing quite well.

Neither one of them heard the doorbell ring over the loud music that was coming from the house.

❧   ❧   ❧

Veronica had decided to quit her job at *Baby Dolls*. She felt dirty after what Greg had done to her and just knowing that he watched her dance in there was enough to make her not want to go back. Bob had found her a job at the studio as one of the receptionists. She would start the following Monday. She still couldn't get very intimate with him and she had nightmares nightly now. He begged her to get help, but she claimed all therapy did was sink a hole in her pocket. She had gone before when she moved out there to try to lay the past behind her but she had not gained anything after going to the shrink for a year. The therapist probably had though. She could've afforded a Porshe from all of the money she had collected from Veronica.

She had all but moved out of her apartment with Sera. She hadn't left Bob's since they had gotten home from the hospital. Bob tried to take her out to dinner, to the movies, anywhere, but she just wouldn't go. She didn't know what she was afraid of, after all, Greg was dead. But she felt like people would know what she'd been through and what he'd done to her and they would scorn her for that.

Bob was at work and she was finally feeling an urge to get out of the house. She called him on the phone. "I need to get out of here. I think being cooped up like this is just making everything worse. I keep reliving that night over and over again and it's making me crazy."

"Why don't I come home early and we'll go out to dinner? Tomorrow I'll make hotel reservations in Santa Barbara and we'll go down there for a few days."

"That sounds wonderful. What time will you be home?"

"At 3 o'clock," he said happily. She was finally coming around again.

※　　　　　※　　　　　※

The back gate opened and James came around the side of the house. Nothing could've prepared him for what he saw. The pain in his heart tore through him like a dull knife.

"I see you've moved on," he said through clenched teeth.

"Omigod! James!" She pushed Jason off of her and sat up.

His back was rigid. "No, please don't stop on my account. I rather enjoy watching my friend and my girlfriend get it on." There was fire in his eyes and she knew at any moment he would explode.

"James, I'm sorry." She ran over to him but he pushed her down.

"Don't take it out on her," Jason said, angry that James had knocked her down.

"Fuck you. How long has this been going on?"

"There is nothing going on." Jason said calmly.

"LIAR! How long?" He turned to Sam but all she could do was shake her head and cry.

He bent down and pulled her up by her arm. "HOW LONG!"

Jason pulled her away from him and James caught him in the jaw with a left hook. Jason swung back and before Sam could blink twice, they were engaged in a full-blown fight.

"STOP IT!" She screamed, trying to get in between them, but James threw her across the yard. She got up and ran into the house through the sliding glass door, grabbed her things and took off in James' car. She headed to Bob's for she had nowhere else to go. She opened the door with her key and saw Veronica sitting in the kitchen at the small glass dinette table.

"Hey," Sam said, trying to act as casual as she could.

"Hi," she said as she tried to calm herself down from the sudden burst of energy that came into the door. "Bob's not here."

"Yeah, he's probably at work, right?"

"He'll be home soon. We're going to dinner. Do you want to join us?" She was happy to see Sam. She had wanted to talk to her but hadn't had the courage to call her at James' house.

"No. I just needed somewhere to go. I'll be fine. But thanks anyway."

"Something happen between you and James?" She noticed the tear stains on Sam's cheeks.

"It's a long story," Sam said, walking outside. She lit up a cigarette from a pack Bob kept in the living room and sat down on the back step. She didn't know why she did that. She didn't smoke when she wasn't high and it really tasted like crap. Old habit, she guessed.

"If you want to talk, I'm here." Veronica followed her outside. "I've been having a really hard time with all of this too," she said, hoping to open Sam up. She knew things couldn't have been easy for her, either. "I have nightmares every night."

"Yeah? Well my problems seem to outweigh that." She looked at Veronica still wondering how she could put up with all that pain in her life. "I'm in love with two guys. I can't pick which one I want because I want both of them, only I can't have both. You know, it had been going so good too." She realized she needed a line and her things were at James' house. If she couldn't have either man she would have to do something to take her mind off of them. She left the house leaving Veronica to wait for Bob.

❦ ❦ ❦

After they were done fighting, they both sat on the lawn trying to catch their breath. Finally Jason spoke, "I'm sorry, James, but I am in love with her."

"Well, so am I, and I believe I laid claim to her first."

"Then I'll back off," he lied. He knew he wouldn't be able to. "I don't want to see her hurt anymore than she already has been." He would never be able to be the bigger man, but he could at least pretend to be.

"And you think I do?"

"I don't know, James, do you? I don't think she would have come to me in the first place if you were able to make her completely happy."

"Do you want to be the third wheel, Jason? Do you want to always be her second choice?"

"Who says that I am?"

※　　　　※　　　　※

Sam went to James' house to find her stuff. She figured after today James wouldn't want to see her anyway, so she may as well take all of her belongings as well. At least that decision was made and she didn't really have to make it. She wasn't sure if it was exactly what she had wanted to happen though.

She opened the door with James' keys. She couldn't remember if she had left anything lying around but she looked in her shoes—none, she looked in her pants—all gone, she looked in the kitchen and the living room. "Damn it! Where the hell is it," she screamed. She looked through the place that James used to hide it. It was cleaned out completely. She searched through the couch and end tables then she went into the bathroom and started throwing things out of the medicine chest and looking in bottles. She threw the towels out of the closet and searched in there. Then she went into the bedroom. She looked through all the drawers in the dressers and then the closet. When she opened the nightstand drawer she saw a small box. She opened the box hoping to find something that would relieve her anxiety. What she found was more than she was hoping for though. She looked at the diamond and fell to the floor on her knees. She leaned back against the bed and stared at it. It was so beautiful. It sparkled off the light shining in through the window. She tried it on and it fit perfectly. She knew it was for her. She had broken James' heart today. Now, she found an engagement ring. He wanted her to marry him. He wanted to spend his life with her. The thought of that made her excruciatingly happy but it also closed her chest on her. She wasn't sure that was what she wanted. It might be fun at first but what about after she got bored with him. She knew she would. She got bored with everything. She constantly needed change in her life. She could not stand monotony. Or maybe even monogamy for that matter.

"What the fuck happened here?" He yelled from the other room.

She hadn't heard the front door open and she quickly tried to put the ring back but she had banana fingers and couldn't get it back in time.

He walked into the room. She was sitting on the floor with the ring box in her hand. The room was thrashed—hell the whole house was thrashed for that matter.

"Were you looking for something?" He asked, taking the ring from her hands. "I found your stash and flushed it."

"No. I just came to get my clothes," she said, getting up.

He sat on the bed and pulled her to him, bringing her face down to his. "I love you so much more than I ever thought was possible, Sam. When we're not together it's like my heart is missing. You make me whole."

She looked at him with tears in her eyes and cut him off before he could say any more. "Don't ask me. Please don't ask me." She took his face in her hands and kissed him on the mouth and walked away.

CHAPTER 44

On the first day of July, Sam turned 26 and started filming her first movie. Her excitement overflowed into everything she did. On the first day, she even got to the set early and tried to help set things up. Jacob had finally come to her and told her she was part of the cast and not the crew. Everyone found her so easy to work with. She didn't have any demands or even any requests. She didn't balk at anything and she was very patient, even after twelve hours on the set.

Sam's role was that of a young girl trying to make it on her own. The girl, Sophie, had been in and out of foster homes her whole life and had escaped the system at age 15 in order to get away from a foster father who was molesting her. She took a bus from San Francisco to L.A. to try to make it in show business. Only she didn't want to be in front of the camera, she wanted to be behind it. It was based on the true story of one of the biggest women producers in history. A woman who battled depression and eating disorders to be one of the most respected women in Hollywood.

The filming started with Sophie on the bus to L.A. All of the filming was on location in L.A. Sam had resembled Sophie a little bit and that had helped her get the part, but once Jacob started working with her he was very pleased at his choice.

Sam found a new apartment down by the beach. It was the first story of a three-story complex. She had ocean access right out her back door and a parking space right outside the front door. She had fallen in love with the place the first time she saw it, but was hesitant about living by herself. But, since Amber and Lance had broken up and Amber was looking for a place to live, she told Sam that she would move in with her, so everything had worked out.

Things always seemed to work out for Sam even without her really having to try. All in all, she was a pretty lucky girl. The money she won in Vegas and getting a movie role off of her first audition ever. Even finding such an awesome place to live. Everything seemed to fall into place for her. Everything, that is, except love. She had a really hard time in that department.

She hadn't seen James or Jason in a long time. They had both quit their jobs to work on their record. They hung out at *HotShots* still but Sam didn't go there anymore. She and Amber hung out at a dance club on the other end of town and when Amber worked, Sam went out with Bob now that he was single again. The day before their trip to Santa Barbara, Veronica bolted. She took all of her stuff and just left. No note or anything. She had just disappeared. Bob had been heartbroken.

That night while Amber was at work, Sam was getting ready for bed. She was just pulling back the white down comforter from her bed, revealing her Ralph Lauren moon and star sheet set, when she heard a pinging on the window. She froze with terror. It was the first time she had felt unsafe since she had been in her new apartment. She thought for sure somebody was trying to get in. She turned off the light and walked over to get the phone. She was about to dial the second number when she heard somebody singing. She put the phone down and held her breath so she could hear. It sounded like *Van Morrison's Brown-eyed girl* only it was revised to be *Green-eyed girl*. Completely unaware of what was happening, but not afraid anymore, she walked over to the window and looked out. James was standing there with a bouquet of roses and a bottle of champagne serenading her. She was surprised at how happy she was to see him out there.

"Hi," she croaked as she opened the window.

"Hi back. Did I scare you?" He asked, smiling up at her in the moonlight. Even though she was on the ground floor, her window was still a good 10 feet off of the ground.

"No," she lied. "Do you want to come in?" She asked, this time able to get the right sounds to match the words.

"Do you want me to come in?" He asked.

"Yes," she said, surprising herself again.

He came around the front and she let him in. He was so happy to see her that he picked her up and swung her around. He was even happier when he saw she was only wearing a bra and panties.

"I see you were expecting me," he said, referring to her lack of clothes.

She looked down at herself and was a little embarrassed. She grabbed the wine and the roses from him, found a vase and put them up on the bar that faced the living room. She opened the champagne, noticing a gold bracelet wrapped around the bottle.

"For me?" She asked as she pulled it off the bottle. It was engraved on the inside with the words, *all my love, all my life.*

"Yes." He told her as he held his breath.

"What's the occasion?"

"Happy Birthday."

She scrunched her nose up wrinkling her brow, "You remembered?"

"How could I forget?" He came up to her from behind while she was pouring the champagne into the glasses and put his arms around her waist. "It's been long enough. If you want to stay here that's fine but I can't be without you anymore."

She turned around in his arms. "It hasn't been that long."

"It seems like forever to me. I keep busy all day and sometimes all night but when I come home to an empty bed and remember what it was like when you were there, it almost kills me. And waking up alone is even harder."

She was fighting the emotions off with a stick now. On the one hand she wanted him so badly. She wanted to make love with him and never let him go, but on the other hand she was doing so well now. She was clean—on her own-she was happy, but she **was** lonely. She hadn't been interested in dating anyone, not even Jason. She missed James so much. She missed the way he looked at her. She missed the way his strong arms wrapped around her. She missed the way his soft lips felt on her body. She missed the way he knew how to hit the right spot every time they made love.

"I know what you mean," she moved over to the couch and sat down on the arm. "It hasn't been easy for me either. But a lot has happened in such a short time. I don't know if I'm ready to spend my whole life with someone."

He didn't want to hear her say that but he went on with his speech anyway. "I don't care what happened between you and Jason. I don't even want to know anymore. I'm not here to ask you to marry me or make a commitment that you aren't ready to make. I'm here to see if we can start over, do things differently this time."

She thought about it for a moment. That sounded all right to her. She wasn't promising anything to him after all. They could start over with a clean slate, without the drugs and without the interferences. "I think I could do that." She smiled at him taking a sip from her glass.

"Let's consummate that," he said. Plucking the glass from her hand and lifting her off her feet, he carried her to the bedroom.

CHAPTER 45

❁

James woke up at 4:30 unaware of where he was for a moment. Then he looked over and saw Sam sleeping soundly. She looked like an angel. He didn't have to be at the studio until late so he curled up next to her and fell back asleep.

Sam jerked awake at 5:30. She sat up in bed covered in sweat. It was the first time she'd had a nightmare since she moved out of James' house. This time, though, she couldn't remember a single detail when she woke up. The sun was coming up and she looked over and saw James sleeping next to her. That calmed her down a bit but she couldn't understand why she had another nightmare. She got up, put on some clothes and decided to take a run on the beach.

🍁   🍁   🍁

Sam was gone when James got up again. A little note on his pile of clothes had told him where she had gone. He decided to take a quick shower and then make breakfast for her. He went into her bathroom and took a shower. When he got out, he looked in the medicine cabinet to find some mouthwash and saw a prescription bottle. It was a prescription for speed.

"What are you doing?" She asked, walking in and undressing for the shower.

"I could ask you the same thing," he said, showing her the pill bottle.

"I needed to lose weight for the part and I was tired of snorting meth." She said it as though it were as simple as forgetting to pick up milk at the grocery store.

Last night he had noticed she was dangerously thin. She was at least fifteen pounds thinner than when he first saw her and she was too thin then. "Sam this is just as dangerous and you've lost more weight than you were even supposed to. Who did you get them from?"

"I met someone on the set whose doctor gets her the stuff all the time. She said it wasn't addicting." It was true though. She had lost more weight than was required for the part.

"Like hell it isn't. Have you looked at yourself in the mirror?" He pulled her in front of the mirror. Her bones seemed to poke out from under her skin and her face was gaunt.

"Look," she stared at his reflection in the mirror, "I had to lose weight for the part."

"Good, then you've lost the weight, now you can quit using the pills."

"No, now I have to maintain the weight," she said, reaching for the bottle.

He held the bottle higher. "Are you even capable of making it on your own?" He shook his head in disbelief at her actions. "You are so naïve, Sam. You believe everything anybody tells you. You are sick. You look awful." He stared at her for a moment. "If I have to make it my life's mission to make you healthy, then I will." He took the bottle over to the toilet.

"What are you doing?!" Her eyes grew big as she watched him dump the pills into the bowl. "I need those." She lunged toward him and tried to grab them from his hand but he grabbed her with his other arm, holding her back, and flushed the pills down the toilet.

"Doesn't matter," she said defiantly. "I can get more."

"The hell you will. I'll make sure to that."

"James, please don't do this. I need to be thin for this part."

"Not that thin. You could gain thirty pounds and you would be thin enough."

"You can't just march back into my life and take control." She wanted him to take control and take hold of her and protect her, but it was in her blood to defy that.

"The hell I can't. I just did."

He went out into the kitchen and cooked her breakfast. He practically had to force it down her because she didn't want to eat. After breakfast she got ready for work and he drove her to the studio.

"I'm going to stay with you for awhile. You might want to let Amber know."

"What?" She swung her head around to meet his eyes.

"I can't trust you to take care of yourself, Sam. You will die if you stay on the path you are taking now."

"Fuck you, James."

"Never mind, I'll call her myself," he yelled after her as she slammed the car door shut and huffed her way into the studio.

❦   ❦   ❦

She walked into her dressing room and immediately called Jason from her cell phone. She hadn't talked to him in a long time but it seemed to be an immediate reaction to any fight she had with James.

"Hello?" A very feminine voice answered which caught Sam completely off guard.

"Um, hi," she stammered. "Is Jason there?"

"He's in the shower. Who's this?"

"It obviously doesn't matter anymore." She hung up the phone feeling as though somebody had stolen her sunshine. It shouldn't have mattered anyway, after all she just kind of left him hanging. He should have moved on by now and she should be happy that he moved on, after all, it appeared that she had James back. But she didn't really know if that was what she wanted.

She put the phone on the dressing table and turned around to look at herself in the mirror. James was right, she looked like shit. She looked up and saw his reflection in the mirror.

"You left this in the car." He handed her purse to her.

"Thanks."

"Jason has a new girlfriend." He said, hoping to dissuade her from calling him again.

Shit! He had heard her calling him. "Really? That's nice," she said trying to play dumb, as she pulled the scrunchie out of her hair.

"I heard you calling him." He looked disappointed that she was trying to beat around the bush.

'Well…"

"It doesn't matter. Nothing I say about it is going to matter. You always do what you want anyway."

"It does matter. I was just calling to say hi."

"No, you were calling because you were pissed off at me about the speed. If you wanted a friend to talk to, why not call Bob? Don't you think Jason is sick of you running to him every time we argue?"

"I'm not running to him. I haven't even seen him since that day at his house. He sent me those," she pointed to the vase of flowers. She didn't really know who sent the flowers but it sounded good to her and gave her an excuse.

He walked over to the flowers and picked up the note, *Missing you,* was all it said. He threw the note down and without even looking at Sam, he left the room without another word.

❦ ❦ ❦

Jason got out of the shower and asked the naked girl in his bed who had called.

"I don't know, but she sounded a little upset."

"It must've been Sam," he said grabbing the phone and hitting a *69 to get her number.

"Who's Sam?" She asked. But he was already out the patio door dialing her number.

❧   ❧   ❧

"James, I don't have anything more to say to you," she picked up the phone and snapped into it.

"It's Jason."

"Oh! Hi. I didn't expect to hear from you. How did you know I called?"

"My mom said some girl called and sounded upset. You are the only girl that ever calls me so I hit *69 and got your number."

"Your Mom? I thought it was your girlfriend."

"I don't have a girlfriend, Sam."

"James said…oh, well it doesn't matter. I called to thank you for the flowers."

"I didn't send any flowers. I am trying to stay out of your life because I thought that was what you wanted."

"You didn't send the flowers?" The disappointment was obvious in her voice.

"Sorry, I wish I would've." He paused. "So you are seeing James again?"

"Well we kind of got back together-sort of-last night," she didn't know what to say. Hearing his voice had sparked those feelings again. *Damn it, why did I even call. I knew this would happen. When am I gonna get a clue?* she asked herself. Then without even thinking she said, "I'd like to see you again."

"How about dinner?"

"Well, James has kind of moved in temporarily. How about a late lunch? Say, three?"

"I'll pick you up. See you then." He knew he was treading on thin ice just talking to her, but he couldn't help it. He would do anything for her.

She hung up the phone, feeling worse now than she had before. She shouldn't be seeing Jason, not if she wanted to work things out with James. Did she though? She didn't know. Things seemed less complicated when he wasn't around.

Sam received another phone call on her cell phone right after she hung up with Jason.

"Hello?" She asked, hoping it was Jason calling to knock some sense into her.

"Sam, it's Jonathan. I've got another job for you; it's a movie that could possibly be up for an Oscar next year. The supporting actress was fired and they called me to see if I had a replacement. Can you be at *Omar Studios* tomorrow at 7 a.m.?"

"Wow! Absolutely. What exactly are they looking for?"

"It's a comedy part. Different from what you are doing now. The character is a young girl with a dry sense of humor, but she is also very deep emotionally. I'm sending over a synopsis of the part so you can familiarize yourself with it. You will be auditioning with Thomas Bennett."

"Omigod, Jonathan! He's the hottest star in Hollywood right now. I can't possibly audition with him." She was freaking out now. Thomas Bennett had taken Hollywood by storm with his last two movies, not to mention the fact that he was extremely handsome.

"You can do it, Sam. By the way did you get my flowers?"

"Flowers? Oh, you sent the flowers." Now she was wondering why **he** sent the flowers. "There wasn't a name, the note just said *Missing You*."

He sensed the puzzlement in her voice. "Oh, well, they must have gotten that message mixed up at the flower shop." Feeling a little embarrassed now he added, "it was supposed to say *Wishing You The Best*."

"Well, thank you very much they're gorgeous. I've got to go into makeup now," she added quickly. She was getting an awkward feeling from the conversation. "I will talk to you soon and let you know how it goes tomorrow."

"How what goes?" His mind was elsewhere now. "Oh yeah, the audition. That's fine, Sam. Talk to you soon." He hung up the phone, hoping he sounded convincing about the flowers. He certainly had read her wrong when she came to his office last time thanking him for the part. He thought she was hitting on him the way she hugged him and batted her eyelashes, but he could tell by her voice today that she was a little disturbed by the fact that he had sent the flowers with that message. Disappointed as he was, he still couldn't stop thinking about her.

CHAPTER 46

❀

Jason picked Sam up in front of the studio at three o'clock sharp. The excitement she felt at seeing his car pull into the parking lot surprised her. She realized just how much she had missed him. He took her back to his place for an early dinner, which he'd had catered in. He made her wait in the car while he lit candles and put on some Enya to set the mood.

When she walked into the house she was overwhelmed at seeing all the trouble he had gone to for her.

"Did you make all of this?" She pointed to the exquisite spread on the table.

"Only the best for you, baby."

"Then you must've had it catered," she said and then giggled. She knew he didn't like to cook, besides the fact that his skills didn't go far beyond dropping an egg into a skillet.

Sam sat down in the chair Jason pulled out for her and then helped herself to some lobster stuffed mushrooms as he poured a glass of wine for her.

"Where's your mom?" Sam asked, after Jason sat down and joined her.

He had just stuck a bite of mushroom in his mouth and almost choked at her question, but recovered quickly with a gulp of wine.

"My parents are staying at the Beverly Hills Hotel," he said, as he cleared his throat from any remaining debris. They are in town for just a few days. My mom came over to cook me breakfast this morning."

"That's so sweet." Sam didn't know anyone in her family who would do something like that. The Brady Bunch they definitely were not. She inquired more about his family as she bit into her second mushroom. She was surprised at how hungry she was. She hadn't eaten well in the last month and this tasted like something out of a dream.

As they started on the main course, Sam lifted the lid off one of the platters. Instead of food there was gift-wrapped box.

"What's this?"

"Happy belated birthday."

"You remembered?" She was touched.

"How could I forget?" He smiled as she ripped into the gift. "I'm so glad you called me, Sam."

"Omigod! OMIGOD!" She screamed, as she discovered the contents of the box. Inside were two round trip tickets and hotel accommodations for a week in the Bahamas.

"The Bahamas? You remembered that, too."

"Of course."

"I also remembered that you didn't like jewelry, that's why there wasn't a diamond ring under there," he mused, even though he was totally serious. He wanted more than anything to spend his life with this woman. Even if it meant leaving the band, he would do it in a heartbeat just to have her with him forever.

"Yeah," she said, looking at the bracelet on her wrist. "But I can't accept these, Jason. I know they cost a lot and I'm sure things are tight right now."

"No, actually we all got advances. Maybe you can take James." Though he hoped she wouldn't.

She looked at him dully. "Take him to the Bahamas? I don't think so. It would definitely put a damper on my fun."

"Things not going so great huh?" He decided a little reverse psychology was in order when he added, "it's only been one day, Sam, give it time."

She didn't understand why he was pushing her towards James. Didn't he still want her?

"He's starting his control shit again. After being away from it, I realized how sick of it I was. My weight has always been an issue with him and now this role I'm playing requires me to be less than thin. Though I'm done with meth, I did get some legalized speed from a doctor. He flipped out when he found the bottle of pills in the bathroom and he dumped them in the toilet." Anger flashed in her eyes as she remembered the scene from that morning.

"Well, Sam, you don't look well. I'd have to agree with James—you are too skinny." That was the only thing he agreed with James about. That asshole had come into the studio that morning yelling at him to stay away from Sam when he hadn't even done anything. He wouldn't have been surprised if James had sent the flowers just so he could see if Sam would've called him, and he told her just that.

"They were from my agent, only the cards were mixed up at the flower shop." She explained to him what the card had said. She couldn't understand why Jason thought James would go to such extreme measures just to pick on him.

The next question that came out of Jason's mouth was one he'd been practicing for a while. He wasn't sure exactly how to ask it so he just blurted it out, "Sam, how much do you really know about James?"

"What do you mean?" She drew a blank to his question. "We've discussed his family, his childhood and the band. I probably know everything there is to know."

He wondered what she would do if he told her that James had slept with a groupie the night they were in Vegas and how he had gone out with a few women since Sam had left him. Of course he wouldn't tell her that, but he would tell her some other things.

"Do you know anything about his parents?" He asked.

"I know they sell real estate. They own his house."

He picked up his glass of wine and swirled the contents around. He watched the motion with deep interest as he went on to talk about James. "His dad died when he was really little, and when his mom remarried, his step-dad didn't want anything to do with him so he was sent to live with his aunt in California when he was fourteen.

Sam's stomach dropped as she listened to Jason. "Oh my God. How awful. Why didn't he tell me?"

He went on, ignoring her question, "and he probably told you his sister is a lawyer," he popped a shrimp into his mouth. "Hardly. She doesn't practice law she hides from it. She owns a discreet escort service in Miami Beach. Sort of like Heidi Fleiss."

"What!!" She was confused and was starting to feel ill. "I don't understand. Why would he lie to me?"

"Probably didn't want you to think he was from a less than perfect family. He had to go to anger management classes after he and Veronica broke up. Did he tell you why they broke up?" He was on a roll now.

"Because she was crazy, threatened a waitress, and was really jealous of him."

"I think it was more the other way around, but she caught him cheating on her."

"Yeah, she mentioned something like that." Sam said quietly as she stared down and pushed the food around on her plate.

"He also followed her for several months after they broke up."

Sam raised her head to make eye contact with Jason. "What do you mean followed her?"

He was reaching now. "I mean he stalked her. He couldn't let go of her. Finally she called the cops on him and he had to go to therapy for a year. I would've warned you but that was over three years ago and I figured he was a little more stable now."

"Why are you telling me all of this now? What makes you think he hasn't changed?" She didn't understand why he had been silent for all of this time and now he was dumping all this on her.

"Because he's mentioned some things at rehearsal that have made me wonder if he wasn't doing the same to you.

"Following me?"

"He said something about your beach house right after you moved in and then when he was asked later about it, he claimed he didn't even know where it was. He said he's seen you and Amber at a dance club down by the beach but he doesn't dance. Just little things I pick up on. I'm telling you this because I care about you and I don't want him to hurt you, or scare you for that matter."

Sam downed the rest of her wine in one gulp. She couldn't believe this. She had been with someone she didn't even know. He had lied right to her face without even batting an eyelash. He had this make believe life in his head. She felt really spooked now. If he were capable of all of these lies what else would he do? Her face got hot as anger flooded her veins. She wanted to call him and yell at him. Tell him she knew the truth; that he was fucked up. But she couldn't, not without telling him she was here with Jason. Not without telling him that Jason had told her all of this stuff. She wouldn't do that to Jason.

Jason ate while Sam toyed with the food on her plate. Neither of them spoke for the duration of the meal. Afterwards, Jason took Sam back to the studio.

"I'm sorry I upset you, Sam, but I just wanted you to be aware of what you are getting yourself into. I could be wrong about everything and I hope to God that I am-but I want you to be careful." He wanted to say, *don't go back, please just stay with me. I love you so much,* but he didn't. Then he added, "you didn't think your meeting

James was fate did you. You knew it was premeditated right? He followed you to that bar you met him at." He had set the bait and now all he had to do was wait for her to take it.

Sam looked out the window not wanting to hear anymore. It was all such a shock to her. "This is a lot to digest in an hour, Jason. I need some time to think about what I'm going to do." She leaned over and kissed him lightly on the cheek. "I appreciate you looking out for me." She got out of the car and walked to her dressing room. She called Bob before she had to go back to work.

"What's up?" He asked.

"Can you come over to the studio after work, I need to talk to you."

"Sure, is everything okay?"

"I just found out some information about James that kind of puts me in an awkward position with him."

"Okay, I'll be there in an hour."

All of the relationships he'd had in his life had been a joke. He couldn't seem to settle down with one person for long. He got bored. Sam wasn't that way. She always kept him on the edge of excitement. He could not imagine being without her. His obsession with her had grown bigger than he ever could've imagined. No matter what it took he was going to get her back for good. And as long as she didn't find out about what he'd done, everything would work out fine.

"What's up? Bob asked, walking into Sam's dressing room. She was leaning back in a chair, knees bent, feet up on the makeup counter and deep in thought.

"How much do you really know about James?"

"I probably know less than you do. I mean I hung out at the bar quite a bit and we became friends that way but I never had real in-depth conversations with him. What's going on? Who has you all riled up now?"

"I had lunch with Jason today and he told me some things about James that I didn't know, or actually that James had lied about. James came over last night and is trying to work things out but, after today, I don't know if I can." She was rubbing her temples with her fingers trying to straighten out her thoughts.

"Well, what kinds of things did he lie about?"

"His parents, his sister, his past relationships. I don't have any reason not to trust Jason."

"Do you have any reason not to trust James? You don't know if what Jason is saying is true. I mean James doesn't seem like he is trying to lead a double life. Besides he's been infatuated with you before he even met you."

She stopped all movement and looked Bob in the eye, "what do you mean?"

"I showed him your picture one day and every time I came into the bar he wanted to see it. He was head over heels for you."

"Really?" It made Sam smile to think that, but it also made her wonder if maybe their meeting hadn't been chance after all.

"Did he know I was coming to L.A. before I got here?"

"I had told him if things didn't work out in Okieville, that you would be on the next flight out. I was at the bar the day you called from the airport."

"Did Veronica ever mention anything about her relationship with James?"

"Just that it had been great at first but got pretty volatile near the end."

"Did she ever say that James had followed her after they broke up?"

"No."

"I don't know what to do. These two guys have me tied up in knots. If I choose one, what if I can't let go of the other? What if I make the wrong choice?"

"Sam, the answers have always been right in front of you. Follow your heart."

"I did that once and all it did was get broken."

"That wasn't love, Sam. That was high school lust. Small town comfort. This is real life. This is where the choices we make matter the most."

"I wish I was like you. You always have the answers to everything."

He laughed at her naïve comment. "If I did, Veronica would still be here."

Sam could tell he was still heartbroken over her. She wished she could make the pain go away for him. It almost made her cry to hear the sorrow in his voice. "Remember when we were in college and my boyfriend broke up with me? Remember how you used to sit on the end of my bed and we would all watch TV? I never wanted you to leave; having you there next to me was such a comfort to me at that time. I wished you could have slept there all night because it made my loneliness disappear. It made my heart stop aching."

"I remember you asked me not to leave," he said, smiling at the memory. He wondered why she had brought it up though. "Where did all that come from?"

"I just wanted you to know how special you have always been to me and one day you'll find the perfect person. And even if you don't, I'll always be here for you. You are my very best friend in the whole world." She got up and gave him a big bear hug and kissed him on the cheek. "Having you in my life has made such a difference for me."

"Me too." He said, and got up to leave before she made him cry.

🍁   🍁   🍁

James got back to Sam's place at six o'clock. Amber was at work and he was going to make a romantic meal for Sam. She said she would be home around seven, so he had plenty of time. He was so happy she was allowing them to have another chance. He was so lost without her. He had gone out with two other girls while she was away but only to get her out of his mind. It didn't work though. She was intoxicating and had made her way into his heart. He couldn't get rid of her now even if he wanted to.

At 10 o'clock Sam walked in the door, blatantly drunk.

"Where have you been?" James asked her as he helped her through the door.

"Doesn't matter. I'm here now, right?" She slurred, pulling her arm out of his grasp and stumbling into the room.

"Okay," he scratched his temple. I had dinner waiting for you. You could have called." He didn't want to fight with her.

"I could have, but I didn't." She looked at him through thin eyes. "Look, you said you wanted to try, we tried and it's not working so let's just end this now." She walked over to the couch and sunk down into the plush blue-striped fabric.

"What are you talking about?" He asked, dumbfounded.

"Well you know, us—we aren't working." Her subtlety killed him.

"I don't understand. Why don't you start from the beginning?"

"Yeah, let's start from the beginning. You knew I was in L.A. when I got here, you knew who I was before we met and our meeting wasn't fate, was it? You followed me didn't you?"

"Followed you? Are you high, Sam? Do I look like a stalker?"

"I don't know are you one?" She pulled her head back from his face. "You followed Veronica around didn't you? Couldn't let go. Maybe you still can't let go of her. I can't play second fiddle to someone else."

He had no clue what the hell she was talking about, but he was tired of her nonsense. He got back in her face again and pointed an accusing finger at her, "you don't play second fiddle to someone else, I do. I play second fiddle to you. Everything in our relationship has been about you. Your drug habit, your neediness, your tears,…your cheating," he figured he may as well add fuel to the fire. "You're always waiting for someone to put you together. To wipe away the tears, to rescue you, to calm your fears, to fill your needs. I have done all of that and more. Every time we have gotten into a fight, I'm the one that comes crawling back to you. I'm the one that wants to fix things. I'm the one trying to put us back together. Maybe you just don't care." His pain was showing now and his voice was breaking with every syllable he spoke.

"Maybe I don't." She said, trying as hard as she could to push him away so the decision would be made for her.

He stared at her in disbelief and without saying another word; he grabbed his keys and walked out the door, just missing Jason who was standing in the shadows. He was so angry and hurt that he didn't even get to say half the things he wanted to say. He needed to take a drive and he didn't really care if he ever came back. Without her, there was nothing to come back for.

🍁   🍁   🍁

Jason walked in the house and Sam was pouring herself a glass of wine from the bottle that was on the table. She drank it as though it was water and as she was about to pour another drink, he walked over and grabbed the bottle from her hands.

"I think you've had enough to drink tonight, sweetheart."

She pulled the bottle back from him. "I will decide when I've had enough." She couldn't even stand up anymore. She almost fell over as she pulled the bottle back from him.

"C'mon, Sam. Don't you have an early audition? You need to sleep this off."

"It really doesn't matter does it? I'm so fucked up that it just doesn't matter. James was right. I can't even stand on my own two feet. I'm involved with two men, my career is about to take off, I've got great friends, a nice home, a Mustang that I suppose I have to give back now, and I am an emotional wreck. At least when I was wired all the time, I didn't have to feel. There was no pain. I can't take this hurt anymore. My whole life has been full of pain and I don't want to feel it anymore." She took a drink out of the bottle and Jason pulled it away from her when she was finished.

"You need to go to bed. Besides being drunk, you're tired and angry." He helped her into bed and he sat next to her until she fell asleep. There were still tears on her eyelashes when she finally dozed off. He sat there looking at her for a long time. He wondered how a person could be so different from day to day. She was usually like a breath of fresh air, bursting with new ideas and hopes and dreams. But when she cried, it tore his heart out. He wasn't sure if Sam would be able to accept her decision to leave James or not, but he was going to try and make it as easy for her as he could.

CHAPTER 47

❀

The alarm went off at 5:30. The loud beeping noise blasted through Sam's ears, giving the pain that thumped against her skull more leverage. *Now I know why I don't drink anymore,* she remembered. When she tried to sit up, the pain grew more intense, so she slid off the side of the bed and crawled into the bathroom, barely making it before her stomach announced it's bitterness with her for all the wine she drank the previous night.

Jason heard her from his makeshift bed on the sofa and walked into the bathroom to see if she was okay.

"No, I'm not okay. My head feels like it was crushed with a ton of bricks, I can't stand up, and I have a very important audition in a little more than an hour."

He helped her into the shower and waited for her wash up. He dried her off with a towel and helped her into the bedroom to get dressed.

"We should've had sex last night."

"I'm not disagreeing, but why do you say that?"

"It cures hangovers. Didn't you know that?" She attempted to smile but the movement of her face made her head hurt even more.

"No, but I will make a mental note of it for next time." He watched while she got dressed. "Why don't we go to the café on the corner and get something to eat?"

She gave him a funny look, "how did you know about that place?"

"I saw it on the way over here last night."

She couldn't remember which way they had come home so she had no right to challenge him. "I don't think I can eat anything," she moaned, as she fell back onto the bed. "I need more sleep. I don't ever want to drink again."

"You need something in your stomach. C'mon let's go."

🍁   🍁   🍁

Bob had thought all night about what Sam had told him. He wished he could find Veronica but he didn't have a clue where she went. James seemed so straightforward and honest that he just couldn't believe he would've lied to Sam like Jason claimed he did. He had a good mind to go over to James' house and straighten this mess out. He wasn't sure if Sam would want him to do it or not, but she was really hurt and he had an instinct to want to fix that for her.

🍁   🍁   🍁

James had driven all night. He ended up in San Diego and thought about going into Mexico but he didn't have his birth certificate and didn't want to get stuck down there. He pulled over and sat for a long time on a deserted beach. Listening to the waves crash up on the beach helped to clear his mind. He needed to fix things with Sam, find out what she was so upset about. She had obviously been talking to someone and that person had made her upset. He had to straighten things out with her. He walked back to the Jeep and pulled out onto curve. That's when he heard the loud honking and the last thing he saw were the headlights of the truck.

🍁   🍁   🍁

After breakfast Jason took Sam over to *Omar Studios* for her audition. He waited outside for her while she went in. When she finally walked out, she had her million-dollar smile spread across her face.

"You got the part?"

"Yeah, I got the part." She jumped into Jason's arms and hugged him.

"Guess you're feeling better, huh?"

"Guess so."

"So, tell me about it."

"Well, I auditioned with the lead actor and we did a screen test and they are going to work around my schedule. Should be done in about a month."

"Looks like you were meant to be here, Sam."

"I'll keep my fingers crossed."

"We better get you to work and I've got to get to the studio."

She looked at him after she got into the car, seeing more than she had let herself see before. She realized how much he did care about her. She wondered if he was in love with her. "Thank you for taking such good care of me. I don't mean to fall apart on you all the time."

He smiled at her. "You're welcome." He started the car and then added, "I know things are hard for you now, but we'll get through them."

Funny, she thought, *that's the same thing James said.*

🍁   🍁   🍁

The band waited until ten o'clock for James to show up. Kevin tuned his guitar about 50 times, Lance mindlessly tapped the drums and Jason sat in the corner reading a *Rolling Stone* magazine. They had tried James' home phone and his cell phone several times. Nobody had heard from him since the day before.

"He and Sam had a fight last night, maybe he's taking some time for himself," Jason said aloud, offering an explanation for James' surprise absence.

"What do you mean they had a fight?" Lance asked.

"They broke up again."

"Again? How do you know?" Kevin was interested now.

"Well, apparently they got back together and then broke up again."

"And how do you know this, Jason?" Lance asked, a little tired of Jason's bullshit.

"Because I was there."

"So maybe he isn't gone because of Sam-maybe it's because of you. It would be nice if you would keep your nose out of their life. Otherwise, we may not be here much longer."

"Lance, maybe you should mind your own fucking business." He threw the magazine down and walked out of the room.

"Take your own advice, dude," Lance sneered after him.

"Lance—phone," a voice from the other room called.

He walked out of the room and picked up the phone, "hello?"

"Lance, it's me." Even though they had broken up, he and Amber still remained friends so he wasn't completely shocked to hear from her.

"What's up?" He asked.

Her voice was shaking as she announced her reason for calling, "there's been an accident."

"Oh my God! Are you okay?"

"It's not me," she breathed, trying to stay calm. "A truck hit James this morning down near San Diego. He's in critical condition. They called my apartment, I guess they found the number in his wallet."

Without so much as even a breath, Lance dropped the phone and ran into the other room and repeated to the guys what he had just learned.

They all three immediately poured into Lance's truck and left for San Diego, not giving anyone or anything else a second thought.

CHAPTER 48

Sam sped down the freeway 80 miles an hour in the Mustang. Tears streamed down her face as she tried to keep her focus on the road and the cars around her. She couldn't believe James was hurt. It was all her fault. If she hadn't been such a bitch to him, he wouldn't have taken off.

"Sam, slow down." Amber told her as she clutched the dashboard. Amber had gone over to the studio to break the news to Sam after she had called Lance. She wasn't aware of what had gone on the previous night.

They arrived at the hospital at three o'clock after driving around in San Diego for close to an hour. When they walked into the ER, Lance, Kevin and Jason were in the waiting room.

"You could've driven down with me." Sam snapped at Jason and then went to find a doctor.

After several tries, she found someone who could be of help to her. He was a young resident who slightly resembled Denzel Washington. He also looked like he had been up for about two days.

"Are you a relative?" He asked Sam.

"Fiancé," she lied.

"He was brought in early this morning. He suffered a collapsed lung and we had to repair his spleen. He also has some major head injuries." He pulled her into a nearby chair to give her the rest of the news. "He's in ICU but he hasn't woken up yet. There's a good chance he may be in a coma."

"No," Sam whispered, as she buried her head in her hands and sobbed.

"Is there someone here for you?"

"Me," Jason said, walking up and kneeling next to Sam. "Baby, it's not your fault. Don't blame yourself for this. You were only protecting yourself last night, you couldn't have known this was going to happen."

The doctor got up and put a hand on Sam's shoulder. "I will update you more later. You can go see him in a few hours."

Jason pulled Sam to her feet and took her outside. They sat together on the curb and she cried in his arms for a long time. At last she pulled her head up and let the sunlight pour onto her face, causing the tears to glisten on her cheeks.

"I wanted someone to make my decision for me, but I didn't mean like this." She sniffled as she picked up a small rock from the pavement and tossed it.

"What decision?" Jason asked, confusion in his voice.

"Which guy. You or James. I didn't want to choose. I wanted the decision to be made some other way. This wasn't what I had in mind though. I brought all of this on. If I would've just stayed away from you and ignored my spontaneous feelings, this wouldn't have happened."

"Sam, you don't know that," he was hurt by what she had said. "Is that what you wanted, though? To ignore me? Because I can leave. If you don't want me in your life, just say so."

"That's not what I meant."

"I hope not," he got up and walked away angry.

Sam didn't even bother to follow him. She didn't have the energy or the desire to chase after him now. She sat on the curb and watched the sun fall behind the palm trees. A soft breeze cooled down her body in the 90-degree heat. She couldn't feel anything on the inside. She felt numb, like her whole body was asleep. She didn't even think she could move until Amber came out and told her that she could see James.

James was lying in bed as still as the night when Sam walked in. If she hadn't known otherwise, she would have thought he was dead. He had tubes in his veins and one down his throat. His head was bandaged and he had cuts and scrapes all over his face.

The nurse smiled at Sam solemnly and walked out of the room to give her some privacy.

"Hi," she said, as if he were capable of carrying on a conversation with her. She sat down in a chair next to his bed and grabbed his limp hand, the one he strummed the guitar with.

"I wish I knew what to say, but for once I'm speechless. I know that's hard to believe." She chuckled as tears welled up in her eyes. "So much has happened to me in the last few days and I don't even know what's going on anymore. Things are so confusing right now. I wish I had handled things differently last night. I am so sorry." She leaned over and put her head on his chest and listened to his heartbeat, more for comfort than anything else. She had listened to that rhythm so many nights before. It had gotten her to sleep after the nightmares, now she may never have that comfort again and that scared her more than anything. She loved James. She loved him more than anything in the world. She knew that now. For the first time in her life, love became clear to her. But now, she may never get the chance to tell him that. She prayed that he would come out of this, that he would be okay. Even if he didn't want her back she still wanted him to be okay.

The nurse came in 15 minutes later and told Sam that she had to leave. She pulled her head up off the gown he was wearing and kissed him softly on the cheek and whispered, "I love you."

❊   ❊   ❊

Everything was so dark. He couldn't see anything but he could hear voices. He wasn't sure whose they were. His eyelids were so heavy. He wished he could open them but it was like trying to lift a hundred pound weight with his pinky. He heard another voice, one a lot more familiar. It was Sam's voice. Why was he hearing Sam's voice? She had made it clear that she wanted him out of her life. Where was he anyway? He wished he could talk to someone to find out. He felt Sam's head on his chest just like old times. His shirt was getting wet, she was crying. Why was she crying? What was happening? He felt something soft on his cheek, like a feather. She told him she loved him. She still loved him. That was all he wanted to hear. That was enough to help him find his way out of the dark.

CHAPTER 49

Sam drove home that night with Jason and Amber. She had wanted to stay, but they told her it could be days, weeks, or even months before he came out of the coma. She didn't want him to be alone but his mother had shown up. After what Jason had told her, Sam had thought his relationship with his mother was rocky, but emergencies seemed to bring people closer and maybe that's why she was there.

They pulled into the parking space at the apartment and Sam noticed something moving on the porch. It was way past midnight and all she could think of, was that someone was trying to get into the apartment. Amber was asleep but Jason noticed the movement too, and told Sam to stay in the car while he checked it out. Within seconds he was running back to the car.

"There's a little girl up there."

"What?!" She quickly flung open the door and ran up to the front porch, completely unprepared for what she was about to find. "Max!" She shouted. Maxine ran into her arms. She was shaking uncontrollably and sobbing.

"Mommy left me here and told me to wait for you. I was scared, Sammy. When is mommy coming back? It's scary here." Her chestnut pigtails were all tangled and her cheeks were stained with dirt and tears.

"Shhh," she comforted her little cousin, picking her up and bringing her into the apartment. She noticed a small suitcase was on the porch. After Maxine was inside, she brought the suitcase in.

She sat down next to Maxine on the couch. "It's going to be okay, Max. We'll find mommy okay?" Jason and Amber walked in quietly so as not to scare the little girl.

"Max, these are my friends, Jason and Amber." Sam introduced her cousin to the people in the room.

Jason knelt down in front of Maxine. "Hi, Max. Can I call you Max?" He asked her.

She nodded her head.

"Max is a very cool name. I had a puppy named Max once, but you are sure a lot cuter."

She smiled at Jason, "you had a puppy?" She had always wanted a puppy to play with.

"Yeah. He was very cool."

"What happened to him?" She was interested in the puppy story now and had forgotten about everything else.

Jason had told her all about his puppy. Sam was grateful he had gotten her attention. She was surprised at how well he did with her. It was amazing. She took Max's suitcase into her bedroom and set it on the dresser careful not to knock over the pictures she had framed of her and James. She picked up her favorite one of him from their trip to Las Vegas and brought it to her lips. Then she said a silent prayer for him and replaced it back in it's spot. She turned back to the suitcase, opened it, and discovered a small envelope with Sam's name on it. She opened the letter and read it.

Dear Sam,

You always thought you could do a better job with her——so here you go.

It was Shelly's handwriting. Enclosed was a newspaper clipping about Greg and what had happened. It stated that Sam was an up and coming actress and had almost had her life taken short. That must be how Shelly found her. *Shit! What am I going to do now? I can't take care of a child*, Sam thought.

"Everything okay?" Jason walked into the room. Amber was fixing Max something to eat.

"No," she sighed, slumping down onto the bed with the note in her hands. "No, it's not okay. Shelly has taken off and left her with me." Sam explained who Shelly and Max were.

"What about her father?"

"Yeah. I could call him," Sam hadn't thought about that. "I'll do that in the morning."

After Max ate, Sam got her ready for bed. "Everything's going to be okay, sweetie. I promise." She hoped she sounded more convincing than she felt.

"Okay. But Sam…" she hesitated, rubbing the edge of the blanket between her fingers. "Will you sleep with me tonight?"

"Of course. I'll be back in just a little while."

She had planned on taking Jason home, but he insisted that he could stay on the couch. Before she walked back into the bedroom, he pulled her to him and kissed her softly.

"What was that for?" She asked, pulling back.

"You are amazing. You take the world on and never buckle under pressure. I don't know how you do it, but I admire you for it."

She smiled at the irony of the situation; she had felt completely opposite. So much was dumped on her shoulders and she didn't feel like she was dealing with anything very well. "Thank you," she smiled at him. A strange feeling had come over her when he kissed her. It had been a long time since her lips had touched his and she had forgotten what it felt like, but it just wasn't the same now with James in the hospital.

"I…," he was cut off by Max calling for Sam.

"I'll see you in the morning," she said.

He lay down on the couch and wondered if all the pain was really worth it.

CHAPTER 50

❀

"Is Rick there?" Sam spoke softly into the bedroom phone so Max wouldn't hear her. Max was having breakfast with Jason in the kitchen. Amber was still in bed.

"Who's this?" The female voice demanded.

"This is Max's cousin, Sam."

"Oh, are you looking for Max?"

Sam was disturbed by the voice so she played it down. "No, I was calling to find Shelly, but I can't get a hold of her." She figured that much was safe to say.

"Well, we're in the middle of a crime scene investigation here, so if you have any information that could help us, you'd better come down to the station.

"I'm sorry, I don't understand."

"Who are you trying to get a hold of?" The female voice inquired.

"Rick Fielding."

"I'm sorry to have to tell you this, but he's dead. He and his girlfriend were murdered two days ago." A pause. "Where are you calling from?"

"Los Angeles, California. I, uh…I…" Sam hung up the phone. She didn't want to get involved any more than she already was. As long as Max was safe, there was no need for her to be talking to the police.

When Sam walked out to the kitchen, the color had drained from her face. "I need to find a newspaper."

"Here's the L.A. times," Jason said, tossing her the paper. Then he noticed how pale she was. "What's wrong?"

She pulled Jason into the bedroom and told him what the cop had told her over the phone.

"We can look for it a lot faster over the Internet. You're going to have a hard time finding an Oklahoma newspaper in L.A." He should know.

In only five minutes, Jason had the information pulled up on the screen. Sure enough, Rick, and his girlfriend, Darla, had been shot. And to Sam's surprise, Shelly was a suspect and was missing.

"I can't believe this. This is insane." Sam paced the room, running her hand through her hair and pulling it, when she reached the length. "I have to call the studio. I can't go to work."

"No, you don't. We won't be in the studio for the rest of the week so I'll stay with her until you figure out another arrangement."

Sam looked at him, shock in her eyes. "You sure?"

"Of course, we'll have lots of fun." He turned to Max as she was finishing her breakfast. "Do you like to swim, Max?"

"Yeah."

"She doesn't have a suit," Sam whispered.

"Then we'll go buy one."

Sam pulled out some money for him but he pushed her hand away.

"I'll take care of it. I really don't mind. Now go get ready for work so we can swing by the studio and get my car." He gave her a small pat on the butt to get her going.

"Okay, okay," she laughed as she went to the bedroom.

🍁 🍁 🍁

Bob hadn't been able to get a hold of James. He also hadn't been able to get a hold of Sam either which gave him hope that they were together working things out. James was a good guy and he really wanted Sam to be with him. He knew that James could make her happy. Sam came off as hard to please, but she really wasn't. She only wanted a few simple things in life. Bob knew James could give her that.

He called Sam on her cell phone. She was in her dressing room getting ready for the day's scenes. She told him everything that had happened. She seemed to be holding up well considering all that was taking place in her life at the moment.

"Is there anything I can do? I could drive down and check on James if you want."

"His mother is there and the doctor told me he'd call if there was any change. You can go see him if you want to, but don't do it for me."

"What are you going to do about Max?"

"I don't have a choice. She has to stay with me. I'm not going to send her to live with anyone in my family-I can't do that to her. Besides, I'm the only one she's close to and I have the financial ability to take care of her."

"What are you going to do with her while you work?"

"She's with Jason for the rest of the week and then I will have to figure something out."

"Call me if you need anything."

"Of course. How about lunch next week?"

"Sounds good. Take care." He hung up the phone in disbelief at their conversation. *Poor Sam*, he thought. He knew she was trying so hard to mask her feelings and not give in to the heartbreak that was eating at her.

Sam worked all day until 7 o'clock. When she got home Max and Jason were playing a game on the floor in the living room and Jason had ordered in pizza.

"I feel like I just walked into a television sitcom," Sam said as she walked into the apartment still warmed by the daylight. Her life had completely changed in 24 hours but it really didn't bother her. It almost gave her a sense of stability to come home to a family.

"How was your day?" Jason asked from his game of *Candyland*.

"Good, and yours?"

"We had lots of fun today didn't we, Max?"

"Oh, yeah. We went swimming and we ate ice cream and we played at the park and we bought this really fun game," she said, pointing to the game she was playing with Jason. Her big brown eyes were all smiles now; the fear had seemed to disappear.

"That sounds like a lot more fun than what I did." Sam walked into the kitchen to get dinner ready. "Why don't you come and eat dinner, okay?"

"I already ate. I was hungry and couldn't wait for you. Sorry, Sammy."

"That's okay, sweetie."

"How about you?" She asked Jason.

"I waited for you," he said, coming up to her and pulling her into his arms.

"I'm glad for that," she smiled at him. Having him around instead of James still gave her an odd feeling in the bottom of her stomach.

"Max, why don't you go play with your doll while Sam and I eat dinner."

"Okay."

"Doll?" Sam asked.

"I bought her a few things today."

"That was sweet of you. Thank you." She plopped two slices of pizza onto a plate for him and handed it over. "You surprise me. I would have never pictured you the kid type."

"I have nieces and nephews that I get to see and spoil on occasion. She's a really good kid Sam. She's really smart too."

"I know. Amazing isn't it. Especially when her mother was such an idiot." Sam's blood boiled just talking about Shelly.

They ate dinner and Sam put Max to bed after her bath. She was able to sleep in the bed by herself as long as Sam left the door open and a light on. Jason and Sam sat down on the couch, each with a glass of wine.

"So what are we going to do?"

She cocked her head at him, wondering if he realized what he'd just said. Or maybe she was hearing what deep down inside of her she wanted to hear. Someone was going to be there for her. "Raise her. Financially it won't be a problem. I will have to make some changes in my life and I talked to my makeup artist today, her little girl is Max's age and she goes to preschool. She said she'd get me some information about it and bring it in."

"I will help you do whatever you need me to. I called our manager today and he said if James isn't better in two weeks, we have to go in and finish the album without him. I'm going to have to take over the vocals and lead guitar. We'll have to get someone to fill in for the bass."

Sam's throat closed up just thinking about James in the hospital bed. His life, possibly over. She needed something to divert her attention from the misery she was causing herself thinking about it. She quickly changed the subject. "I need to find a two bedroom apartment. I need to get her clothes, toys, and a bedroom set. She won't be in school until fall so I don't have to worry about that for a while. I'm going to pay Amber six months rent, so that gives her plenty of time to find a roommate." Sam felt like she was rambling now but there was so much in her head and she felt she needed to say it out loud to make it real.

"Why don't you move in with me?"

"What?"

"I have a three bedroom house. There's plenty of room. You can have your own bedroom and so can Max."

The knot in her stomach grew tighter. "I can't do that to you. You have a life and we would be imposing on you. Besides, I like living by the beach."

"Okay, then let's get a place together by the beach. I want to be there with you. I want to help you. Today felt so right. I haven't felt this good in a long time. I love you, Sam." There, he said it. For the first time he said it out loud. He finally told her what he'd wanted to tell her since the day he met her.

Sam was stunned at those words. She could never get anybody to fall in love with her in any of her previous relationships and now she had two men in love with her. Two very hot, soon to be very famous, men.

"Don't say anything," he put his finger to her lips, "just listen to me. I have loved you since the first time I saw you. I didn't want to get in the way of you and James. James is my friend, but I also hate him with a passion sometimes. I wasn't willing to risk the band's success before. Sam, James may never come out of that coma and if he does there's a chance he may be brain dead. You know that. I don't want to waste anymore time worrying about him or the band. I know right now with all of my heart that I love you. That's all that matters to me."

She had dreamed of someone saying those words to her for what seemed like a lifetime. Now someone was saying them to her, but it wasn't the someone she had wanted. For a moment she wished that James and Jason had traded places. That Jason was the one in the hospital and James was here helping her, taking care of her. But it might never be that way. She knew James' chances were slim. Could she settle for Jason? From the way she felt at this moment, she thought she could never love him as much as she loved James. But she also knew there was the chance that her feelings stemmed from guilt and the fact that Jason was here and James wasn't. Always wanting what she couldn't have. Never accepting what life offered her.

He leaned in to kiss her. It was so gentle, yet so firm. She wanted something to take her mind off of James and her feelings for him. She needed a distraction from the pain she had been in. But for once, she couldn't give in. She pulled back from him and told him she needed time to think. She walked out the door and onto the beach, leaving his desire to burn out on it's own.

CHAPTER 51

❀

The next few weeks proved to be trying for Sam. On top of two films, she had Max, Jason, and a move to make. She had enrolled Max in an all day preschool program and she seemed to really like it. She enjoyed being around other children her own age. *Cruel* had gone back to recording their album. Jason took over vocals and they hired a guitar tech to fill in for the bass. Jason and Sam had found a beach house and were set to move in the following weekend. Sam had decided to take him up on his offer to move in together. She would have her own room and she made that clear to him. She just wasn't ready to get into a full-blown relationship with him. But she did need someone to help her with Max and he had been the one to offer.

On July 26th, Sam took the day off work and flew down to San Diego to spend it with James. She had arranged it with Jacob before because it was James' birthday. She hadn't told Jason she was doing this and hoped he wouldn't find out. It wasn't that she owed him anything but, whenever she mentioned James to him, he got distant and quiet, which put a strain on her.

She walked into the hospital room and James' mom was in there with him.

"Hi," Sam said to the well-dressed blonde on the other side of the room. She looked like she should be running a corporation from an office with a view on the upper west side of New York. She was slender, sophisticated and very well kept.

"You must be Sam," the woman said, getting up from her chair. "I'm Marla, James' mother." She held out a well-manicured hand to Sam.

"It's nice to meet you," Sam said, unsure of how to act since Jason's stories.

"James has told me a lot about you."

"Really?" Sam asked.

"You sound shocked." Marla smiled at the surprise she found in Sam's eyes.

"Well I guess I kind of got the impression that you weren't very close with him."

"What would give you that idea?"

"I guess because he never really talked about you or his father that much."

"Well, we've had our ups and downs over the years, I won't deny that. But things have gotten better for us over the last year, especially since I left my husband."

"You aren't married anymore?"

Marla looked down at her lifeless son. "Sometimes we do things in life because we want what's best for our children. We have to look ahead and see what we can do now that will produce the best outcome for them."

"I thought you sent James was sent to live with his aunt after you remarried."

"Not necessarily sent. He was already there."

"Excuse me for being so abrupt, but how's that doing what's best for him?"

"Let's go get coffee and I'll explain it to you," Marla looked up at Sam and they left to walk down to the cafeteria. They sat down and Marla explained things to Sam.

"James' father, Charles, died of cancer when James was five. Not only was it a blow emotionally for us but financially as well. He had used the money he had inherited from his father to set up his own law practice. We had nothing left. The cancer came fast and the life insurance policy we had was minimal. When Charles died we moved out to California to live with my sister and her kids. It was a big help for me. I hadn't worked the whole time Charles and I had been married and now I was sort of forced to go out into the world and start over." Marla stirred some creamer into her coffee.

"Soon, I found a job in a real estate office as a secretary. After about four years, I decided to go after my real estate license. A year later, we got a new partner at the firm and he and I started dating. His name was Andrew. James got along well with him until we got married. It was around the same time James hit puberty and then he developed a big attitude problem." She took a sip of her coffee, noting that Sam was not a stranger to the attitude James sometimes still displayed.

"Julia, my daughter, liked Andrew but James held a grudge against him for, doing what he saw as, trying to replace his father. Anyway, Andrew wanted to start another office on the East Coast and James didn't want to go. I gave him a choice of staying in California with his aunt or moving to Boston with me. He chose to stay here. He was already really into his music and had some friends he played with so it was probably best for him to stay here with my sister. Julia stayed to finish her senior year and then moved to Boston."

"What does Julia do now?"

Marla smiled shyly at the question, not sure how to answer it. "She went to Harvard Law School. Andrew and I made enough money to be able to send her there. James had the option of going to college but he claimed school wasn't for him. I had to agree. If all he wanted to do was play music, then I thought he should focus on that. Andrew completely disagreed with me on that aspect but that's beside the point." She waved her manicured hand in the air. "Julia had wanted to be a lawyer because her dad and her grandfather had been lawyers. She felt she should carry on the family tradition since James wasn't going to. After school she practiced for a year but she didn't care much for the firm or the long hours. Anyway, to make a long story short, she now owns an escort service in Florida. We'll save that story for another time though."

Sam didn't really know what to say. "Does James know what Julia does?"

"Why? Did he tell you that she still practiced law?"

"Yes."

"Don't take it personally. He's almost ashamed of her. She had been such a big influence on him growing up and now that she's doing what she does James almost feels let down. He feels her talent is wasted. Plus, he loves his sister and wants to protect her integrity. He doesn't feel it's a very reputable occupation."

"Why are you and Andrew separated?" Sam was always interested in the whole story.

"Our marriage was more of a business merger," she said, adding cream to her second cup of coffee. "Oh, I loved him at first and we were great friends. We had a lot of fun together. By the time we got married the kids were almost grown and I didn't really want to be alone anymore. Plus, I knew that what I was going to accomplish financially would work out for both of my children. Julia was able to go to Harvard Law and I was able to buy James' house for him. I was able to send the kids monthly allowances so they could have fun. Plus, I have three houses of my own not to mention what Andrew has."

"So that's how James got his cars," Sam said. "I didn't think bartending was that lucrative."

"Ah, yes, his cars," she smiled at Sam. There was something very charismatic about this girl and Marla had immediately liked her. She went on to talk about her son,

"James still has a lot of pent up anger inside and he doesn't always direct it the right way. He's still angry with me for a lot of things and I don't blame him. But I believe with all my heart that what I did was best. I don't know if he'll ever see it but I hope one day he can. Our relationship has gotten better over the last year. I didn't see him much on account of Andrew's behavior every time I mentioned James' name. He thought I let James get away with too much and didn't raise him right. He just didn't understand James and vice versa. It was a hard struggle for me to live in that kind of situation. But eventually the romance fizzled and in actuality it ended up to be more of a business partnership than a marriage. I needed more. Apparently so did he. I found out he was cheating on me and that's when I filed for divorce. I actually came out on top."

"Sounds more like a corporate split than a divorce."

"It kind of was. But that's okay," she shrugged her shoulders at the concept. "Andrew and I had fun, in fact we're still friends, but Charles was the only man I ever really loved. Probably the only man I ever will. It took a long time, but I discovered that I don't need a man to be happy. I am dependent on myself and only myself."

Sam wished she felt that way. She was never happy unless there was a man present. She didn't know what to do with herself without one. "I admire your tenacity, Marla." Sam told her when they were done with their chat.

"James loves you more than anything in the world. He told me that himself and I know he's sincere. He would want you to go on with your life though if he doesn't get better," Marla had tears in her eyes now. She could see the struggle in Sam's eyes as they were talking and she sensed that she was torn between James and something or someone else.

"Do you think he will get better?" Sam asked, fighting back the tears.

"God, I hope so, honey," she touched Sam's hand for support. "But at this point, no one knows."

They walked back to the room and Sam spent some time alone with James. She sat with him and held his hand and fought herself over the decision she had to make. She couldn't hold Jason in a second place spot forever, knowing that if James came to she would run back to him. She knew that eventually he would expect more from her. Right now she was just biding her time. She was also angry with Jason for making it sound as though James had lied to her, which he really hadn't. She was going to have to sit down and have a long talk with him about it. But just thinking about having to confront him made her sick inside. She didn't like confrontation and knew in the end that she would wimp out.

"I wish you'd come back to me," Sam whispered to James through choked sobs.

He heard her voice again and wanted to reach out to her but his arm wouldn't move. He tried to speak her name but there was something blocking his throat. He wished he could find his way out of this world he was trapped in, but he was lost. He felt like he was walking circles in the dark. He tried again to move his hand but it was no use the weight on it was too heavy. By the time he was able to move it, there was nobody there to see it.

That week at the recording studio had been tough. All the guys were on edge and everyone was blasting each other with insults and stabs. James' birthday had been a really rough day for Jason. Lance finally blew up at him.

"What's your problem, dude?" Jason asked him after a nasty insult.

"I've just been thinking that James's accident has done nothing but benefit you."

"What are you talking about?"

"Well, you've got his woman, his job—seems like you've come out on top."

"Are you implying that I caused the accident? Because I didn't force James to drive off that night and I sure as hell couldn't have caused the accident if I didn't know where he was." Jason glared at Lance.

"Maybe not directly, but indirectly-yes. You obviously had some influence over Sam breaking up with him."

"Why do you say that?"

"Amber told me."

"Look, I told Sam some things that I figured she needed to know."

"That he was a stalker? You know that's bullshit, man. If anything Veronica made that shit up to get you to feel sorry for her and fuck her. He's not like that man. YOU KNOW THAT." Lance had been pissed when Amber told him that. She hadn't said anything to Sam but she had known James for a while and didn't think it was true.

"Did you ever ask him about it?" Jason asked.

"You know it's a fuckin' lie. She was a freak, man. She was always high, and—fuck, dude-she was a nut case. Somebody from the strip club was probably following her but it wasn't James. He didn't want anything to do with her." Veronica had smoked a lot of pot when she was with James and that had sparked quite a bit of paranoia within her. Of course, Lance now knew what that stemmed from.

"I just wanted her to be careful. I care about her."

"Maybe you care a little too much. She is James' woman and you should have stayed away from her. You can't just go around and take people's girlfriends away. You can't be so obsessive about things that don't belong to you, man." It was no secret that Jason was obsessive about his music, but Lance had picked up on his behavior towards Sam along time ago. He had only wished now that he had said something earlier. But he too was afraid of breaking up the band over it. Now his silence had made things worse. His best friend was lying in a hospital bed and might never make it out.

CHAPTER 52

When Sam got back from San Diego, she met Jason over at his house to help him pack his things. He picked Max up from school since he always finished his day earlier than she did. Jason started in the bedroom and Sam started in the kitchen while Max played outside. She was emptying out a junk drawer and looking at all the pictures and mementos that were in it. There were pictures from Vegas and pictures of the band.

There was even a picture of Sam and James together at *HotShots*. She wondered why he hadn't given it to her before. She quickly tucked it into her bag and went back to work. He had beer bottle caps and playing cards, tools and other little odds and ends. When she tried to pull the drawer the rest of the way out though, it got stuck on something. She reached back up inside and pulled, what seemed to be, some small papers out. They were ticket stubs from flights. She noticed the dates were for March and April of that year, before she had even come to L.A. Then she noticed the destination. Her stomach dropped and she felt as though she were going to faint. Her head was getting dizzy and she couldn't breathe. It wasn't a coincidence. It couldn't be a coincidence, because if it were, he would have told her.

When Jason walked into the room Sam was pale and she looked as though she'd seen a ghost. "What's wrong?" He asked, worried by the look on her face.

She decided to confront him. "Why didn't you ever tell me you went to Tulsa, Oklahoma?"

"Why is that a big deal? I had a friend in Sand Springs. I flew into Tulsa and drove to his house from there."

"You went to see him three times in a month?" Sam asked, trying not to sound accusing.

"He was sick. I wanted to spend as much time with him as I could. He died two weeks after my last trip there. Is there something wrong with me going to Oklahoma?"

"How come you never told me?"

"I didn't know it was a requirement. Besides the fact that it happened before I knew you. Did I do something wrong?" He could tell she was upset with him.

"I moved here from Tulsa," Sam informed him.

"You never told me that."

"Yes I did." Sam said matter-of-factly.

"No, sweetheart, you didn't. This is the first I've heard of it."

Sam was scanning her brain trying to remember if she had mentioned it to Jason. She was sure she had. But maybe she hadn't. She had a bad habit of not remembering very many things she said. More often than not, it got her into trouble. Of course, she felt silly now.

"What did you think? That I was stalking you in Tulsa?"

Sam laughed a small laugh. She didn't really know what she had thought. It seemed ridiculous now that she had even been upset about the tickets in the first place. "I don't know what I was thinking," she said, as she finished packing up the box.

He was concerned about her now as she tried to brush him off and finish what she was doing. He gently grabbed her arms and asked, "are you okay?"

"Yes, of course. I just want to get as much of this done as possible." She really wasn't okay. She had been thinking about the conversation she'd had with Marla earlier that day. Marla was definitely a motherly woman. Sam had felt an immediate connection with her when they met. Sam had never been close to her mother, and when she met people like Marla, it made her feel good inside. To have a mother-daughter connection with someone filled a hole in Sam's soul. Of course it would be temporary, it always was, but it made her feel good all the same. Those thoughts brought her back to James. Was she doing the right thing by trying to move on without him? But could she wait for him? What if he never got better? On the other hand what if he came to tomorrow? What would she do? Maybe she only felt that she loved him so much because he wasn't there.

CHAPTER 53

During the next few days Sam and Jason got the house packed up, They moved into the beach house over the weekend, which happened to be just down the street from where Sam had lived with Amber. They went out and bought furnishings for Max's room along with a whole bunch of toys and more clothes. Max seemed happy to Sam. A lot happier than she had been living with her mother, and Sam was glad she could give that to her. She deserved it. It felt strange to Sam that suddenly she had a motherly instinct toward Max and that it filled her with so much joy inside. She never thought that that was where her happiness would come from.

The house they rented was about a hundred yards from the beach. It had three bedrooms, a large kitchen, a family room, two bathrooms and a huge redwood deck with a sunk-in hot tub. It had a small white picket fence that went all the way around the house. The lawn had been well taken care of and there were several flower beds in the front and the back. Sam had to have it the first time she saw it. Luckily, Jason liked it too. The neighborhood was pleasant and there was even another little girl next door that was Max's age. For once, Sam had felt like she'd made a good decision.

❦   ❦   ❦

On Monday, Sam had lunch with Bob.

"How are you holding up?" He asked her as they sat down at a table.

"I'm doing well. Things aren't so bad anymore. Jason and I moved into the house this weekend. Max is doing great, the film's going well." She had told him she was moving in with Jason the previous week. He hadn't felt right about it but didn't tell her that. She always jumped into everything she did head first. She never took the time to think about anything. This was definitely another of those situations.

"Okay, sounds good, but you still didn't answer my question. How are you doing?"

She sighed and set her sandwich down. "I don't know how I'm doing. I don't even know how I feel anymore. Things are moving so fast in my life that I can't quite sit down and take a look at what's going on." She hadn't really expressed her feelings to anyone. She mostly kept them hidden from Jason because things were going so well between them. He was trying hard not to push her but she felt obligated to be with him just the same. Then she blurted out in a half choked up sob, "I miss James so much."

"I know you do. I can see it in your eyes."

"I met his mom and from what she told me, James didn't really lie about anything, he just sort of hid the truth a little bit."

"You spoke with his mother?"

"I went to see him on his birthday. I didn't tell Jason so don't say anything, but she was there and she told me about his childhood and how they had been in the process of repairing their relationship when his accident happened. She told me James loved me more than anything and that he would want me to get on with my life if he didn't get better. I still have this nagging hope that he will get better though. I can't let go of him for some reason."

"And what about Jason?"

"Jason is wonderful. He has been so supportive and so good to Max. I just don't know if I love him. When I look into my future I don't see Jason, I see James."

"That's a hard situation to be in." Bob didn't envy her one bit. He could tell she was struggling over it. "What will you do if James gets better?"

"I don't know. Part of me doesn't want him to get better just so I won't have to deal with the situation when it arises. I just don't know what I'll do. I mostly try not to think about it because it consumes me when I do."

They finished their lunch and Bob added, "sometimes the price you have to pay for what you want can be high. But I'm sure in the end you'll find that it's worth it.

"Yeah, I guess dreams aren't made of cotton candy and bunny rabbits. It's more like vampires and monsters. The funny thing is though, I've never not felt pain and so this is normal to me. I wouldn't know what to do if there wasn't pain inside eating me up all the time. I guess when the pain goes away I know I've stopped living."

"Or just started," Bob advised. He wished there was something he could do for her. But he knew she was on her own here.

Sam went back to work and tried to focus on her lines and her scenes. She was having a hard time for some reason today. It was one of those days where you just felt like you forgot something all day. Like there was something you were supposed to do but you couldn't quite remember what it was.

When Sam got home that evening Jason had picked up Chinese and had it all set out on the table for them.

"I'm gonna have to teach you how to cook or you'll go broke feeding us."

"We can always get a cook, you know."

"After the money starts pouring in," she joked. "I'm not exactly in a situation to start living high on the hog." She had gotten a good salary for her film with Jacob and they were going to pay her well for the other film she was doing, but after the SAG fees and taxes she wasn't ready to start hiring help and driving Ferrari's.

She only had time for a quick bite tonight though and then she had to go to *Omar Studios* and work on the other film, *Everything Roses*. She was exhausted and wished now that James hadn't thrown her pills in the toilet. She didn't want to go back to the doctor because it wasn't time for a refill and he would probably think she was either selling them or addicted to them. James had thrown out about a 90-day supply. She didn't want to ask Jason for any speed because she didn't think he was using and their last conversation about it had told her that he didn't condone her use anymore. She ate dinner and showered and was back out the door in less than an hour.

Tonight was her first shoot at the studio itself and she was trying to find her dressing room. When she thought she had finally found it, she walked in on Thomas Bennett. He was snorting a line and she immediately apologized and walked out. He came out after her.

"Samantha," she turned around. "Not a word to anyone, okay?"

"No problem, I used to do it a lot myself. I was just looking for my dressing room."

"Three doors down on the left. Would you like a line? I've got plenty."

Sam hesitated for a moment. She was really tired and she could use one for tonight. It would really help her. One time wasn't going to get her hooked again. It wasn't like she was buying any. Just one line would be okay.

"Yeah, I would." She went into his dressing room and snorted up her nose what he had laid out for her on the mirror. She dropped her head back and swallowed and probably could have had an orgasm just from how good it felt.

"Been awhile?"

"Hmm, too long," she said, enjoying the instant rush she felt. "I better go get ready." She left the room and went into hers. She couldn't believe she had just done meth with the hottest star in Hollywood. The rush made her forget everything else and everyone else. There was no doubt in her mind that if he wanted to take her to bed, she would go in an instant.

CHAPTER 54

❈

Sam got home after midnight that night and Jason was waiting up for her.

"How'd things go?" He asked as she walked in the door.

"Great," she said avoiding eye contact. "Looks like they may wrap things up early. The director loves me, which is a big plus for future projects, and Thomas is wonderful to work with."

Not something he had wanted to hear. "Well, maybe you'll get to do more projects with him." Sam could hear the jealousy in his voice.

"I didn't mean it that way," she said. "He's just a great actor, has his shit together and is very professional. You don't find that too often." She walked over and gave him a kiss on the mouth. She was feeling great now with the speed rushing through her system.

He responded passionately to her kiss by picking her up in his arms and carrying her to the bed. He put her down on the downy soft comforter and removed her shirt and her shorts kissing every inch of her body as he did. He gently slid his fingers into her, bringing her to intense satisfaction within minutes. Then he plunged into her, eventually bringing them both to a high he had never imagined. He loved being with her and every time they made love it was better and better. He had never been with anyone who piqued his interest like Sam did. She was the first girl who he'd never run away from out of boredom. He'd had quite a few relationships with different women over the last ten years. He'd dated models, strippers, aspiring actresses and even a porn star once. With most of them, the sex had been good but that's where his interest ended. They were all boring, self-centered, always worried about what they looked like and who was watching them. He had never attempted to even try living with any of them. Sam had been the first one. She had an alluring quality, a vivacious character, a passion for life, and a big heart. From the moment he laid eyes on her, he knew she was the one. His golden-haired beauty. He knew now, without a doubt, that she would be worth any fight he might encounter along the way.

"I love you," he said to her as she curled up in his arms.

"Hmmm," she couldn't bring herself to say it back to him. The guilt she felt inside over her recent actions was eating her up already. Why had she given in to the moment again? When would she learn? She whispered, *I'm sorry*, and then lied awake most of the night, not falling asleep until it was almost time to get up.

❦ ❦ ❦

Sam felt like crap the next morning and luckily Thomas had given her some extra speed, "just in case." She'd been hesitant to take it, but now she was glad that she had. If anything it would erase her feelings for a while. She would just do one line this morning and then, after a good night's sleep tonight, she would be back on track tomorrow. She got Max ready for preschool and then after breakfast they left to start their day.

Half an hour later Jason received a phone call from Lance.

"James has made progress. He moved his hand last night."

"That's great. Is he awake yet?"

"No, that's why I'm calling. Sam needs to go down there and spend some time with him. The doctor says that could make a big difference in his recovery. Is she there?" He knew his request would piss Jason off, but he didn't care.

"No, she just left for the studio, but I'll call her on her cell phone and make arrangements for her to fly down a.s.a.p."

"Thanks, dude. See ya later," Lance was so happy. Maybe Jason really did care about James. If James woke up, then they could get the band back together the way it was supposed to be. Even though James had a bad temper and they all bickered quite a bit, he still missed the way things were. James was the heart and soul of *Cruel* and without him, it just wasn't the same.

Jason hung up the phone and went to shower and shave before he had to leave for the studio. He never picked the phone up again that morning.

🍁 🍁 🍁

"Did you get a hold of her?" Amber asked Lance as he lay in bed next to her. The doctor had called Amber's number, which had been Sam's old one, to tell her the good news. Lance had taken the call and immediately called Jason.

"No, she'd already left. Do you think Jason will give her the message?" Lance was concerned now that he had hung up.

"I'm sure he will. You can always call her on the cell phone if you want to." She nuzzled on his neck. "But I'm thinking of a lot more fun things to do right now." They had gotten back together the night that James was admitted to the hospital. He had been spending a lot of time at her apartment and things seemed to be better for them this time. It was funny how tragedy brought people together. He took her up on her offer and forgot about Sam and James until he reached the studio at ten o'clock.

🍁 🍁 🍁

Jason was late and when he arrived Lance asked him if he had called Sam. He told her he had and she was in the process of making arrangements to get down there as soon as she could. Lance and

Kevin had a really good day that day, but Jason was completely off on his vocals and the riffs. The news about James had really ruined his day and now that was all he could think about. He was going to have to fight for Sam, which after last night shouldn't be hard to do, but he was going to lose his spot in the limelight and he knew Lance and Kevin wouldn't back him up. They both wanted James back so badly it was pathetic. He didn't know how he was going to keep his new job and that really scared him.

Ever since he joined the band two years ago, he lived in James' shadow. Since the other three had known each other for about seven years, Jason was a newcomer. They'd always played pranks on him and had treated him as though he were rushing for a fraternity house. He'd gotten through it though, and figured he'd proved himself to the band. However, James was never open to anything Jason wanted to contribute music-wise and he wouldn't even look at the songs Jason had written. James instigated a lot of the anger Jason kept inside. Then Sam came along and Jason was sure he was finally going to have something James wanted, but couldn't have, until James practically pounced on her that day in the parking lot of *The Rambler*. It seemed he and James had competed over everything and Sam had been no different. Only now he had her and he wasn't about to let her go.

❦ ❦ ❦

By noon, Sam had to have another line. She was extremely tired and getting more and more impatient by the minute. Jacob noticed that she was acting strange and approached her at lunch.

"Is everything okay?" He asked, bringing her over some yogurt and a bagel. He had a fatherly concern for Sam. She was the same age as his oldest daughter and between their first meeting and now, he had grown to love and respect her as if she were his own.

She noticed the concern in his blue-gray eyes and she felt bad for not opening up to him, but she didn't want to go into it anymore.

She figured it would be best if she could just forget about James and try to move on with her life. And she definitely wasn't going to tell him that, after being clean for over a month, she had come to crave her addiction again.

"I'm fine. I just haven't slept well the last few nights and last night I was out until after midnight for the other film."

He'd known that this other film was going to be too much for Sam, especially now with everything else going on in her life. He'd had the conversation with her before but she was determined to do it all. It sounded like her life's goal to wear herself thin. He did admire her for her drive though. She was by far the easiest going actress he'd worked with. She always made everyone smile and she never demanded anything. She was very self-sufficient.

"How's James?" He asked.

"No different, I assume. I haven't heard anything new," she sighed as though talking about him at all was a big weight to bear. He understood though. He knew how much she cared about him.

"Well, if you need anything let me know." He walked away and she went into her dressing room and pulled out another line setting her lunch aside. Within moments she was feeling good again and ready to finish the rest of the day.

At six o'clock Sam decided to swing by *HotShots* to say hi to Amber. She hadn't seen her in over a week and she missed the late night conversations they used to have when they were roommates. She walked into the bar and Amber was shocked to see her.

"What are you doing here?" She asked.

"I know it's been a week but I thought we were still friends." Sam replied with a look that said, "what the hell is your problem".

"You're my best friend, Sam, but why aren't you in San Diego?"

"Why would I be there? Is there something I should know?" She feared Amber would tell her that James was dead. She sat down and took a deep breath.

"James moved his hand last night and the doctor called this morning. He wants you to go down there to help with his recovery."

"Why didn't anyone tell me?" Sam was pissed now.

"Lance called Jason this morning after you left, he was supposed to call you."

Sam's heart skipped a beat. "He didn't. Oh my God, I have to get down there." She was frantic now as though every minute wasted was critical to James. She didn't know how long she'd be there but she needed to go. It didn't matter, but now she had Max to think about and she couldn't just up and abandon her. She had to go by the house and get her but she knew she'd have to confront Jason and she didn't want to do that because then they'd waste time arguing.

Sam sped home and walked into the house casually. She told Jason she was taking Max to get her haircut, that she'd forgotten about it and had just remembered.

"Do you want me to go?"

"No, it won't take long. I'll bring home something for dinner on the way home."

"What about work?" He asked.

"I'll have plenty of time," Sam said, rushing around.

"Okay," he kissed her on the mouth. "See you in a little while."

She got Max into the car and headed for the airport hoping there would be a flight when she got there.

She called the director for *Everything Roses*, Emme, and told her the situation. She apologized profusely and told Emme she'd try to be back tomorrow night. Emme told her not to worry about it and wished her luck. She'd call Jacob later.

When she got to the airport she booked two tickets for the next flight. She got Max something to eat and tried to explain the situation to her.

"Where are we going?" Max asked, gobbling down the hamburger Sam bought her.

"I have to go see a friend in San Diego who's sick and needs my help," Sam explained.

"Where's San Diego?"

"Down by the beach, kind of like where we live."

"Where's Jason?" Max asked wide-eyed. She had come to love Jason like a father. Sam felt bad for taking her away from that, but she had to make sure that Max was safe. She couldn't just leave her with Jason if they were fighting.

"He's at home working. This is just a special trip for you and me."

"Are you going to leave me there like mommy did?"

Max's question brought tears to Sam's eyes. "Oh, sweetie, I'd never do that to you. I promise," she grabbed Max's little hand and gave it a squeeze.

The plane left on time and they were there before nine o'clock. Sam hailed a cab from the airport and went directly to the hospital. When she walked into the room, Marla was there holding James' hand.

"Sam," she stood up. "I'm so glad you're here. What took you so long?"

"I didn't get the message until late. How is he?"

"He hasn't moved again, but I'm hoping you can change that." Then she added with a smile, "who's this?"

"This is Maxine, my cousin. She lives with me now." She looked down at Max, "can you say hi to Marla?"

"Hi," Max said shyly, standing close by Sam's leg.

"You look like you could use a bowl of ice cream, young lady," she looked at Sam for approval, "do you mind?"

"How's that sound Max?" Sam asked her cousin.

"Good," she smiled.

Marla and Max went down to the cafeteria and Sam stayed with James.

"Hi, baby," she walked over to the bed and kissed him on the forehead. His cuts and scrapes were gone now but he had a few faint scars. "I know you can hear me and I wish you'd just wake up. I need you." Tears rolled down her cheeks. "I need you so bad. I need you to hold me and kiss me and make love to me. I need to be in your arms when I go to sleep at night and wake up to the sound of your voice. I need to hear your songs and watch you play the guitar." She put her head on his chest once again to hear his heartbeat. "I love you so much, so much more than anything else in the world. Please come back to me."

The emotional effects of the last few days had taken a toll on her especially combined with the drugs that were in her system. As she lay on his chest she closed her eyes and drifted off to sleep for a few minutes.

"Sam," she heard a faint voice. She looked up, but no one else was in the room. She figured she must have been dreaming.

She laid her head back down and heard it again. She looked up at James and saw his eyelids fluttering.

"James, baby, are you talking? Are you waking up for me?" She put her hands on his cheeks and kissed him. His eyes slowly came open and she stared at him unable to believe what was happening. She pinched herself to make sure she wasn't dreaming.

"Sam," he whispered.

"Oh, James," she broke into a full sob now and he reached over and put his hand on her cheek like he'd done so many times before.

"He's not what he seems," he whispered again, barely audible to Sam.

"What? What are you saying?" She looked at him but his eyes had closed again and she was yelling at him now. "James wake up. Wake up!" She was shaking him when the doctor came in.

"He was awake. He spoke to me." She sobbed harder now. "He was here, I promise you," she looked at the doctor as he examined James.

"Did you fall asleep? Maybe it was a dream." The doctor tried to console Sam.

"NO! He was talking to me. I swear," then she looked at James again, her knuckles white as she gripped the bed rail. "Wake up, dammit! Don't do this to me. I need you!" The doctor put his hands on her shoulders and gently guided her out of the room.

Once outside he spoke to her, "that's not going to help anybody, Sam. I need you to settle down."

Sam clenched her jaw to fight back the tears, "he touched me. He wiped the tears from my cheek. I wasn't dreaming."

"I don't think that's possible, Sam." He left her to sit in a chair outside the room and he went back in to check James' vitals. He picked up his right hand and he noticed the inside of James' right thumb was moist.

He checked him out but there was no indication that he had ever woken up.

CHAPTER 55

❀

Jason was angry. He had called all over the place to see if anyone knew where Sam was and when he finally reached Amber, she told him that Sam had flown to San Diego. He couldn't believe she had lied to him like that. And then to take Max, like he was going to hurt that little girl that he'd grown to love so much. He just couldn't believe that she would take off like that. He had a good mind to fly down there and talk to her but he felt that would be ridiculous and would accomplish nothing. So he waited at home for her to return. It was a long wait.

❦ ❦ ❦

Sam and Max flew home late that night and got home after midnight. Max was fast asleep as Sam carried her into her bedroom. She walked quietly into her own room, trying not to wake Jason, but the light turned on just as she started to remove her clothes.

"That must've been some haircut," he looked at her blankly. He was still fuming over her flying to San Diego and lying to him about it.

"Look," she said as she saw the anger in his eyes. "Obviously you know where I was. It's been a long night, let's discuss it in the morning." She was too tired to argue with him tonight and she had to be on the set early in the morning.

"I want to discuss it now. I've been waiting over five hours to discuss it. Why did you lie to me?"

"Why did you lie to me? You were supposed to call me and tell me about James and you didn't. Why not? Are you afraid of him waking up? Are you afraid if he does that I'll go back to him?" She was angry now. Angry that James was no better off after she flew all the way down there. Angry that she didn't understand what he'd meant when he had spoken to her. Angry that Jason had tried to conceal the information about James from her and angry that he thought she owed him an explanation.

"I know you aren't going back to him if he does wake up because I'm never going to let you go."

His words were so poisonous, it gave Sam goose bumps to hear him speak. The way he looked at her was so malicious that she was almost afraid to sleep in the same house with him.

"Whatever. I just want to go to bed now. Please leave." She crawled into bed and curled up on the edge trying to stay as far away from him as possible when he didn't obey her request.

※ ※ ※

The next morning she got up, showered and got ready for work. She left Max in bed and asked Jason to let her sleep as long as he could before taking her to school.

"You take her," he said, as he sat down with the paper.

"I can't take her, you know that. The school isn't even open yet." Sam was close to tears now as she tried to explain to Jason why she couldn't take her. Lack of sleep and the events of last night had left her frazzled.

"Not my problem," he said. His voice chilled her as she sat and watched him. He hadn't even looked up from the paper to acknowledge her.

"I thought we had an arrangement. I thought this was the family you wanted to take care of," she said, choking back her sobs.

He turned around in his chair to look at her. "You lied to me and you betrayed me. This arrangement works for you, not me." He stood up and walked over to her. "You can't have your cake and eat it too. You need to let go of James. He's not coming back." He glared at her and she had never seen so much hate in his eyes. She walked away and went to get Max up. She would have to take her to the set with her.

When they got to the set, she fed Max some breakfast and let her lie on the couch and watch TV in the dressing room. Sam's hairdresser, Daphne, had offered to take her to preschool so Sam didn't have to interrupt her schedule. Jacob had gotten a glimpse of Maxine as Daphne walked her out to her car. He commented to Sam how beautiful she was, and told Sam she should have some headshots done.

"She's only four, Jacob, she's not ready for this crazy life." Sam was not ready to get Max into acting. She had been through so much already; acting was not going to give her a peaceful life.

"Well, think about it," he said, and then inquired about James and her trip down to San Diego. Sam told him all that had happened and then went onto the set to begin her day.

When Sam got home that night, Jason wasn't home. Relief flooded her when she saw that his car was gone. She wouldn't have to deal with him for a while at least. She fixed Max a sandwich for dinner and then sent her off to play. Sam decided a little housework would take her mind off things. She went into Jason's room to put his shoes away when she saw a photo album in the back of the closet. She picked it up and sat down on his bed. Some of the pictures fell out when she opened the maroon cover. On the first page were baby pictures of Jason. In spite of her fury with him, she smiled at how cute he'd been. She skimmed through more pages and at about the middle of the book she noticed a funeral announcement that had been cut out of a newspaper, and a few other things referring to a Patricia Ann Chase. Chase was Jason's last name so she figured it must've been his grandmother or an aunt. As she read down the eulogy, she realized it was his mother. For an instant she had felt sorry for him and sad that he had never told her, but then she remembered when she had called him after she had received the flowers from Jonathon, he had told her that his mom had been there. Now she wondered who that woman had really been.

"Find something interesting?" He asked and she dropped the book at the sound of his voice. She hadn't heard him come in.

"I was just looking at your pictures." She closed the book and placed it back in the closet. "You were such a cute baby," she said, trying to hide the uncertainty in her voice. He was still cool and aloof and she couldn't believe how much he'd changed over the last 24 hours. "How was work today?" She wanted to change the subject before he suspected what she had seen.

"Fine," he walked into the bathroom that connected their rooms and stripped off his clothes to take a shower. It was hard for her not to look, he had such a nice body.

But then she remembered the photo album and quickly turned her head still wondering why he had lied to her.

She walked into the living room, thinking of what she was going to do with Max for the evening while she worked. She called Amber to see if she was home but she wasn't. Then she called Bob, if nothing else maybe he would watch her on the set. He happily agreed to let Max come over for the evening and Sam was getting their stuff together when Jason walked out.

"Going somewhere?"

"To the studio," she said quietly. "I'm taking Max to Bob's house while I work." She suddenly felt very tired and had wanted a line but she'd decided she was going to quit, even if it killed her. She couldn't run around on drugs forever because eventually they would kill her.

James had told her that before, but she hadn't given it much thought until Max entered her life.

"I think tonight you could stay home, don't you?"

"I have to work. I missed last night."

"Yeah, because of James, tonight you can miss because of me."

"Jason, I can't do that." She didn't understand his actions. It wasn't as though she had even told him she wanted to be with him. She had definitely not made any promises to him about their relationship. She started to walk away to get Max but he grabbed her, shoving her up against the wall.

"Why do I always come last?" He was starting to lose his temper now. He had taken himself off of his medication two days ago. He had quit cold turkey and he wasn't able to control the severe withdrawal symptoms that he seemed to be having. And the meth only made it worse. This was why he couldn't quit before. He didn't want to scare Sam or hurt her, but he was tired of playing left field to everything in her life.

He had startled her immensely, mostly because he'd never become violent with her before. Her first instinct was to push him off of her, but she wasn't strong enough and he just squeezed her arms harder. "Let go of me," she said through gritted teeth.

"You need to understand something, we are together now. You, and me, and that's the way it's always going to be." She was shocked at his sudden possessiveness over her. He had never acted that way before. He released her and she quickly got Max and left. When she dropped Max off at Bob's, he could sense something was wrong but she didn't have time to talk to him. She was already late.

When she arrived home that night Jason was not waiting up for her, in fact he wasn't there at all. She carried Max to bed and then went to bed herself. She had a lot on her mind so it was hard for her to sleep. She couldn't understand why Jason was acting so weird and furthermore, why he had lied about so many things to her. Sam wondered who that girl was at his house that day she had called. It was obvious now, that it wasn't his mother. Finally, at about one a.m., tired from contemplating her situation with Jason, she dozed off to sleep.

❦ ❦ ❦

She felt someone on top of her, pulling at her pajamas. She twisted and turned and struggled to push away the intruder but he was too strong for her. She tried to focus on him, get a good description, but it was so dark she could barely see him. But she could see his eyes. There was something vaguely familiar about his eyes. The way he looked at her, it was the same look she'd seen when she was raped before. Pure rage. He pulled off her panties and she pushed at him harder, but he grabbed her wrists with his hands and pried her legs apart with his own. She screamed out for James. She didn't know why, it wasn't as if he could hear her. It wasn't as if anyone could hear her. He covered her mouth so she wouldn't scream again. As he began to pry her legs open again, Max's bedroom door opened. The intruder turned his head at the sound and jumped off the bed running through the bathroom that adjoined Sam's bedroom with Jason's. Max walked into Sam's room and Sam quickly led her back to her own room and put her back in bed. Then she did a thorough search of the house. Satisfied that the intruder was gone when she saw the open bathroom window, she went back into her bedroom and shut the door. She sunk back into the comfort of her bed and cried.

❦ ❦ ❦

He awoke with a start. He heard someone scream his name. His eyes popped open and he didn't know where he was. All he could see was a tiled ceiling. Some moonlight filtered in between the crack in the thick, polyester curtains. His whole body ached like he hadn't moved in forever. The voice he heard was so familiar. He looked around to see if anyone was there. He thought for a moment, trying to remember the voice. Sam. It was Sam's voice. She was in trouble. He could feel it. He tried to speak out to someone but his mouth was so dry, he couldn't get the words out. Finally the door opened slowly and he saw a figure walk in. Light poured in from the hallway and he could see the petite figure of the nurse walk toward him. She checked the machines by his bed and then looked at him. She nearly jumped when she saw that he was looking back at her. She quickly ran out of the room and within seconds was back in with the doctor. Several other people came in and the doctor was checking his eyes and his heart and then he said, "I know someone who is going to be very happy to see you."

CHAPTER 56

Jason came in at around four a.m. and Sam was still awake. When he got home all the lights were on in the house and Sam was sitting on the bed curled up in a ball, crying.

"Sam," he came over to her and sat down next to her, concern in his eyes. "What's wrong, baby?" He seemed to be the Jason she had remembered. The one that cared about her.

She looked up at him through swollen eyes and just shook her head, "where were you?"

"Out driving around, hanging with some old friends. Giving you space," he picked up her hand and she quickly pulled it away. "Is something wrong?"

"No, it's just been a rough night and I need some sleep before I go to work." She turned off her bedside lamp and lay down in the bed.

"I'm sorry, Sam. I know I've been a jerk the last few days and I'm sorry. Things are really rough for me at the studio. The guys are blaming me for James' accident and…well, let's just say not everything is rosy in the band." He pulled the blankets up around her like he'd done so many times before and kissed her on the cheek. She needed him now, she needed someone to hold her, but she was still so angry with him for the way he had been acting. She couldn't bring herself to let her guard down as he curled up beside her in bed. She still got bad vibes from him–like something just wasn't right.

The alarm went off at six and Sam dragged herself out of bed and into the shower. Jason was sound asleep, so she got ready quietly hoping not to wake him. She would've given anything for a line at that moment but she was beginning to form some strength against that habit, and even though she still had some from Thomas, she felt it was not the right thing to do. She got Max up and they headed out for the studio. At least she had been successful in not waking up Jason. She didn't want to deal with him this morning. In fact she didn't want to deal with anyone today. She just wanted to lock herself up somewhere and never come out. It would be better that way. No one could hurt her then. And she couldn't hurt anyone either.

At seven a.m. her cell phone rang, she was tempted not to answer it because she figured it was Jason. When she saw the number though, it wasn't even an L.A. area code so she picked it up curious as to who it might be.

"Sam?" He asked as soon as she said hello.

"Yes," she hesitated, not recognizing the voice on the other end.

"This is Dr. Green from Tri City Medical Center. Do you have a minute?"

"Yes, what is it?" She figured it was more bad news about James, so she braced herself for the inevitable.

"I've got some good news for you. James woke up early this morning. He is alert; his brain seems to be functioning normally. His heart and his breathing are stable and he's asking for you. Can you come back down today?" He was smiling into the phone as he thought about the good news he was able to deliver to her.

"Omigod!" She yelled and she almost dropped the phone. "Yes, yes I'll be there as soon as I can." She was so happy that she had forgotten about last night and started making plans to go down there. She called Amber, telling her the news, and asked if she could take care of Max. She happily agreed to do so. Then she called Bob and told him the news. She spoke with Jacob briefly, begging him to let her go and he did so only if she promised to be back the next day. She drove to the airport as fast as she could and took the next flight to San Diego. She could barely sit still the whole flight down there. She hoped this wasn't some kind of fluke or something. She hoped he wouldn't fall back into his coma, and then with nothing else to do, she worried about that the rest of the flight.

※　　　※　　　※

Lance was ecstatic as he ran into the studio that morning. He hugged Kevin, who didn't like to be touched by anyone, and then sat down to bang on the drums for a while. He was too giddy to play any real music that day and didn't have the concentration. However, when Jason got there later, he was ready to start recording.

"Why is everyone so happy?" Jason asked, as he threw his guitar strap around his neck and shoulder and tuned it.

"Didn't Sam tell you?" Lance asked, wondering what in the hell was actually going on between those two anyway.

"Tell me what?" Jason was getting sick of these games that everyone was playing.

"James woke up this morning. She's on a flight down there."

"That's great," Jason said, trying to sound convincing, even though he was angry that Sam was going back down there without him and especially that she hadn't told him. He knew his relationship with her was falling apart and with James back in the picture he was going to lose. Well, he had to make sure that didn't happen. He had everything he wanted now. As long as he remained stable he was fine. He couldn't let James take that away from him.

※　　　※　　　※

Sam arrived in San Diego at 10 a.m. She hailed a cab and was at the hospital by half past. It took all her control to not run into the hospital and down the hall to James' room. When she was outside his door she took a deep breath and walked in. His mom was in there, along with a few nurses. As soon as he saw her his face brightened.

"Hi there, sweet girl," he smiled at her. God how she'd missed that smile.

"Hi." She tried to swallow the lump in her throat but it was too big. Tears streamed down her face as she walked over to him.

"Now, now enough of that. C'mere you," he reached out to her and she buried her face into his neck, so happy he was conscious again. The nurses and Marla took a cue to leave the room.

"I don't understand. I was here just the other day and I swore you woke up and spoke to me and the doctor said you hadn't. What happened?" She had so many questions she knew he couldn't answer but they were burning in her mind.

"I don't know. I had a dream that you were calling for me. I actually heard you scream my name. Then I woke up and I was here." He kissed the top of her forehead as she lifted her head and stared at him. Her face went white.

"You heard me scream for you?"

"Yeah, it was quite a dream." Then he looked at her, sensing something was wrong. "What happened?"

"I screamed your name at about 2:30 this morning."

"What? You did? Why did you do that? Even more importantly, how did I hear you?" He was puzzled now, but even more so as to why she screamed for him.

She didn't want to tell him but she knew she couldn't keep it inside much longer. He was here now for her and he deserved an explanation as to what made him snap out of it. "Someone broke into my house last night," she started to cry again. She didn't want to tell him that she'd been so stupid to almost let the same thing happen to her twice. "He was on top of me and I couldn't get him off. I screamed for you. He heard a noise that scared him away but he was about to…." She put her head in her hands as if she were ashamed of herself for something that was completely out of her control. "He almost raped me."

His face hardened at the word rape. He couldn't believe she had almost been victim to this crime twice. "How?" He didn't understand.

She decided to start at the beginning. She told him about Max and about all the events that had gone on. She told him about her and Jason, with reservation of course. She told him about the house and about the funny way that Jason had acted. "I thought you were gone. He offered to help me with Max. It was kind of like having a real family. We slept in separate bedrooms," she wanted to make that point clear to him. "It was fun for awhile, but when I came to see you the other day he started acting really strange. I hardly knew who he was, then this morning he was back to his old self again."

James was disappointed to hear her stories about Jason. He couldn't blame her for trying to move on without him, even though that wasn't what she had implied, she would have done it eventually and that deeply hurt him. He had wanted to be the one there for her, but fate had moved in and had taken him from her just when she needed him most. She had obviously been through a lot in the last month and he could see her strength was starting to fade. Enduring much more at this point would be inconceivable.

"When I was here the other night you told me, 'he's not what he seems'. Do you remember that?"

He tried hard to think and he had a vague recollection of something but he couldn't really remember.

"What did you mean? Who were you talking about?"

"I don't know." He looked at her for answers to her own questions but there were none.

One question that had been invading her mind recently was about Jason's mother. She knew she could ask and get an answer from him.

"Is Jason's mother dead?"

"I believe so," James recalled a conversation he'd had with Jason a few years ago.

"Do you remember that day I called him from the studio about the flowers?"

He racked his brain, "sort of."

"A woman answered the phone, he told me it was his mother."

"Didn't I tell you he had a girlfriend?"

"Yeah, but I didn't believe you. Anyway, I had lunch with him that day and he told me some things about your family that I didn't know. I later found out from your mom that some of it was true but I believe Jason had misconstrued everything to make you look like a liar."

"Jason's good at that. He lives in another sort of world. One that seems to be far from reality sometimes. What exactly did he tell you?"

"He told me that your mom hated you and that your sister ran a Heidi Fleiss type business. He also told me that when you and Veronica broke up you stalked her for months."

"Bullshit!" James shouted, startling Sam. He couldn't believe that Jason had said that to her. It was more like the other way around only Veronica had used Jason to get back at him. He had known she had run to Jason when they broke up and he also knew they had slept together. He never let Jason know he knew about it. It was better that way. But the last thing he'd wanted to do when she left him was see her again. He had purposefully plotted out the whole cheating thing so she would leave him. He knew he couldn't get rid of her any other way.

"Don't get upset, please. You don't need to do that." She was concerned about him and she didn't know if she should have told him all of this stuff so soon after he had woken up. On the other hand she needed to get it off her chest.

"Is that why we got into that fight the night I took off?" He was curious if Jason's lies had contributed to her breaking up with him.

She felt guilty now. It was all her fault he was here in the hospital. She dropped her head, staring at the marbled tile floor not wanting to answer that question, "I suppose so."

"Why didn't you just come to me in the first place? Why did you believe him?"

"I don't know. Because I was mad at you for dumping my pills in the toilet. You came back into my life with such force that I was confused," she tapped her foot in between the tiles on the floor. "I didn't think he would lie to me. He always seemed to have my best interest at heart. I thought he was telling the truth."

"You trusted him more than me?" That was a hurtful question for him to ask her, but she figured she deserved it.

"Sometimes I guess I'm really naïve," she looked down at her feet again avoiding eye contact.

"Yeah, Sam, you are. I can't believe you think that I would lie to you and even more than that, you think I would try to hurt you." His disappointment was obvious. Once again she had gone about things the wrong way. She always wanted to believe everything everyone said to her. That's how she always got into trouble. Always giving everyone the benefit of the doubt. She always ended up hurting herself in the end.

He grabbed her chin and pulled her face towards him, "I love you, baby girl. I have since the moment I saw you. I always will."

"You mean you loved me since the moment Bob showed you my picture?" She was inquiring about his motives now.

"He told you, huh? I figured he would. Every time he came into the bar I wanted to see that sweet angelic smile. It warmed my heart to look at that picture of you. Your beautiful curls blowing in the breeze, you looked like you were having so much fun in that picture. How could I not want to see it every time? You are so beautiful. Do you even realize the effect that you have on people?"

She laughed at him shyly. He always made her feel so good about herself. "I have to know one more thing. Jason told me that you followed me to that bar the day we met? Is that true? Was that premeditated?"

He grabbed his own chin this time rubbing the overgrown goatee. "I suppose in a way it was. I had gone to Bob's that day to see you, I knew you were here and I wanted to meet you. I had even taken the day off. He had told me he'd bring you into the bar but I couldn't wait any longer. He was going to set us up. When I was driving over there I saw you standing at the bus stop. You weren't hard to miss," he raised his eyebrows and smiled at her. "Then you got on the bus and I followed it until you got off. Truth be told, I'd never been to that bar before."

"You mean you didn't get ripped off by the bartender? You didn't 'fuck him up' like you said?"

"Hell no. I was just lucky you hadn't caught his name, because I made that up too."

"And the drugs? How did you know my drug of choice?"

"You didn't have track marks on your arms, so I knew it wasn't heroin. Marijuana was completely out of the question; people just don't get that upset over pot. You don't look like a crack whore, and so the last obvious choice was speed."

"Did Jason see my picture at the bar too?"

"Yeah, he used to hang out there all the time. He stared at it once and then that was it."

"So he knew I lived in Oklahoma, right?"

"Yeah. Why?"

"Does he have a friend in Oklahoma, someone who died recently?"

"Not that I know of. Is that what he told you? Why would he tell you that?" He thought for a moment, "I suppose it's possible. He's kind of reserved; doesn't always open up to people, but I think I would've known about it." Sam figured she better not tell James about the tickets she found. She was going to handle it on her own. She changed the subject and sat with him for the rest of the afternoon talking about her movies and what she knew about the band. She also talked about her new house and where it was. He enjoyed just sitting with her and being able to talk to her again.

The doctor came in and told Sam that James needed his rest. He would need to stay in the hospital for a few more days, but as long as he continued to progress they could let him out. She kissed him on the mouth for the first time in over a month and he had never felt anything so wonderful in his life. She told him she'd be back as soon as she could, but definitely by the time he was released.

🍁   🍁   🍁

The flight home was rough for Sam. All she could think about was the fact that now, she had to approach and confront Jason about things. It was something she completely dreaded. She had never been good at confrontation. It was time now, though, to get some balls and face it. Jason had been lying to her and he needed to know how she felt.

Max was staying at Amber's for the night in case Sam got back too late. When she got home, Jason was sitting on the couch reading a book.

"Hi, how's James?" He asked her immediately without even glancing up at her.

"He's doing well." She took a deep breath, not willing to postpone the inevitable any longer. "Jason, we need to talk." She sat down in the easy chair on the opposite side of the couch, keeping her body straight, not allowing herself to be swallowed up by the situation at hand.

He put his book down and sat up, preparing to defend his ground. "What's up?"

She could tell this wasn't going to be easy. But she had better get straight to the point rather than pussyfoot around it. "I'm just going to lay it all out." She took a deep breath folding her hands together and bringing them up to her chin. She closed her eyes for one more small pep talk and said, "you lied to me. All those things you said about James were lies. Plus, I know your mother is no longer alive and the girl that answered the phone that day was someone you were sleeping with." She wasn't ready to broach the subject of Oklahoma just yet.

He put his head down in his hands not sure of what to say. In his mind he hadn't really lied about James, it was more like he stretched the truth some. As for his mother, he knew eventually he'd get caught in that one. The girl was just some chic he'd picked up at a bar the night before. Someone to replace the pain Sam had caused him. He knew this was going to cause a fight and he didn't want to fight with her. He loved her so much. He just wished she could see he was trying to look out for her best interest. James was only going to hurt her. James couldn't take care of her as well as he could. James couldn't love her the way he did. He knew all these things and he had tried to make Sam see them too, but she was too damn stupid to realize it. He would be damned if he'd lose her to that son-of-a-bitch. "I'm only looking out for you, baby."

"My ass! You are looking out for yourself. I just don't understand why you would cause all of this hurt and pain." She stood up and walked to the window. *Deep breaths, deep breaths,* she told herself. But it was too late. The emotion was there and she was not going to conceal it for his sake. "Your lies caused me to fight with James, which in turned caused him to almost die! How do feel about that?" She was yelling at him now. She hated it when people acted as though their actions were no big deal when they really were. He was so smug and calm about everything. God, how she hated that.

"Are you blaming me for James' accident too?" She was the second person to say that to him. Why was everyone blaming him when he had nothing to do with it?

"I guess I am. You know, Jason, I thought you were different. But you are just as full of secrets as you said James was." She was going to let it all out now. "Let's talk about Oklahoma. You don't have any friend there, do you? You knew who I was a long time before we met, didn't you? James told me you saw the picture of me. You knew where I lived. You lied to me about that too. You told me I'd never told you I was from Oklahoma. But Bob did." She gripped the windowsill with both hands behind her back. "Why were you really in Oklahoma?"

He couldn't take anymore of her shit now. He had to get out of there before he did something he regretted. How could this all fall apart? It had all been going so well. What had gone wrong?

He grabbed his keys and walked out the door just like James had done the previous month.

She couldn't believe he couldn't even face her. He was walking out on her like a coward. She just stood there looking after him and then sank down on the couch and cried. How could she have been so stupid? *Because,* she told herself, *he was so charming. He made me feel loved and cherished.* Now she didn't even know who he was anymore. She was afraid to stay by herself, so she packed some clothes and headed over to Bob's. She needed him tonight.

Bob listened as Sam wept and yelled and laughed while she told him the story of the last few day's events. The only thing she left out was the recent intruder. She figured he didn't need to know that and she didn't want his pity, she wanted his friendship. He sat on the bed while she fell asleep not daring to get up until she was in a deep sleep. As he sat and watched her sleep he was afraid for her, there was no telling what Jason might do once James was back, if he was as crazy as Sam made him out to be.

🍁 🍁 🍁

James lay awake in bed, his thoughts focused on Sam. He certainly wasn't tired and hadn't wanted her to go. He couldn't believe she had almost been raped again and after looking over the *L.A. Times* from the past few days, he was sure there wasn't a rapist on the loose. He was upset about her moving in with Jason, but he was sure Jason had persuaded her with charm, which wasn't hard to do if he offered to give Sam what she really wanted, which was stability. He was starting to remember when Jason hadn't been around those weekends back in March and April. He hadn't told anyone where he'd gone, just that he'd gone to visit friends. But Sam had asked him if Jason had a friend in Oklahoma. *Why would she ask me that?* he wondered. He also remembered that Jason had asked Bob a lot of questions about Sam. He also wanted to know how Jason had known he'd followed Sam to the bar that day. He certainly hadn't told anybody about that and the only way he could've known, was if he was following Sam as well. It was late, but he decided he'd call her anyway. He needed to know some more things. The phone rang four times and then on the fifth ring someone answered.

"Hello?" He answered. He was wide-awake, snorting lines to keep the anxiety at bay.

"Where's Sam?" James asked.

"Oh, hi, James. How are you feeling, man?" He acted as though they had just spoken the other day.

"I don't want to discuss how I am feeling with you because I might just reach through this phone and rip your head off. You are an asshole, you know that? I can't believe you would move in on her like that, especially when you know how vulnerable she is. What in the hell are you doing anyway?"

"Staking my claim man. Sam's with me now. She's not going back to you. I won't let her."

Those words made James sick to his stomach. What kind of freak was he anyway? How the hell did they ever find him and think he was so normal? "Let me talk to her."

"She's sleeping right now. We just made love and she was all worn out from the flights today. It's okay though, I'm gonna take good care of her."

James slammed down the phone. He knew Jason was lying. He'd never heard him act that way before. There was definitely something wrong with him. And if his instincts were right, Sam was in danger.

CHAPTER 57

❀

For the next few days, Sam went to work and took Maxine with her. She hadn't seen Jason since the night she came back from San Diego. She had hoped he would just go away but she knew that wasn't likely. Apparently he'd been at the studio during the day because she hadn't heard from anybody over there.

On Friday night when she came home Jason still wasn't there. She and Max ate dinner and then she sent Max outside to play while she paid bills.

🍁　　　🍁　　　🍁

James was checking out of the hospital that evening. He and his mom were going to fly back to L.A. and he was going to surprise Sam. He couldn't wait to see her face. He was so excited just thinking about being with her again that he could barely get through all the discharge papers.

🍁　　　🍁　　　🍁

At 8:30, Sam put Max to bed and read her a story. She always had so many questions when she went to bed at night; Sam thought it was just so she could stay up longer. Tonight though, she asked about Jason and where he was. Sam really didn't have an answer so she told her that he was out of town for a few days visiting his family. Max really loved Jason and Sam had to admit, he had been good to her despite the last week. But Sam knew she was going to have to get Jason out of their lives no matter how much it hurt Max to do so. She didn't feel safe around him anymore and he'd told her too many lies. But for now, she'd just let Max think he was coming back.

And just as she hadn't hoped, he came home a little after midnight. Sam had been asleep but had been startled out of it by a noise in the hallway. She turned on her light and peeked out into the hall from the bed. She didn't see anything, but she left the light on just in case. She was still a little scared at night, with good reason, but she was able to get to sleep without lights on. She had told herself to be brave, but she slept with the gun loaded and within arms reach. When she awoke the second time, the light was off and someone was hovering over her. Her eyes popped open as she saw the knife in the intruder's hand. Forgetting about the gun and hoping to get away, she rolled over to the other side of the bed, but he caught her with an iron-clad grip. She pulled her leg and kicked with the other one but without any success of getting out of his grip. Finally, she pulled hard enough and he let her go but she fell backward onto the floor. She stumbled to her feet but he was right in front of her. He had a black ski mask on and she wondered if this was the same person who'd been in there the other night. She tried to scream but he quickly put his hand over her mouth and shoved her up against the wall. She kneed him hard in the groin and he bent over clutching his manhood. She pulled the mask off and he stood up knocking the wind out of her with a right hook to the chest. She sunk to the floor looking up into his bright blue eyes. The same eyes that had made her once feel so loved and cared for, were now staring back at her with hate. She was finally able to catch her breath.

"Why?" It was the only word she could get out as she struggled for another breath.

"I can't live without you, Sam. If I can't have you then I can't let anyone else have the pleasure." His eyes looked so oddly familiar when he said that. They were evil looking, not the way they normally looked, but she knew she'd seen that look before.

"I don't understand. You said you loved me."

"I do love you. I love you more than anything in the world. But if I can't have you, I can't stand it. You are the first woman I've ever really loved and I can't let you go. There will never be another one like you, Sam. I can't just let you walk out of my life."

Sam decided to play along. Maybe if she could get him to think differently, he wouldn't hurt her. "Nobody said I was going to leave you. Why are you saying that?"

He smacked her across the face. "Bitch." That was familiar too. Then she remembered. His actions mimicked Greg's, the night he had raped her. "If I can't have you, then nobody can." Same words Greg used. This was all like deja vu to her.

"It was you, wasn't it. That night in Oklahoma, it wasn't Greg who raped me. It was you." She felt her body go weak as she came to the realization that she'd been sleeping with the man who raped her for the last four months.

"It wasn't supposed to happen that way. I just wanted to talk to you. I just wanted to meet you. I'd been up there for three weekends trying to get your attention but you just ignored me. I finally got the courage to talk to you that last night I was there and you thought I was Greg. You didn't even give me a chance. Then you started yelling at me and cursing at me. I couldn't handle it, I snapped. I had quit taking my medication, hoping for a normal life, and had been doing way too much speed. So, once I got going, I couldn't help myself." He stared at her as he confessed. "I got lucky with leaving Greg's wallet there though. That was an accident as well. He had dropped it on his way out of the bar and I grabbed it. I was going to give it to you, but when I got back up to the bar I forgot about it."

"What medication?" She didn't know he was on medication. In fact, come to think of it, she didn't know very much about him at all. Just what they'd talked about in Vegas, but that had been shallow things.

"I'm a manic depressive. I have been on medication since I was a teenager. It started a few years after my mother died. I'm tired of taking medication to be normal. I just want to do it on my own. Can you understand that? I can't live like this anymore. I thought it would be easy, that I could do it on my own. I'm tired of not feeling anything. It shows in the way I play and I just can't do it anymore." He started to cry, but caught himself, not wanting to seem weak in front of her.

"Why didn't you tell me?" She wanted to help him, despite all he'd done to her.

She felt sorry for him, seeing the pain in his eyes. He was like a lost little boy. But then, she reminded herself, this could all be another one of his games.

"Tell you I'm fucked up? Who wants to be with someone who's that fucked up, Sam? Do you? No, you want to be with the lead singer of a heavy metal band. You want to be with James. So I tried to make him sound fucked up so you would want me instead. But my plan backfired." He wiped the sweat from his brow in frustration.

She figured that was true. If he'd remained normal, she'd have stayed with him. Of course the illegal drugs he was putting into his system didn't help either. His nose was running profusely and his eyes were black as night. Sam figured he was using intensely now because the medication was gone and he couldn't function. Of course she'd known him when he was using both together. That really scared her knowing that she was living with a time bomb waiting to explode. What about Max? What would he have done to her?

He pulled up to the address that Lance had given him over the phone. It was a nice place, but awfully dark. He walked up the path that led to the house and noticed that the Malibu lighting was out. He walked further and noticed the front door standing wide open. The house was pitch black and James heard voices coming from the inside. He walked in with caution and dread. He felt his way around the furniture so as not to make any unnecessary noise. As he neared the room where the voices came from, he silently walked through the doorway.

"I always have to play second best to James and I'm tired of it. Even Veronica used me to get back at him. I'm so tired of living in his shadow. He is so domineering and won't give me a chance. Then when you came along I was supposed to get you." He moved closer to her face causing her to push harder against the wall. "You were supposed to be mine."

"That's why you followed her around town when she got here." Sam looked up with relief at the sight of the man she loved more than life itself.

Jason's stature shrank at the sound of James' voice. His shoulders slumped forward and his eyes narrowed. "Yeah, I followed her to the bar that day and you beat me to it, just like you always do."

Sam was angry now. They were treating her like she was some sort of prize, like she was a competition to be won. "You guys are pathetic. I'm a person, not something you win at a carnival." She gave James a quizzical look. "Why can't somebody just love me for who I am and not for what I look like? You didn't even know me. You just saw a picture and immediately got a hard-on from it."

"Sam, I love you for everything you are. That was testosterone talking back then. I may have fallen in love with your looks the first time I saw you, but I fell in love with your person the first time I met you." He was looking at her but also keeping a close eye on Jason. He hadn't realized what a mess Jason was until now.

Jason slowly got to his feet and then quickly grabbed Sam. He had a knife in his hand and held it to her throat, causing an indentation along her jugular. "I'm sorry, buddy, but if I can't have her neither can you. If she's out of the picture things can go back to being the way they used to be. We can get on with our album and start touring. She has caused too much pain in our lives."

James was amazed at how quickly Jason had gone from wanting one thing to the next. "Whether she's gone or not, nothing will ever be the same. I don't want you a part of my band. You can't just go around fucking up people's lives. Whatever the hell is wrong with you, you belong in a mental hospital. You obviously cannot function in the real world. I'm just sorry I misjudged you."

Jason grabbed her tighter, lightly slicing her neck, "fuck you, James. You think you're so much better than me. You think you're so much better than anybody. Well, I've got news for you. I was able to give her what you couldn't. We had something stronger than the two of you ever did. I love her and I won't let you have her."

Sam gasped for breath. She was hyperventilating and James knew he had to do something fast. He lunged forward smashing Jason's nose with the ball of his hand. Jason fell backwards onto the bed and dropped the knife. Sam fell to the floor and blood streamed down Jason's face. He started to get up but James was on top of him, releasing all of his pent up anger. Sam had to pull him off so he wouldn't kill Jason. Then she called the cops and they both made sure Jason stayed put until someone arrived.

❦ ❦ ❦

As she watched them handcuff Jason and read him his rights, she felt sick to her stomach. She realized now that he was the one who broke in to the house the other night. He was the one who raped her in Oklahoma. Greg was dead for what Jason had done to her. In the end she supposed that Greg got what he'd deserved, but she had triggered him by accusing him of something he hadn't even done. Jason had ruined so many lives. The cops hauled him away and tears fell down Sam's cheeks as Jason looked back at her.

"Don't," James pulled her away from Jason's sight. "He's not worth it." He wiped the tears away and Sam realized that Max was in the other bedroom. Frightened that she may have heard or seen something she shouldn't have, she walked over and opened the door quietly. Amazingly enough, she was still asleep. James walked up behind her as she watched Max sleep.

"Another little angel, just like you." He put his arms around her pulling her to him and she turned around burying her face in his chest. She let it all go this time. The tears streamed down her face and soaked his t-shirt. She had so much to be sad for and so much to be thankful for that the tears were doing double duty.

CHAPTER 58

Over the next several months, Sam's life was chaotic to say the least. Sam and Max moved in with James at his house. It was closer to work for Sam, but she missed the beach horribly. Both of her movies were in the theater by Thanksgiving and Max had started Kindergarten. Sam hired a nanny while she was filming to take Max to school and pick her up and spend afternoons with her, so she wasn't at the studio all the time. *Cruel* finished their album, hiring a new bass player that didn't appear to have any secrets lurking in the closet. They were starting a tour in January opening for *Kid Rock*. Sam was very apprehensive about James being gone so long. She knew there were going to be hundreds of girls at each concert waiting to get a piece of him. It made her sick to think about it and it affected her moods as well as her appetite. She started losing weight again just from the stress of it, and by New Year's she was so thin that James was worried she was using again.

"I'm not using. I quit while you were in the hospital and I haven't touched it since," that was the truth. No matter how bad she craved it, no matter how much she had felt that desperate need to be high, she wouldn't let herself get sucked in by the temptation.

"What's going on then? You're nervous all the time. You've lost weight Your pants don't even fit anymore. I know you don't need to lose weight for your new part. What's the matter with you?"

Sam was in a new movie that would start filming in February. It was a thriller and she played the part of the bitchy wife who was trying to have her husband killed. She was excited about it and couldn't wait to get into character.

She was tired of him asking her what was wrong all the time and she hadn't wanted to tell him before, but now as she was getting ready for rehearsal, she snapped at him. He had finally worn her down. "You leave for your tour in a week and I'm scared. I haven't been away from you since you were in the hospital. I haven't slept alone since the night Jason was taken away and," she walked up to him and looked him in the eye pointing her finger at him, "do you know how many beautiful women are going to be waiting for you after each show? They get picked out of the crowd for God's sake, just to meet you backstage."

James sat down on the edge of the bed and laughed at her. He hadn't laughed so hard in months. Max had heard him and came in to see what was so funny. He tickled her until she left screaming with laughter. Then he looked at Sam. "C'mere baby." She walked over to him and sat down on his lap. "There could be 250 supermodels backstage and I wouldn't give them the time of day. And if I did, all I would see is your face. You are the only one I want to be with. Forever." He said that with hesitancy because he'd been reserved about talking about their future together. He knew Sam was still scared and the fact that she never said anything about it, confirmed that. He had been waiting to propose marriage to her in the right way and had finally found the perfect way to do it. And one month later his plan had started to take form.

On February 5, Sam received a phone call from Jonathan asking her if she would like to be a presenter at the Grammys. Needless to say, Sam was on cloud nine for the rest of the day. She would be presenting the award for best new artist but she was disappointed to learn that *Cruel* had not been nominated. She knew James had hoped they would be in that category, but there was a lot of competition this year.

On February 25, Bob picked up Sam at her house to accompany her to the Grammys. Max was staying the night with Amber and would be watching the night's events on television. When Sam came to the door she was wearing a black, spaghetti strap gown with silver trim. The slit rose high to expose her thighs and the black heels that boasted a diamond strap that she had searched endlessly for. Her hair was done in a French twist with a few tendrils falling down in the back.

"Aren't you a sight for sore eyes." Bob whistled as he followed her into the living room.

"Thanks, you look mighty nice yourself." He was wearing a black tux with a deep purple vest. For the first time, Sam realized how handsome he was.

A limo picked them up at 5:30 and they rode to the Staples Center drinking the complimentary champagne. As they stepped out of the limo and onto the red carpet, reporters and interviewers bombarded Sam. The crowd went wild when they recognized her. She hadn't even been aware that she was that well known yet. She knew the movies had taken off and she was nominated for an Academy Award for best supporting actress in *Everything Roses*, but she hadn't really thought she was that big of a star yet. Apparently she was wrong.

The sat in the fourth row, directly in the middle of the stadium. Thomas Bennett was also seated in her row and welcomed the chance to catch up with her on her recent life events. He had grown fond of her when they worked together and even though she had resisted his advances at her, they remained good friends.

At 8:30 p.m. Sam went on-stage to present the award for Best New Artist. Most of the other presentations were done in pairs but her companion had backed out at the last moment, leaving her to present this award solo. She was nervous, as she slowly walked up to the podium, and prayed that she wouldn't fall or say something stupid. Before she started her introduction, there was whispering in the audience and someone came up behind her.

"Hey," he smiled, as if it were the most natural thing in the world for him to be standing there.

She glanced back casually and then flipped her head back again. "James! Omigod what are you doing here?" She blushed at the embarrassment she felt from not being prepared for him.

"I just flew in from halfway around the world and that's all you have to say to me?" The audience laughed as he played up his part. She stood there dumbfounded as he continued to speak into the microphone. "Before we go on tonight, there is something I want to say and the producers have graciously allowed me the time to do it. Proof that money can buy you anything." The audience laughed again and he turned to Sam and grabbed a hold of her hands. "This last year has been the best year of my life. You brought something into it that I thought only existed in the throes of fiction. Everyday when I wake up and see you lying next to me I know that, no matter what the day brings me, I'm the luckiest man alive."

Sam looked at him with tears in her eyes, still not completely understanding why he was there, but glad, nonetheless. She watched as he pulled something out of his pocket and held it up in front of her, "Samantha, will you do me the honor of becoming my wife?" It was the same ring she had found in his nightstand.

The whole auditorium went silent as they waited for Sam's response. Astonishment covered her face. She thought she'd blown it the first time she told him not to ask her, and figured he'd never ask again, and for him to do it, not only in front of the people that were in the auditorium, but the millions of viewers that were watching from their television sets, shocked her even more. He didn't like to bask in the glow of the limelight. He was such a private person and he never really wanted to be a part of the public eye or the tabloids. But apparently tonight he had let his guard down.

She looked at him longingly and blinked back the tears that threatened her makeup. "Yes," she choked out and the crowd went wild. They all stood up and clapped and cheered and James picked her up and kissed her, which made the audience whistle and yell even more. They introduced the nominees and gave out the award for Best New Artist. He carried her off the stage and she breathed into his ear, "you have made me the happiest woman in the world."

"It's about time," he said, as he kissed her again.

CHAPTER 59

❀

A month later Sam was preparing for the biggest night of her life. The Oscars. James was still on tour and Bob accompanied her once again. This time she wore all white, as if to signify her virginity in the business. The halter-top satin gown with tiny diamonds around the neckline (made just for her so she wouldn't have to wear a necklace) flattered her figure immensely. She wore the diamond studs that James had given her for Valentine's Day and open-toed white heels. She wore her hair tied back loosely at the nape of her neck and when Bob saw her, he knew without a doubt that she was the most beautiful woman he'd ever laid eyes on.

Amber had come over to help her get ready and when Max saw Sam, she told her she looked just like an angel. It brought tears to her eyes to hear the same words James had told her so many times. She was so glad that she had Max in her life. She made Sam's life a lot less lonely, especially now that James was touring. She never asked about her mother and father anymore, and Sam came to the realization that maybe she was a lot better off without them. She had never pictured herself as a mother before, but when Max was left for her she had taken on the role heroically. As did James. He was even better to her than Jason had been, if that was even possible. He loved her like a daughter and in a lot of ways Max had changed both of their lives for the better. Max still missed Jason though and asked about him on occasion, Sam just told her he had gotten sick and had to go to a hospital for awhile. Which wasn't far from the truth.

With all of the things Jason had wrong with him, his family had decided he needed hospitalization and he was put in a mental hospital up in Washington state. Sam had fought with James about pressing charges. He had demanded they do so, but she didn't think prison would benefit him at all. She had talked to his father and his two sisters and they agreed that a mental facility would be best.

His condition started after his mother had died. A true mama's boy, he had gone into a deep depression once she had died. He had been on several different medications since he was fourteen years old. His father had paid him a large sum of money to leave home after several violent crimes had pointed the finger at him. One involving the lead singer of the last band he was in. When Sam had entered his life, he thought he had found the one person that could make him better. She had reminded him so much of his mother, that for him, Sam was like getting the life, and the love back, that he'd lost at such a young and impressionable age.

She still felt sorry for him, though she'd never tell James, but he had been a special person when she met him and he had brought happiness to her life, even if it was just for a little while. That meant a lot to Sam, because deep down she knew he really cared for her, he just couldn't show it like most people.

Without James' knowledge, Sam had called to check on Jason a few weeks after he'd been hospitalized. He'd admitted to everything she thought he'd done and more. When Sam had moved out onto her own, he had followed her, broke into her home to be near her. His therapist had made her privy to this information because it was something she felt Sam needed to know for her own safety. She needed to know that there wasn't someone else out there who was after her. His therapist had also told Sam that because Jason had lost his mother at such a crucial age it had almost destroyed him. His mom was the most important thing in his life. He dropped out of school at age sixteen and that's when he started getting into trouble. It had broken Sam's heart to hear the story but she knew Jason was getting the help he needed. Even though he'd done some awful things to her, deep down inside her heart still went out to him. She knew his intentions were good, he just couldn't control his behavior. As for Oklahoma, she'd never really know why it happened or what triggered him to go there, the therapist had chalked it up to obsession. But Sam thought differently. He had already known a lot about her and seen her picture. He was looking for something he hadn't been able to find in over ten years. Unconditional love.

When they walked the red carpet together, Bob was very proud to be on her arm. She was hailed by all of her fans as the most glamorous star of the twenty-first century. By now people couldn't get enough of her. She was called daily for interviews with magazines and television shows. When she went out there were people everywhere begging for her autograph. She knew as soon as James came home they were going to have to buy a more secluded house. People were starting to follow her home and she had to hire a bodyguard to stay at the house 24 hours a day. She had to hire another one to stay with her when she went out.

She was working on a new movie and had another one on deck for the fall, which she would be earning ten million dollars for. She had not wanted to take her money for granted or spend it unwisely, so she had started a project to help kids who wanted to be actors. The kids had to be 18, have completed high school, and be in need of the money. There were no other requirements. This fund would pay for acting classes for them and get them headshots. Then they would meet with Jonathan and he would represent them, which also helped boost his business. She sponsored a new kid every month and then she would help them get a part in film or television, even if it was small, it got them exposure. She was proud of her little scholarship program and it made her feel good to know that she was giving support to kids to help them make their dreams a reality. She didn't have any support through her youth when she so desperately wanted to become an actress, so this was extremely important to her. James had loved her idea and was planning on setting up a program for musicians when he got back from his tour.

At 8:00 the awards ceremony started. Sam's nerves were on edge, as she was in one of the first categories. Bob held her hand as Mel Gibson and Tea Leoni presented the award for Best Supporting Actress.

As the camera shot over to her during the reading of the nominees, James was so proud at how beautiful she looked. He was watching with Lance, Kevin and Eric from their hotel room and even Kid Rock had come by to party with them as they watched the show. He crossed his fingers and paced the room, almost having to leave the room as they announced the winner.

"And the winner for Best Supporting Actress in a film is," the suspense was killing her, "Samantha Steele." Bob jumped up as Sam stood up unsteadily, resting her arm on the back of the seat in front of her as Kevin Costner and his girlfriend turned around to applaud for her. She was shaking so badly she was afraid she wouldn't make it to the stage. Bob hugged her tightly and she kissed him on the cheek thanking him for being there with her. When she got up to the stage she was amazed at how nervous she was as she looked out over all of the famous people. People who'd been acting for twenty years and knew everything there was to know about the movie business. People who had won many awards for their talents. She felt like a baby up there on the stage. So young and so new to the world of Hollywood. This was the moment she'd been preparing for all of her life.

Standing in front of the bathroom mirror as she gave her acceptance speeches. It had been good preparation for her. She swallowed back the lump in her throat as she started to read her speech.

"I came to this amazing town a year ago," she looked out to the audience hoping she could make the speech meet the time requirements. "I had dreamed of becoming an actress since I first saw *Flashdance* in the movie theater, but I didn't get up the courage to try and make it a reality until fifteen years later. When you have a dream, it's important to try and accomplish it because dreams are what we live for," now she was speaking mainly to the people on the other side of the television sets, the ones who planned their lives around this event. "They keep us going through the bad times. Sometimes it may seem hard, maybe too much effort, but if you believe in yourself, then anything is possible. You may have to cross some big mountains and swim some wide seas to get there, but you will make it. Tonight, I want to thank the people who gave me the confidence I needed to cross those mountains and swim those seas." She looked over to her best friend in the audience. "Mr. Bob, my best friend in the whole world. You've seen me through many tough times and we've been through even better times together. My agent, Jonathan, thank you for giving me my first taste of Hollywood," she smiled coyly, "and then tracking me down to make it up to me. Jacob Byrnes, you made me a star, enough said. Jason, you were there for me through the worst and you helped me recover. I wish you well. To my fans, I appreciate your love and support. And most importantly, to the love of my life, James. You have given me so much in the last year. Things I would never have found if it weren't for you. I love you forever, baby." All of the people she had mentioned looked at her admiringly. She had such class and style.

🍁　　🍁　　🍁

As James watched her from the hotel room, he had a tear in his eye. He was still amazed by her success in Hollywood. It took most people years to accomplish what she had done in only one. Seeing her on TV had made him miss her so much, now he wished he hadn't watched the show. It would be two more months before he saw her again and that would be for their wedding. The tour would be taking the month of June off and starting again the second week of July in the states. It worked out well because then James and Sam could take their honeymoon right after the wedding and be gone for a month. Marla had happily agreed to take care of Max while James and Sam were gone.

❦ ❦ ❦

After the awards show Bob and Sam went to a few parties. She met some exciting new people and introduced herself to some new contacts. Because of tonight, she would be sought after for years to come. When she got back home it was just shy of four a.m., so she decided to call James. It would be afternoon where he was.

"Hello?" He answered the phone.

"Guess who?" She asked him, a throaty growl to her voice.

"Jill, no. Kate...doesn't sound like you either. Maybe Christy. Or how about Cindy," he loved to mess with her like that and it always made her laugh.

"Very funny," she laughed at him. "Did you watch the show tonight?"

"What show?"

"Ha ha!" She laughed at him again.

"Of course, we all watched it. You were gorgeous. You didn't even look nervous."

"Well I was," she wondered if he'd say anything about her words to Jason, she didn't want it to upset him, but she felt it was only right to say something about him.

"I liked your speech and I thought what you said about Jason was really nice," he knew she'd be afraid it would make him mad but it hadn't. He knew Jason had been good to her and he helped her out a lot. She owed him that mention in her speech.

"I'm glad. I wanted to let you know that the wedding's coming together perfectly and we are set for June 7. So just make sure you are here."

"I'll try."

"James!"

"I'm kidding. I love you, Sam." He doodled her name combined with his last name on the pad of paper by the phone.

"Not as much as I love you," she smiled into the phone.

"Not quite as much but maybe close," he joked with her. "You better get some sleep the phone will start ringing soon."

"Okay, bye, baby." She hung up the phone and lay back on the pillow to sleep. She didn't have to worry about nightmares anymore; since Jason was taken away she hadn't had another one. She drifted off to sleep enjoying her success and dreaming of her perfect June wedding.

CHAPTER 60

❀

As James predicted, the phone rang for three days straight, right up until Friday night. She had movie offers, television offers, interviews, charity events and the list went on. Sam figured she would have to hire an assistant to help her keep track of her schedule and help plan her wedding. She wouldn't have time to do it if she accepted all of these offers and she wasn't sure what she should do. She needed to get a manager as well. She needed someone who could help her decide what she shouldn't do and what would be a good choice and what would boost her career in the right direction. *Maybe Bob knows of someone,* she thought.

On Saturday night Sam and Bob took Max out for her favorite food, pizza, and Sam asked him if he had any good recommendations.

"What about me?" He asked when the waiter brought their salads.

"What about you?" She wasn't completely sure what he was asking.

"For a manager I mean. How about me?"

She almost dropped her fork on her plate. "Are you serious?" She asked, looking at him. "My God, you are serious aren't you?"

"Well, yes."

"What about your job at your uncle's studio?"

"I can do both."

"Do you know anything about that sort of stuff?"

He tried hard not to laugh at her question. Sometimes she said the most ridiculous things. "Sam, I've been in this business for quite a few years now and I know enough to know what you should and shouldn't do."

She thought about it for a moment. "Well, I guess it would work. When can you start?"

"Monday," he said, swallowing a tomato.

"Monday it is. The first thing I need you to do is decide what I should do," Sam gave him a pathetic smile to accompany the request.

"Thanks a lot," as he looked at the two-page sheet she handed over to him. It had been messages from the phone calls she had received since her award. "I might have to quit my other job just to keep up with your requests. Did we negotiate pay yet?"

"I'll double what you make now."

"In that case, I'll give my two weeks tomorrow." He toasted her with his beer.

On Saturday afternoon Sam asked Amber if she wanted to become her personal assistant. "You are so organized plus you wouldn't have to deal with all the drunk assholes at *HotShots*," Sam knew about them. She'd had to fend off a few when she worked there. Luckily, James was always right behind her to back her up. Sam threw Amber a figure and it was more than twice as much as she was making currently. She accepted and then immediately went to see Lonnie to give him her two weeks. In the meantime she would start working for Sam on getting her wedding coordinated and returning phone calls. She was excited. She had come to love Sam as a sister and was sad when she had left their apartment in Huntington Beach. And she loved Max to death. It would be great hanging with Sam all the time again. She couldn't wait.

The three girls went to the beach that afternoon and Maxine played in the sand and the waves while Sam and Amber worked on their tans. By four o'clock they had to leave, as the crowd of admirers was getting increasingly larger and Sam's sun was replaced by shadows of bodies hovering over her.

On their way home they stopped to get gas and Amber was in line at the mini mart to pay when she noticed the cover of the *National Enquirer* and who was gracing it. She purchased the gas and the magazine and ran out to the car.

"This ought to brighten your day," she said, tossing the magazine into Sam's lap.

On the cover were pictures of Sam and Jason, Sam and James, and a picture of Sam and Bob. She was the focus of the cover story, which was titled, *Samantha Steele and Her Many Love Affairs.*

"What the fuck is this?" Sam asked, ignoring her rule of not cursing in front of Max, who was sound asleep in the back anyway.

"Somebody has it out for you," Amber said, grabbing the magazine back and opening it to the story. She read aloud:

Samantha Steele, is definitely America's sweetheart. The sweetheart of America's men that is. According to reports; the sexy golden-haired siren, famous for her role in "Everything Roses" has been seen out and about with several men lately, even though she is engaged to rock-star, James Jordan. She attended the Grammys and the Oscars with longtime friend and lover Bob O'Brien. She has also been spotted with ex-lover Jason Chase at his new home in Washington. According to medical reports released to the Enquirer, Sam has a sex addiction and will go to any length to satisfy it.

On the left of the article was a picture of Sam when she went to the supposed "swimsuit audition". It was a video camera picture of her and the two bi-sexual bimbos in the room with her.

"This is going to ruin my career. Nobody will ever hire me again. My reputation is ruined." Sam drove down the freeway towards her home with extreme speed.

"Slow down, girl," Amber said, gripping the roll bar on the Jeep. "Nobody believes this crap. It's all lies. Doctor's aren't allowed to release medical information without your consent. Get a lawyer and sue the fuck out of 'em."

Sam calmed down a bit. "Maybe you're right." But when she walked into the house the machine was blinking with ten messages and the phone was ringing. Sam ran to the phone and picked it up.

"Hello?" She said into the mouthpiece.

"Have you seen it yet?" Bob was on the other end asking about *The Enquirer* piece. They had tried to interview him for the story two weeks ago but he had ignored them. He hadn't told Sam about it because he didn't want to upset her.

"Yeah, it was the highlight of my day."

"Ignore it and it will go away. Bad press is still press."

"This is going to ruin my career, Bob. It's all lies, but everyone is going to buy into it."

"Who cares? This is not going to ruin your career anyway. This is going to bring you more publicity than you ever dreamed of. As your friend and your manager I am telling you to just ignore it." Bob was sitting at his uncle's desk at the studio sipping a whiskey sour. He was leaning back in the plush brown leather chair with his feet up on the desk, very much enjoying his new job.

After Sam hung up the phone she called for a pizza and took a quick shower. While she was in the shower she came up with an idea as to what she was going to say to the press who she knew, would be outside her door in the morning.

Amber listened to the messages and jotted them down while Sam was getting cleaned up. There were four messages from James, three from Jonathan, one from Bob—whom she already had talked to, one from *Entertainment Tonight* and one from *Access Hollywood*.

Man, they sure are quick, Amber thought. When Sam came out she told her to call James because he sounded upset.

"It's two in the morning where he is, I doubt he's still up." Sam fixed herself and Amber a glass of wine and then poured some strawberry Kool-Aid for Max. The phone rang again. Amber answered it and immediately passed it to Sam.

"Hello?"

"Sam," it was James voice. "What is going on? Where do they get this bullshit?" He sounded angry and upset and tired.

"Honey, why are you up at this hour?"

"I haven't gone to sleep. I've been waiting for you to get home."

"Oh, well Amber and Max and I went to the beach today. We just got home about twenty minutes ago. I was going to call but I thought you would be sleeping."

"I'm not. What is all this crap about you and Jason and you and Bob?"

Sam laughed out loud. He sounded like a heartbroken child who had just lost his dog. "It's crap. That's exactly what it is. I don't know where they get their information. Probably the same place they get their alien abduction stories and four headed dragons—out of their ass! Don't worry, though. I have everything under control. By the way, did I mention that I hired Amber to be my personal assistant and Bob to be my manager?"

"No, but I think that's a great idea," he felt better now that he was talking to her and that she didn't seem to care about the story. He had been freaked out when he saw the cover at the newsstand in the lobby. He bought a copy, read the story and sat by the phone until he got a hold of Sam. "You need all the help you can get. How's Max?" He was always curious about Max. He loved her as if she was his own child and she certainly loved him as well. She asked about him daily.

"She's good. She had lots of fun at the beach and she has marked her X on the calendar to count off another day until you come home."

"I bought her some toys from local vendors around the cities. I shipped a box today for her. You should get it next week," he yawned and then said, "I'm going to go to sleep now. We have an early start tomorrow. I love you, baby."

"Right back at ya," Sam smiled into the phone. Tears were welling up in her eyes because she missed him so much. Sometimes it was more painful to talk to him than to not.

After dinner, Amber went home and Sam put Max to bed. Then she crawled into her own bed with one of James t-shirts held closely to her cheek, and fell into a deep sleep.

CHAPTER 61

❈

Just as Sam had suspected there were several reporters and photographers outside in the front yard waiting for her to make an appearance. After two hours of making them wait for her, Sam walked outside in cut-offs and a halter-top. Her hair was tied back into a messy knot. She had no makeup on and she certainly didn't resemble her glamorous alter-ego that everyone expected to see. She brought out blueberry muffins and coffee and offered it to the reporters.

"I know y'all must be hungry after spending most of the night out here, so I made you some breakfast." She gave her best southern belle drawl as she passed out the muffins. Then she added, "is there something I can do for y'all?"

One reporter from *Hollywood Gossip*, the hot new television magazine show, stuck a tape recorder in her face and asked, "What do you have to say about the allegations the *Enquirer* has made? Is the story true? Do you have several lovers other than your fiancée, James Jordan?"

Sam finished passing out the coffee and walked back up to her front door. She turned around and smiled her wholesome small-town girl smile and said, "a wise person once told me to always keep 'em guessing." She walked back into the house as flashes were going off and the reporters shouted more questions at her.

When Sam turned the television on that evening after dinner, sure enough, she was the cover story for the evening. They showed her standing out in front of her house and her brief statement. The anchor had said a few more things about the story in the *Enquirer*. Sam was proud of herself for how she handled it. It wasn't any of their business what she did. The public didn't own her and she would fight them tooth and nail if she had to. It was better to keep them guessing then to let them know too much. She turned off the set and sat down with her wedding checklist and realized she had to pick up the invitations and mail them out that week. She also needed to order the cake and the flowers and get fitted for her dress, which she had yet to pick out. She had to get measurements for the tuxedos, which she hoped James had gotten for her. She needed to book the church. She needed to book the caterer and the Beverly Hills Hotel for the reception. She had a lot to do but luckily now, she had Amber to help her and she wasn't starting her next movie until August.

Wedding's are a lot of work and preparation for an outcome of a 20 minute ceremony, she thought. *I may have to invest in some meth to get me through this.* She laughed aloud at that thought. She had been clean for well over six months and she wasn't about to jeopardize it. The thought of it scared her to death now because she knew if she ever did it again, she would be hooked. Nobody seemed to mind the fifteen pounds she had put on, plus she worked out at the gym four times a week so her body was very svelte and taut. She looked and felt better than she ever had before.

The last week in April was a chaotic one to say the least. Amber and Sam ran all over town trying on dresses, picking out flowers, tasting cakes, listening to bands and so on. Even after they picked

Max up from school they dragged her along for a few errands as well. She was going to be the flower girl so Sam had her try on dress after dress until finally at last on Wednesday evening, they found the perfect one.

Coincidentally, it was from the same designer that Sam had found her and Amber's dresses. Her name was Anna Lin, and she was a designer new to the Los Angeles area. Coming from New York her designs were simple, yet elegant. Not frilly and annoying like the ones Sam had seen all week. The dress Sam picked out was a white silk halter with tiny white beads around the neckline and bodice. It came to just above her knees with a long train of detachable silk coming of the back. She had picked out a tiny tiara veil to wear with it. Amber's dress was a butter cream yellow which accented her tanned skin and dark hair beautifully. Her dress was similar to Sam's but without the train and the beads on the bodice. Max's dress was a smaller version of Amber's.

James had faxed Sam the tuxedo measurements and she had dropped those off earlier in the week and Bob had gone in to get fitted for his. She had booked the outside garden of the church that Bob's uncle and his family attended. She would have a mid-morning ceremony, when the air was clearest and it wasn't so hot. The reception would be held at the *Beverly Hills Hotel*. She had yet to find the band and the caterer for that event though.

Two weeks later, in the middle of May, Sam and Amber had accomplished their mission. The wedding plans were done. Sam kept her fingers crossed that nothing would spoil her big day.

CHAPTER 62

❊

It was four days to the wedding. For the last two weeks Sam had been house hunting trying to find the perfect house for the three of them. She had wanted something out of the way, maybe hidden by gates or walls to keep the press out, but with wide and open grounds. She had found the perfect one the day before but fell heartbroken when she found out it was under contract. It was the house she'd always dreamed of. It had the appeal of a southern plantation with it's wide wrap-around porch and shutters on the outside of the windows. Inside, it was mostly hardwood floors with five bedrooms, a kitchen, dining area, living area, family room, den, and servants quarters. The kitchen was a cook's dream with two granite topped islands, two glass cook tops, a bar, and three different sized sinks. The refrigerator was built into the maple cabinetry. It also had a breakfast area with a bay window overlooking the swimming pool. The master bedroom was almost as big as the family room, boasting skylights, two window seats and two walk in closets with a separate shoe closet for each one. The master bathroom had two white pedestal sinks, a separate vanity, two toilets, a shower surrounded by glass block with two showerheads, and a Jacuzzi tub that was surrounded by windows, which overlooked the garden. The swimming pool had two waterfalls, surrounded by plants and tropical flowers, a slide and there was a built in Jacuzzi about 10 feet away. The house sat on six acres of lush green grass and beautiful flowers. It was the house Sam had waited all her life to have, and now it was gone.

James would be coming home the next day, so she tried to keep her mind off the house and the anticipation of seeing him again, by rehearsing her lines and reading over another script she had been offered. She had two magazine interviews the next morning and then she would be free of obligation until after the honeymoon. Marla would be coming in two days before the wedding and would be staying in the house with Max while James and Sam were gone. Sam had already prepared the guest room for her.

❦   ❦   ❦

After Sam's second interview, she left the *Silver Screen Bistro* in West Hollywood, exhausted from defending herself over that damn *Enquirer* story. She finally told the reporter, "look I don't want to seem rude, but I could care less what anyone thinks. I know the truth, James knows the truth, the people closest to me know the truth and that's all that matters." *She'll probably put that on the cover*, Sam thought, as she got in her car and went to go meet Bob for lunch.

She hadn't been to *HotShots* in a long time, but was glad when Bob suggested it. It was like home to her, comfortable and familiar. However, when she walked in she was not prepared for what awaited her.

The place was decorated with balloons and streamers and flowers. The tables had been rearranged and the music was louder than usual. There was a table filled with fruits, crackers, cheeses, finger sandwiches, and champagne. There was a table filled with gifts and a huge cake.

All of Sam's friends were there. People she had worked with at *HotShots* and on the two films she had already made. Even Thomas

Bennett was there, looking extremely hot as usual. Amber came over and ushered her in.

"Surprise bachelorette party!" She screamed as she hugged Sam. "I figured once James got home you wouldn't leave his side, so I had to do it today."

"You are amazing," Sam smiled at her friend as she walked into the room, exchanging hello's with the other guests. She noticed, as she looked around, that Lonnie had put up the movie posters from her films.

"You're my most famous ex-employee yet, with the exception of James, but all I could get was their CD. Apparently they haven't done any publicity shots yet."

"Oh they have, they just aren't printed yet." Sam gave Lonnie a big hug. He had been a true friend to her in the year she'd known him. "This is quite the party," Sam told him. People were dancing and drinking and eating and having a wonderful time.

Bob came over to her and kissed her on the cheek, "Were you surprised?"

"Of course. Did you have anything to do with this?" She teased him as she poked him in the ribs.

"Nope. It was all Amber's idea. I just had to get you to meet me for lunch."

"I am so lucky to have such wonderful friends," Sam said as she looked around again. "It means so much to me."

"Speaking of wonderful friends," Bob pulled Sam outside where it was quieter. "I wanted to give you this." He handed her a small wrapped box with a ribbon tied around it.

"What is it?" Sam asked as she opened it. Inside was a small gold ring with tiny diamonds set in across the front "I love it, it's absolutely beautiful!"

"It belonged to Marilyn Monroe once. I know you've always been fascinated by her and so I thought that this would be perfect for you. She had a great career in Hollywood and if it hadn't been for her personal endeavors that had gone so wrong, she'd have a had a longer and more fulfilling one." He put his head down to block the sun that glared off one of the windshields. "Anyway, I wish you that much success here and I know you will be another Marilyn."

Sam leaned over and kissed him softly on the cheek, a tear in her eye. He could have given her a rock and it would have been special because she knew he would have spent months trying to pick out the perfect one. She had idolized Marilyn Monroe since she had been in her early teens. It wasn't just her persona, Sam had read a biography about her and immediately had felt a connection to her. They had a lot in common, the way things had happened in their lives. Sam just hoped she wouldn't fall down the same road here on out.

"Thank you. This really means a lot to me." She slipped the ring on her finger. "And it fits perfectly."

"I'm glad you like it."

"Like it? "I love it, this was a wonderful surprise." She eyed the ring again thinking that Marilyn had worn it once herself. She wished she'd known the history behind it. It would be a good research project for her when she got bored. "And speaking of surprises, I have one for you. But you'll have to wait until tomorrow."

"Fair enough." He grabbed her arm and they walked back inside to the party.

After everyone ate, Sam opened her gifts. She received a lot of lingerie, a few books, some gift certificates to several boutiques on Rodeo Drive, plus a whole plethora of other things from candles to sex toys.

The party was still going strong when Sam realized she was going to be late picking James up at the airport.

"Just one more toast." Lonnie said, as Sam rushed around to say goodbye. He handed her a glass of champagne.

Reluctantly, she grabbed the glass. She didn't want to miss James but she didn't want to walk out on Lonnie either. Lonnie raised his glass, and as if on cue, James walked in the door. Sam looked up as she heard the familiar ring of the chime that was attached to the door. She almost dropped her drink when she saw him standing there. She set the glass down and ran over into his arms. He smelled so good, and his body next to hers felt even better.

"God, it's good to hold you again," he said as he buried his nose into her neck, taking in her scent. Sam pulled back and smiled at him with tears in her eyes.

"I know what you mean," she told him, emotion flooding her. "How did you know I was here?"

"It was all planned this way darlin'," he picked up two glasses of champagne and handed one to her. "To us, forever."

"I'll drink to that."

They both mingled with the guests for a while and then left to pick up Max before heading to the airport to pick up Marla.

CHAPTER 63

❈

Wedding Day

Sam woke up in her old bedroom at the beach apartment. She had stayed with Amber the night before per Marla's suggested superstition. She hadn't wanted to, because she had only been able to spend one night with James since he'd been back. What a wonderful night it had been too. They went out to a late dinner by the beach and then walked and talked for hours. Then they went home and quietly made love for what seemed like hours until they both fell asleep from elation. Sam had almost forgotten what it was like to have a body in bed next to her.

They wedding was scheduled for 10 a.m., and Sam needed to be there a half an hour early. Marla was in charge of getting Max and James ready and to the church on time. They had their rehearsal the previous night and then went to dinner at *Johnny Americas* with all their friends and family. Sam had to book the whole restaurant for their party. James's sister, Julia, had flown in from Miami with her boyfriend. Sam had immediately connected with Julia and by the end of the evening, she had a sister. Julia had a darker complexion than James and his mother and she had the most beautiful ice-blue eyes. She had the body and the face of a supermodel and Sam couldn't understand why she was doing escort services when she could easily be on the cover of *Cosmo*. But as James reminded her, she owned the business and she certainly wasn't hurting for money. Besides the fact that she enjoyed the lifestyle she lived.

Sam also had the honor of meeting James' aunt, who had practically raised him. Maggie was a short, stout woman, with a heart of gold. She was as beautiful as Marla was, but a bit wider. She was a devout Christian and certainly the bubbliest person Sam had ever met. Maggie had immediately fallen in love with Sam and vice-versa.

Amber and Sam got ready after breakfast. They both wore their hair in the same French twist and they applied each other's makeup with steady hands. At nine o'clock Bob was there to pick them up. He was actually going to be Sam's best man. She hadn't known anyone longer and he was such an important part of her life. It was a most unusual situation but everyone agreed, it was perfect.

They hung the dresses in the limo and got in to head for the church. Sam was so nervous that she felt like she was going to throw up. She hardly slept the night before and breakfast had been very little. She twisted her engagement ring around her finger as she looked out the window. It was funny that such a special day and important day for her was just an ordinary day for other people.

They got to the church just as Marla, James, and Max were arriving. Bob kept her in the limo until James was safely out of eyeshot. She watched James from the window as he strutted into the church in his tuxedo. He looked so handsome that Sam could hardly wait to rip it off of him.

"I can't believe this day is finally here," Sam said as she sprayed some more hairspray on her hair before putting on her veil. They were in the choir room now, getting the last minute touches done.

"I am so happy for you," Amber told her as she admired how beautiful her best friend looked. "I can't wait until my wedding day." She and Lance were finally getting their dirty laundry straightened out and it looked as though, following James's lead, Lance might make the leap into marriage soon.

"This is the happiest day of my life." Sam looked out the window at the people pouring in. "How many people are coming?"

"I think it was around 200."

"I didn't know I knew that many people. I also didn't know it was possible to be this happy and feel as though your life wasn't missing anything." She looked at Amber, "all of my life I've had this small hole inside. Like something was missing. I'd get this really weird feeling for like five seconds that I didn't belong where I was at. It was the most depressing feeling you could imagine and then it would be gone and I couldn't even remember it. When I met James I never had that feeling again. Today I feel like I have everything I could ever want and if someday I get more," she swallowed hard as she started to choke up. "If I ever get more, I might just burst."

At 10 o'clock Bob walked down the aisle followed by Kevin who was followed by Lance and Amber walking arm in arm. Little Max strolled down the aisle throwing rose petals into the air and watching them land. At seven after, Sam started down the aisle accompanied by Jacob Byrne. Since she had been estranged from her parents for so long, he had been like a father figure to her. Dreading her mother's negative comments, she hadn't even called her parents since she'd been in L.A. It was less stressful for her if they weren't there anyway.

James couldn't stop smiling at Sam as she walked down the aisle. She looked like a queen. He had never seen anyone as beautiful as she was in his whole life. If there had ever been a doubt in his mind about his love for her, it was completely gone now.

Jacob handed her to James and said, "I don't think I've ever seen a more perfect union." Sam kissed him lightly on the cheek as James took her hand and helped her up the step to the altar that was a ten-foot high, by six-foot wide, arbor covered in fire and ice roses. Sam had picked out the flowers to ensure a marriage that was pure and full of love.

"Dearly beloved, we are gathered here today to establish a union between these two people," the minister began his speech. Sam and

James had both written their own vows hoping not only to personalize the ceremony but also to convey their love for each other in front of their guests. Sam began with hers first.

"Once upon a time there was this little girl who dreamed of finding prince charming and living a fairy tale life. But fear of rejection and unhappiness kept her closed to a world full of love and excitement. You opened that door for me, James. When I met you, my life changed forever. You filled a void inside of me that had been there for so long. Knowing you has made me want to be a better person. You have taught me to love and to trust. You are what all my dreams are made of. You are my life, my soul, my love, forever."

Tears spilled down James' cheeks as he listened to the words that had come from her heart. It had taken him so long to get her to open up to him and now, here she was, doing it in front of 200 people. He spoke his vows next.

"You, with the fire in your eyes and the love in your heart, have made my life not only a joy to live everyday, but an adventure to look forward to. I knew from the moment I laid eyes on you that you were the one I wanted to be with for the rest of my life. I never had a doubt in my mind. There is so much we have to look forward to in our life together. So much to do and see and I am so lucky I get to do it all with you. I will never let you down, Samantha. I will never hurt or betray you. I will always be there for you and above all else, I will always love you." James could barely get the last few words out; emotion had consumed him. Tears spilled down onto Sam's skin and her lips trembled as she looked into his eyes.

They exchanged their eternity bands with each other and the minister pronounced them man and wife. As they walked out of the garden, the guests threw rose petals at them. The limo was waiting to whisk them off to the hotel but before they left, they graciously posed for a few photos for the photographers that were patiently waiting outside.

🍁   🍁   🍁

"That was the most beautiful wedding I've ever seen." Marla came up and hugged her new daughter-in-law. She was so happy that James had finally found his soul mate.

Sam was so thrilled that Marla, Julia, and Maggie had welcomed her into their family with such open arms. They were a very close family and a very loving family. It was the kind of family that she had always wished she had. She felt like the luckiest girl in the whole world and to her, the wait had been worth it.

Sam and James danced the first dance and then Sam danced with Jacob, Lance, and then later she danced with Bob and Thomas Bennett. By the end of the afternoon, she and James were on the dance floor for every slow dance. James didn't like to dance to the faster songs, so they mingled with friends during those songs.

After a while, Sam finally spotted whom she'd been searching for all day. She ran over to Veronica, who was standing just outside the room, and embraced her.

"I wasn't sure if you'd make it," Sam said as she noticed how stunning Veronica looked in a lavender silk suit, her dark hair flowing around her shoulders.

"I wasn't sure if I wanted to come," she admitted to Sam as she caught the sight of Bob. He looked so handsome and happy. Maybe he wouldn't want her back.

"Well, I spent a lot of time trying to find you and get you back where you belong. I think you owe it to me." Sam smiled at her friend as she grabbed her arm. "C'mon. I know he's going to be ecstatic when he sees you."

"I don't know about this," Veronica said as Sam led her across the room. She had moved back east with her mother and gone to therapy for a year to learn to cope with what Greg had done to her. She had never told anyone before Bob, and the fact that she had been holing it up her whole life had caused a little bit of damage to her psyche. She felt better now than she ever had in her life and she definitely felt in control of things. She had missed Bob terribly and had thought about calling him or writing to him, but she figured she had caused enough damage to his life and he wouldn't want anything to do with her. She hoped that wasn't the case now.

Sam tapped Bob on the shoulder and when he turned around his natural grin widened. "Oh my God! Veronica!" He pulled her into his arms so fast that Veronica had to catch her breath. She was surprised at how happy he was to see her.

"I thought you'd be angry with me when you saw me," she said as she pulled away, her hands lingering on his arms.

"Why would I be angry? I'm sure you did what you felt you had to do. I was upset, yes, but my feelings for you have never changed. Seeing you now, I know that I still love you." That was all she needed to hear. At last she felt like she was home.

Sam left them to get reacquainted with each other. She was thrilled that he had been so happy to see Veronica again. She knew how much he loved and her and how deeply saddened he'd been when she left. He hadn't dated since Veronica went back to New York and Sam hoped that her surprise for him would make his life complete again. His happiness meant a lot to her and since she was going to be gone on her honeymoon for a month she didn't want him to be lonely.

Before they cut the cake, James got on stage with Lance and Kevin and sang a song he had written for Sam while he was on tour. It was a ballad about two people and the struggles they were faced with as their love grew. It was going to be recorded on their next album. Sam cried through the whole song and figured that was the surprise he had mentioned to her earlier.

Lance and Bob made toasts to Sam and James as they cut the cake. James gently gave Sam a bite of his cake, making sure not to mess up her face. However, Sam smashed her cake into his face. He cut another piece to get back at her, but she ran from him. He finally caught her outside by the pool as they both fell onto the grassy area enveloped in laughter.

James still had cake on his face as he looked down into her shining eyes. "I love you so much," he murmured as he kissed her.

"Let's get out of here," Sam said, catching her breath. It was barely four o'clock, but Sam was anxious to begin her honeymoon.

"Sounds good to me. Let's go say our goodbyes."

After saying their farewell to their family and friends, Sam got into the limo while James spoke briefly with the driver. When he got in, he grabbed a bottle of champagne and poured two glasses. "To the rest of our lives," he said.

"To the rest of our lives," Sam repeated as she clinked her glass with his. The glasses were etched with *James and Samantha Jordan* and little roses all the way around the rim.

Sam had been so busy talking to James and admiring how handsome he looked in his tuxedo that she hadn't realized the house they pulled up in front of, wasn't theirs. The driver came and opened the door and when Sam got out she gave him a puzzled look. Then she looked back at James. "What are we doing here? How did you know about this place?"

"What do you mean, how did I know about this place?"

"Well, I looked at this house about three weeks ago to buy but they told me it was already under contract. I wanted to buy it for your wedding present. When I saw it I immediately fell in love with it. You can imagine how heartbroken I was when I couldn't have it."

"Really? They didn't tell me it was under contract when I signed the paper's for it."

"You what?!" Sam exclaimed as he walked her up to the front of the house. "You mean this is ours?" Sam was so excited she could hardly breathe. She couldn't believe that, despite all the time she spent agonizing over this place, it was now her very own."

James pulled a picture from his pocket that he had found in her stuff and held it up for her. She'd had it in her scrapbook with the title *Dream House* under it. "I found this picture before I left for the tour. I made it my mission to find a house just like it for you. I realize this one is about five times the size of the one in the picture, but I didn't think you'd mind. The minute I saw this place I made an offer and they accepted immediately."

"Guess we're in synch," Sam said as she looked at the picture he held in his hands. She remembered the day she took it. She had been so sad that day. That life now was a distant memory for her as she stood looking at the house in front of her. Her home.

"Well, I guess we'd better do this right," James picked her up in his arms and carried her to the front door. He handed her the keys and she opened the door. In the middle of the door, right above the brass knocker, was an engraved plaque. It said, *What Dreams Are Made Of.*

She glided her fingers over the words. "Yes it is," she smiled. "Yes indeed."

0-595-22436-9

Printed in the United States
69481LVS00006B/13